THE
PROTOTYPE

THE
PROTOTYPE

MATT McCORMICK

First Edition, 2018

Cover design and book design by Kelley Dodd
Cover illustration © Agsandrew | Dreamstime.com

Print: 978-0-9998488-0-7
ePUB: 978-0-9998488-1-4
Kindle: 978-0-9998488-2-1
PDF: 978-0-9998488-3-8
Audiobook: 978-0-9998488-4-5

To Kathy Engman and her family, Beau, Katherine, Audrey, and Clara. Kathy, your faith and your fight are an inspiration to us all.

To my wife, Mary, and my children, Elizabeth, Patrick, Megan, Kevin, and Johnny.

Prologue

Zamtech, a publicly traded Silicon Valley tech company, has been in business for over ten years selling solar panels for commercial and private use. Its latest development is a heavily guarded, patented solar capture technology designed to reduce the total cost of solar paneling and significantly increase the amount of energy that each panel can generate. If successful, it will be able to provide power to most of the world's houses and energize car batteries using solar panels on car roofs. Electric cars can be fully charged by the power of the sun—even on cloudy days. Some of the world's largest companies have already placed preorders for the technology, even though it is still in the development stage, based on its potential scope.

The company is racing against a significant competitor to be the first to market with the technology. While Zamtech's product development is almost complete, it still needs to figure out a way to pass the collected energy from its panels to storage devices. To do this, Zamtech plans to purchase a new type of transmission system for the energy that it has captured. There are two companies considered leaders in development of energy transmission systems: Hodophi, a $7 billion publicly traded company out of Beijing, and ART (Advanced Research Technologies), a thirty-five-person company out of Towson, Maryland. Watching the world's electrical demands increase exponentially and seeing the opportunity to compete, both of these companies began developing techniques in this area several years earlier.

The month of May has been set for testing transmission system prototypes to determine the winner of the contract. Whoever wins the race to develop this new energy transmission system will get a percentage of every sale that Zamtech makes, potentially gaining hundreds of millions of dollars in revenue. Both companies know the significance of what Zamtech has developed and understand that Zamtech would need to resell or embed their technology into everything they are selling going forward. Now the date set for prototype testing is fast approaching, and everyone is working feverishly to win the race.

Chapter 1

Wednesday, March 11
ART Headquarters
Towson, Maryland

I can feel sweat soaking the back of my shirt. This always happens to me when I get nervous. Here I am: the stinking new guy at this company. I'm sure they're going to hate me, but someone is ripping this place off and the people here have no clue—IT security isn't even on their radar, or the person supposed to be doing cyber security for ART isn't any good. I stare at my screen. What the heck is going on? I watch data from one of our servers just walk out the door through a command-and-control channel, right through our firewall. Can I shut down the server? Should I shut down the firewall? Oh, yeah—that'll go over really well. The new guy on the job brings everything to a screeching halt.

I log in as root and kill the command-and-control process.

With the process dead, I start to calm down. But suddenly, the process I just killed is back again.

If I shut down this production server, they're probably going to fire me, but I've seen enough. I roll up the sleeves of my blue Oxford and unbutton another button at the top.

I quickly type "Shutdown -a" and am promptly kicked off the server as it's shutting down. I think for a second and then log into the firewall that the command-and-control channel is using and set it for no incoming or outgoing connections on any port, except the port that email is using, and internet browsing. The command-and-control process is using a high port.

I walk down the hall toward the management's offices. I don't even know any of these guys, really, but I'm sure they're going to be angry with me. I start to tuck in my shirttail and then think better of it. My jeans are pretty ratty. It is the end of my second week on the job at Advanced Research Technologies, and I have to wonder about the genius that came up with the company name. I guess the acronym "ART" doesn't sound too bad, though.

Like many people in this industry, I have a mild case of attention deficit disorder. ADD is funny sometimes; as I head down the hall to get yelled at and potentially fired for entirely disrupting production, here I am thinking about the name of the company.

I graduated from Penn State last year with a degree in computer science and have been living at my parent's house since then. I spent eight months trying to find a job. Hopefully, I won't have to start over after today. A security issue with potentially far-reaching implications causing me to panic is not how I want to end my second week at my new job, that's for sure.

Zamtech Headquarters
Palo Alto, California

Jonathan Jacobs, the chief technology officer (CTO) of Zamtech, looks nervously at Elaine Fitzpatrick after he finishes his last slide. Jonathan is a tall, thin African-American man who is always dressed in a suit and a heavily starched white shirt. He never wears a tie, but he has a quiet intelligence that makes people stop and listen carefully to what he is saying. He runs his hand over his short, black hair and adjusts his glasses.

Elaine is the longest-standing Zamtech board member, and she always asks the hardest questions. She pushes her cropped blond hair off her face, and Jonathan sees from her dark blue eyes that she is thinking hard. Her background is on the financial side, and he feels more comfortable talking about technology. Elaine was once a CEO of a Fortune 500 company, and though she is nice enough, her extreme intelligence makes Jonathan nervous. He has watched her destroy people before with questions, and he thinks people always underestimate her.

The first question comes from another board member at the back of the boardroom. "First of all, congratulations on getting us to where we are. Thank you for that. With respect to the potential delays due to the transport of the energy to the batteries, do you think you can just build this yourself and not rely on third parties?"

Jonathan is comfortable with this question and has an answer already formulated. "We could build it ourselves, but we would have to find a better way to do it, and we would run the risk of further delays. We have tried that with limited success at this point. There are two companies that we have identified with significant technologies around this type of transport. I believe we will get there much faster if we simply use their transportation techniques and innovation. We could potentially integrate what they have and have a solution to go to market by the end of the summer."

Jonathan runs his hand over his hair and sneaks a glance at Elaine. She is scribbling notes furiously on a piece of paper. Another question from the back of the room rings out: "Zamtech sales executives just informed us of the incredible pipeline of deals from the largest electric car manufacturer, traditional car companies, large home building companies, utility companies—you get the point. How will these development delays affect those potential sales?"

"It is my understanding that we have briefed all of those companies that this is a calendar Q3 release, with full production coming in Q4, but we cannot delay it any longer than that," Jonathan replies.

"Any idea when the competition will be releasing?" the same board member asks.

"Everything we have heard says their technology is not as efficient as ours, and the whisper on the street is that a release would be early next year for them. We should be able to beat them to market by a full six months or more without delays and set the requirements for any competitive battles in the future."

Elaine's head darts up. "You mentioned two companies have the technology we need. Tell me more about the companies and whether the competition is also using them."

Jonathan takes a second to think about it before he responds. "We have a prototype test scheduled in May, so both companies have several months to finish what they are doing. That's when we will have a chance to see if they are able to meet our requirements."

He takes a deep breath and continues. "We put out a confidential RFP and tried to make it look like were sending it out to a lot of companies, but in fact we just sent it to three. We have already discounted the third. We have been working with two companies around this specific technology for a while, because we knew they both have some great innovations in this area. The first company is a division of Hodophi out of China, who you all have heard of. Over the last three years, they have invested heavily in the exact area that we need and are the forerunner in this type of technology.

"The second company is a startup company called Advanced Research Technology out of Maryland. Its founder and CTO is considered by many to be the world's foremost thinker about this type of technology. He has developed a unique way to handle the problem."

He is about to continue when Elaine interrupts, "How many people does the startup have? Do you have any idea about their financials? For instance, who has funded them?"

Jonathan is happy to get this line of questioning; he has heard Elaine's questions to other executives over the years and is prepared to answer. "The startup, which goes by the acronym ART, has just over thirty people right now but has received $29 million through two rounds of funding by ESRN Capital, right here in the Valley. ART can continue hiring right now for seventeen months in their current operating plan without any revenue. Revenue would accelerate their hiring, but they are on path to have about eighty-five people by the end of this year. ESRN Capital is a very reputable venture firm and has been responsible for other very successful companies over the years."

"Yes, I know ESRN," Elaine replies. "The next issue I have is outside your area, but surely you have heard the incredible pipeline projected by Sales that moves this from a $3 billion company to a $15 billion company in just three years before accelerating, if—and only if—you can deliver in the timelines you say you can. First of all, do you believe the sales forecasts and understand what that would do to our stock price? And, second, can you deliver?"

Jonathan now speaks with complete confidence and an edge in his voice, "I have been a part of the executive-level meetings for many of these opportunities. Yes, I believe them. This will change the world if we can deliver. The companies that we are talking about are making plans right now to bake this into their offerings. I will let you worry about the stock price, but the sales will be there. As far as if we can deliver, I would have to say that we would not be in this position without the innovation of our technical leaders and their scientists."

He pauses, looks around the room, and then continues, "We have developed something here that disrupts almost every industry, not to mention the world's utility infrastructure and the environment. We are very proud of this innovation; our scientists are the best in the world. The issue now is simply transport of the energy that we are already able to capture. We intentionally focused our resources on developing the energy capture first. We are now focusing on the transport. The companies we have identified may be able to reduce our time to market. We have been watching them closely, and not only will their technology work for us, we need it to achieve our goals."

Chapter 2

Wednesday, February 11
Hodophi Headquarters
Houhai Lake, Beijing, China

Sinh Lee, chairman and CEO of Hodophi, has heard enough.
He has made his fortune by not taking no for an answer,
regardless of the outcome. He stands, appearing much larger
than his five-foot, five-inch frame, and takes a look down the
table. With hate and anger in his eyes, Sinh focuses on his tall,
lanky VP of Engineering. "How could you have gone down
this incorrect path for so long in your development cycle?
This contract could easily be the future of this company,
and you put that future at risk by listening to your arrogant
directors."

Ja Sin, who is quiet by nature and dislikes confrontation
unless he is the one on the attack, has been VP of Engineering for
three years, but he has never set foot in this boardroom. He shuffles his feet and clears his throat. "At every step, from the initial
design through the original alpha product and code, we have not
seen or expected the heat problem. The heat should be dissipated
through our matrix of diodes, as we have seen with other products. We have our best and brightest in the company working on
this problem, and we will get results."

Sinh replies in a low, agonized voice, "If you have the best and the brightest on this problem, how come your competition has resolved it?"

Ja responds, "We do not know their design, but we assume that we are building it the same way as our competitor to meet Zamtech's design specs. We do not know that they have actually solved the heat problem."

Sinh scowls and says, "We have sources saying they did indeed solve the problem, and I would make it your business to find out their design. Do whatever it takes, or we will have to take things out of your hands and into our own."

As Ja leaves the room, Sinh looks over at his brother, Kahn Lee, who acts as his chief of staff, and says, "We will need to handle this ourselves with our people, regardless of what he does."

Khan, who stands about an inch taller than his older brother and has pockmarks all over his face from childhood acne, does not smile, even though he has finally received what he has wanted all along: the permission to really go after that smaller company with his own connections and resources. He looks at his brother and says simply, "Engineering management is not capable of doing what needs to be done here. I am."

• • •

Walking back to the main engineering building, Ja slowly blows a mouthful of cigarette smoke straight into the air. He looks at his best friend, Lan Su, who is the senior director and program manager of Project SUN, the internal project code name at Hodophi, and says, "You and I have been through everything together. We have hired and fired thousands of employees over the years to get the best teams to always deliver on time. Now, we both could be ruined by a small heat issue on a circuit board that we have innovated and created to send our company to new heights. We are one of two companies on earth that have the potential to perfect this circuit board, and yet we are being looked at as failures."

Lan, who is tiny in stature compared to his lanky friend but overweight and perpetually nervous, frowns and darts his eyes from one thing to another. "We have tried everything in the lab, and we continue to get exactly same results."

Ja asks, "Anything new with trying to recruit an engineer from the other company? Our sources all indicate that they have passed every initial alpha test and are actively developing and testing the prototype today."

Sighing, Lan replies, "No, the headhunters continue to try, but the company has been generous with stock options. The employees have a big stake in the company, and they believe they are going to be rich. Our surrounding technology is better. We just need that one fix for the win. We have also tried poking around their networks, but we can't seem to find what we need."

Ja looks up, intrigued. "Interesting. If you can't find their designs on the internal networks, have you looked at the backups?"

Lan replies quickly, "Up to this point, we have just been poking around. We have not put a concerted effort into the activity. If it's not on the production services, I believe we would be able to find a backup of it. The source code is the problem; we have the compiled code."

"Do the people you have poking around ART's network know what they are doing?" Ja asks.

With a smirk, Lan says, "All smart, good programmers. But they are not hackers."

Ja perks up, lights another cigarette, and asks, "Do you know any hackers, or could you find some? I'm talking the best of the best. Cost is no issue."

Chapter 3

Wednesday, March 11
ART Headquarters

My mind is racing, and I'm thinking about the job that I'm pretty sure I'm going to lose. I was hired as a software engineer, but in a small company you really end up doing a little of everything. I have mainly been doing some system administration work—basic Linux stuff, nothing too exciting. We have been building a bunch of servers for an upcoming product test cycle and release.

ART is into some sort of hardware, controlled by software. Honestly, I'm not sure what the final product we are building will do. I'm just building servers right now. I think I'm responsible for the development servers. Some of our work is also done on the Amazon Cloud, but I'm not really sure what goes where.

My random thoughts are interrupted as Chet Hartley, who introduced himself as the head of Software Development, asks me quietly and directly, "Robert, can you tell me again exactly what you saw?"

What kind of a name is Chet? Visions of pastel shirts, popped collars, and polo clubs make me laugh to myself. Really, though, he looked 100% like an engineer. A little heavy, with glasses and huge computer screens in front of his desk. I don't mind

Chet though; he doesn't go nuts when my boss, David Rogers, walks me into his office and has me explain that I shut down his production server in the middle of the day. You could even say he's relaxed.

I answer, "I saw a command-and-control channel that was basically taking everything you had on that development server and sending it out through our firewall. So, I killed the channel, and it came right back and picked up where it left off. There must be another process starting it back up once it is killed."

David is red-faced and upset with me. He says, "Why did you have to shut down the server, and why were you on it in the first place?"

David went to Yale, or Princeton, or one of those schools. To be honest, I really wasn't paying attention on my first day when he was going on and on about himself. I shouldn't have gone into his office to tell him first; he was kind of a blowhard the first time I met him. He is tall, what some people would consider handsome, and dressed better than most people in IT. He always seems to be looking for someone's approval.

I am annoyed at his question. "Didn't I just say someone was stealing all the data from that server and I couldn't stop it? A better question would be why I stopped all inbound and outbound connections to the firewall.

"The reason I did that is whatever malware is in here is probably on more than one server, and if this company has any important information that they would not like others to have, we had to stop it."

There is silence for a minute, and David's head looks like it is going to pop off. He manages to control his temper and says, "Robert, can you head back and finish building those servers that we asked you to complete?"

I slowly get up, and Chet gives me a weak smile and a shrug when David isn't looking.

I add, "Oh yeah, the reason I was on that server in the first place is I was wondering why the firewall would allow an internal server to have a connection through a high port."

David answers slowly, "How did you get the servers' root password?"

Got me. I answer lamely, "Someone gave it to me when I asked."

He said, "Who?"

"I don't know his name, but I can tell you where he sits."

David says, "Get back to building servers, like you are supposed to be doing."

I trudge back to my office believing that I've underestimated David and I should have held my tongue with him. He is clearly angry with me and can easily find some reason to get rid of me. He may not have to look too far, either, as he's probably figuring out that I hacked the Unix server for the password. Good thing the week is half over and this day is almost done.

• • •

In the evening before I go to bed, I sit up and talk to my parents for a while about work and everything going on. My dad enjoys talking about my work, and he is very interested in what we are doing. He is an accountant by trade but loves working on little projects and definitely understands technology. He has worked in downtown Baltimore for years. I would describe my dad as a hardworking family man who is interested in the well-being of everyone he meets. He is not as tall as my brother, William, or I. He is probably too skinny, but he loves to run. He is very soft-spoken and spends more time listening than talking.

My mom is a labor and delivery nurse who can and will strike a conversation with anyone. She always is curious to find out what my friends are up to and seems to care about everyone. She is tiny, but she's a ball of energy and does most of the talking in our family. In general, if everyone was like my mom and dad, the world would be a better place. We don't have a ton of money, but we are always okay. We live in a modest neighborhood that is nice but not over the top.

Monday, March 16
ART Headquarters

Ugh—what a weekend. Although I am new to this work thing (besides my summer jobs waiting tables), I still like to think I have a right to hate Mondays. Mondays stunk at school as well—from grade school right through college. People talk about Monday night football, but I'm usually so shot from drinking too much beer over the weekend that I don't care. Thursday night football? Now that I can get behind.

I managed to make it through the rest of last week simply by building servers and avoiding my boss. I'm counting myself lucky that he hasn't walked in with HR to fire me.

This morning, we are all gathered in a boardroom. It's pretty small, though, so I'm not sure what they really use it for. There are probably thirty-five of us packed in here. I am employee number thirty-five and one of the last hires, so I was proud of my deduction.

I notice a couple of cute girls in the room, which is pretty cool, as there are usually not many in this industry, at least from what I have seen in my computer science classes. I wonder if they are in IT or Marketing? My important thoughts are interrupted by the CEO walking in, which silences the crowd immediately.

"For those of you who are brand new that I have not had the chance to meet, I'm Joe Benfield, CEO and cofounder..." He launches into his speech.

I'm not sure if I am physically capable of sitting for long in this room. I have the Monday-morning blues, and it feels like everyone knows I can't put a sentence together because of too little sleep and too much beer this weekend. Joe is wearing a short-sleeved collared shirt and khaki pants and talking about this technology and some competitive race to get to a prototype. He really looks like a CEO with his graying hair parted on the side. He is on the tall side, but not taller than I am, and he speaks with ease and confidence as he paces the front of the room and makes eye contact with individuals.

Some of what he's talking about, especially about some of the solar applications, is actually pretty interesting. He seems nervous about timelines and is requiring and requesting hard work, blah, blah, blah. Should I raise my hand and ask if I can have opening day off? The Orioles are going to be great this year. Well, maybe.

"As part of this hard work, every employee will receive an additional 20,000 options, valued at 10 cents a share, to be added to what you were given when you were hired," Joe continues.

This catches my attention. People ask a couple of questions; to sum it up, if the prototype wins, we will either try to go public, or someone may try to purchase us.

I do some quick math. With 20,000 shares, if we get sold or go public at $10 a share, that's equal to $200,000; $20 a share is equal to $400,000—funny how math works like that. I also received 5,000 shares when I was hired. Maybe I wouldn't have to split a rental in Federal Hill with my high school buddy George! He's a great guy and all; he'd just probably want to go out every night. It's bad enough seeing him just on weekends.

Joe continues, "The design is almost complete. We are seeing great results in testing, and we need everyone to focus over the next several months. If we are successful, everyone will profit."

Probably not everyone will profit as much as Mr. CEO there, but I'm okay with it. He's giving me a reason to care, which is cool.

The meeting ends, and I'm actually impressed with how much I learned from it. A couple of weeks into corporate America, and I'm saying my first real meeting is interesting? Now I'm back to building my servers in my storeroom of an office. Hopefully soon I'll be able to start programming and actually working on the project they are talking about.

One of the hot girls from the meeting comes up to me. Well, maybe not hot, but definitely a mixture of cute and hot. She is actually extremely pretty with long, dark brown hair, deep blue eyes, and a wonderful smile. She is dressed better than most of the people in the office, in a long blue dress, matching shoes, and a scarf. Not that I notice that sort of stuff.

"Hey, my name is Sarah Donnelly. Do you have a sec?"

I respond, "Hi. Robert Dulaney. Nice to meet you." I can't think of anything cool to say, but I have mentioned I am tired, right?

"I talked with Dave Rogers, and he mentioned you could build me a server."

Dave? I thought his name is David? And what's the big idea? Why is my boss telling people I'll do things for them?

"What flavor server would you like today?" I say, trying to sound suave.

She smiles. "I need a Centos server, something pretty fast and powerful, if you have the hardware."

"I can do that, and I do have the hardware. They seem to be buying it up fast; maybe based on all that cash they were talking about this morning. Round B funding or something."

"Yeah, pretty exciting, isn't it?"

Ugh, I hope she is not too caught up in this corporate junk. I reply, "Sounds like it. How long have you been here?"

She leans back against the doorjamb, looks up, and seems to be thinking. I sneak another glance at her long, dark hair before she finally says, "Seven months. That makes me an old-timer here."

I ask, "Are you working on anything cool related to the prototype he was talking about?"

"No, not really. Some heat dissipation simulation models; we test things in software before putting them into hardware. The work is almost done though, so I'll be moving onto something else. You?"

I reply, "I'm supposed to be doing some machine language programming, but now they have me building servers. I guess that's all they need right now."

With a reassuring look, she says, "Things change quickly around here, so don't worry. When do you think you can have it done?"

"Is tomorrow good?"

"That works. And thanks!"

I watch her walk confidently down the hall, and then I daydream a bit. I believe that is my longest conversation to date at ART, and for some reason for the rest of the day, I cannot stop thinking about it.

Chapter 4

Tuesday, March 17
ART Headquarters

I am still wrecked from the weekend, and here I am in the HR training I had forgotten about when I made my promise to Sarah yesterday. I ended up staying late to get her server done. Do what you tell people you will do—I learned that in grade school, I believe.

I did make her an extremely fast, high-end server yesterday. I really just loaded the operating system with some monitoring tools we use here. My mind wanders now as our HR lady talks about benefits. No matching 401k, okay health and dental... dentist...I should probably go soon. I think the last time I went was in high school.

Back to thinking about that server last night, though. Right when I put it on the networks, something started probing it right away. That's curious. A computer was poking at it from inside our network for vulnerabilities or holes that could be exploited.

Do we have a security person? Or maybe Chet has an IT person doing security after I reported the hack from last week? I noticed some high ports light up right away with some of the monitoring tools I put on the boxes.

I keep thinking about the scans; they're typical really, just scans to see if there were any ports that could be broken into. They seemed to be focused on ports that were not used often. Ports like http are normally on Port 443, and I was originally alerted to the scan by http trying to access a high port.

If I tell someone about it and they ask me how I know all of this, what will I tell them? I guess some of it comes from computer science classes, but most of it comes from dabbling on the "other side" a little when I was younger.

More HR babbling going on...vacation days, sick days...I wonder if the "Irish flu" could be used for such days? There are two other newbies in class with me; both look as bored as I am.

My mind keeps racing. When I say I was on the "other side," I don't mean to imply I was a major hacker or anything. I just liked to poke around corporate and government networks every once in a while. My older brother was really, really smart. He graduated from college about two years before I was in high school. He got a pretty high-flying job in finance and bought himself a great Mac right when they were becoming popular again. He was working and living at home while he and his fiancée looked for a house, which meant I had access to his high-end Mac during the day and in the early evenings.

To stave off boredom, I would play in other people's networks. Nothing big! I would just look at information from big companies, the Department of Homeland Security, the IRS, and other places like that. I never took anything; I just looked. Anyway, I never got caught. I assumed it was because I was good at it and would cover my tracks, but it was probably because everyone else was doing it, too.

Anyway, the HR lady finishes up, and I am on break guzzling some free coffee. One of the benefits of working at a tech startup is the free loot: sodas, Red Bull, candy, and coffee are everywhere in the office. It's not a bad perk, but I notice since I have started working here that I am pretty jacked up, either on caffeine or sugar, at all times.

A fairly large dude comes up to me. He's over six feet tall and looks like he's pushing 250 pounds with a ponytail and a couple of earrings. He's chewing some tobacco during the break. He looks like he is in his thirties, but I'm not a good judge of age.

"Hey, I'm John."

"Robert. Nice to meet you."

"Back at you. What do you do here?"

I chuckle. "Nothing really. I hang out going to HR meetings and corporate meetings, and I walk the halls drinking soda. You?"

He nods and replies, "I'm in QA, or Quality Assurance. When we build software, QA tests it to tell us if it works or if it breaks something else within the code. Software programs reference each other throughout, so sometimes if you make one change to fix one thing, it may break something else entirely unrelated."

I know all that, but I decide not to be an idiot and tell him that. Instead I say, "I'm building servers right now, but I'm supposed to be doing some programming. We shall see."

"Gotcha."

John seems to be a man of few words, so I ask him, "How did you find out about this place?"

"I used to work for the development VP at a previous startup. He's a pretty good guy, and really smart."

"Cool." Now I seem to be a man of a few words, myself.

"Are you that dude who shut down the firewall and production server last week?"

Oh no—I had no idea that had gotten around. "Yeah, that's me."

"People were pissed, and I heard you almost got fired, but anyone with half a brain knew you did good work. They had trouble finding the source and finally cleaned it up."

"Thanks man! I didn't hear I almost got fired. Do you know if we have anyone doing computer security here now?"

"Don't know, but we need it. Not sure if you know, but that was not the first time something like that's happened."

I decide I liked John. Who wouldn't like a dude that chews tobacco and spits into a Coke can during boring HR meetings? I wonder if David did try to get me fired, or if John is just talking trash. I better watch out for that Ivy League bonehead, I think to myself.

Wednesday, March 18
ART Headquarters

Training is over, and I am back to building my servers. Equipment is piling up in the storage room and in the corporate kitchen. They want it built and put into production, development, or QA as fast as I can. Each group seems to have a large need for servers. I continue to see high port scans on every server I bring up. There's nothing really exciting, but I have to assume that we at least now have a security guy who is paranoid. I guess that's why they're in security.

Anyway, they are not going to find many holes in my boxes. I lock them down pretty well. I use a base Linux build, and I take out some services that are rarely used as well. They must be doing some penetration testing as well as just looking for vulnerabilities, because I can see access attempts in the logs. It's funny, because the person doing it actually seems to be pretty talented; they aren't just looking for normal stuff. I have to meet this guy.

I'm tired of sitting there looking at screens and decide to take a walk. I pick up a manila folder, throw in a couple of packing slips to make it look like I am working, and start my stroll.

Our building is four stories tall, and ART is located on the third and fourth floors. Our reception area, executives' offices, and Accounting are on the fourth floor, while Development is on the third floor.' You have to use your security key badge to get to each floor going either way in the stairwells or to get off the elevator on our floors.

I am on the fourth floor in a storage area with computer boxes strewn everywhere. In the back of my mind, I remember the HR woman saying there are over twenty requisitions out for new people. No wonder they hired me; I guess they were having trouble hiring enough people.

As I swipe my key badge to get into the stairwell, I'm thinking that I should at least meet the security dude to let him know that I've noticed he's messing with my servers. He seems to have gotten a lot better in some of the things he has been trying recently; maybe he just has more time. I am pretty sure it is someone in the company because the scanning is always from an internal ART system.

The development team is broken into two areas: hardware and software. There are also groups that work on both hardware and software.

As I walk around the building pretending to be doing something, I notice them clearing out and getting a few more cubes ready. Maybe I'll actually be able to get to move down and do my job one of these days.

Suddenly, I see someone that I can talk with. Sarah is banging away on the keyboard at her desk. Ugh—a Michigan pennant hangs in her cube. Penn State folks don't like Michigan, period. Some think it a football rivalry, but I take it more seriously than that.

"What's shaking, Sarah?"

She turns around slowly but keeps her eye on her monitor for a second longer before answering, "Oh, hi Robert. Sorry. I was just mesmerized by my screen trying to figure out why a subroutine I just wrote to help me with my simulations is not working."

Hey, she remembers my name! I had forgotten how pretty she is. I try to act casual. "How is that computer working out for you?"

She leans back in her chair, stretches out her long legs, and crosses her feet.

"It's great, thanks. Been downloading a bunch of open source apps from the web to help me with simulations. There is some really cool stuff out there for free."

There is that smile again. Her dimples are showing, and her hair looks like she spent hours getting it perfect. She is "dressed down" in jeans and a blouse, but she has a way of making it look dressed up. There is a slight hint of a perfume that smells good, and her cube is decorated in a light, easy manner to match her personality.

"I didn't know you went to Michigan. Nittany Lion here. Are you from there originally?"

She chuckles. "Yep, grew up in Kalamazoo. Ever hear of it?"

"Can't say that I have. Is your family still out there?"

"Everyone but me. My three sisters and my parents never left."

"What brought you out here?"

"A recruiter contacted me through LinkedIn. Sounded like a great opportunity, so here I am. How about you?"

"Born and raised in Baltimore. Well, a little outside in the Towson area. I'm moving down to Federal Hill next month, which I'm psyched for." I realize I need to change the subject before she finds out I live with my parents in the same house I grew up in. "Hey, quick question for you, do you know who is in charge of computer security around here?"

"No, I don't know if we have one. Why?"

"Just noticed some penetration testing going on, and I wanted to make sure it was legit."

"Check with Chet Hartman, last office down the hall. He's one of the original Dev guys and knows everyone around here."

"Cool, thanks. Good luck with that simulation, or whatever it is you are playing with."

She laughs and turns around. Wow, I need to make an excuse to come up here more.

I didn't want to tell her that I already know Chet from getting in trouble the week before. Chet's office is empty, so I do a lap around the office and start heading to the hardware section. The hardware section of the building is pretty neat. A lot of it is glassed in, and there are racks and racks of computers. There are also the hardware sections of the "final product," which is basically circuit boards that will be used to transfer energy.

Our company is only designing one small part of the board: the brains behind load-balancing electricity in a series of tubes. But the amount of software and hardware that goes into that section is mind-boggling. I guess I did pay a little attention in the orientation.

As I take a cruise around the hardware section, I see people with their heads down working, and I take a left down another hallway to QA. I come up empty there as well, so I decide to do the unthinkable: I stop in and talk to my boss. His office is just past QA. Maybe I can make peace with him.

"David, do you have a minute?"

"Hey, kind of in the middle of something, but what's up?" We are all in the middle of something; must be a real important email or spreadsheet he is working on.

"I would like to talk to our computer security guy. I want to see what type of scanners he is running on the systems I am building."

"We don't have any computer security people that I know of. I think IT manages the firewalls. Scott Williams runs IT, let's give him a ring." He dials the phone and gets an answer promptly. "Hey Scott, David here, on speakerphone with Robert Dulaney, who is new in my group. We noticed a scanner running on the systems we are building and wanted to see what you guys are running."

Did he just say "we" noticed? Now I see how this works.

Scott responds in a confused tone of voice, "We are not running anything. Are you sure about what you are seeing?"

I speak up. "Scott, this is Robert. Yes, I'm sure. It's mainly lighting up high ports, but it's every time I put something new on the network. I'm also seeing penetration attempts almost immediately when I put the new servers online."

Scott pauses before replying, "Robert, can you show me?"

"Yep, I'll meet you upstairs. I'm in that storage space outside the kitchen."

David looks at me after we hang up, locks his computer screen, and says, "Let's go."

And here I thought he was busy.

When Scott comes to meet us, I like him immediately. He is tall and skinny with a beard, an earring, and a t-shirt that says "Beer." He is wearing flip-flops and shorts, and I think to myself that I like a company where this dude can run a group. He has long, dark hair past his shoulders that he is always playing with.

I start to walk Scott through what I am seeing. I take a device, change the IP address of it, and reboot it so it will look like I just placed it on the network. Within two minutes, a scan starts.

I say, "I thought this was an internal scan from a security person because it is coming from an address within our company."

I can tell Scott is getting a bit more nervous, and I can also tell he knows what he is doing by the questions he asks. He calls his network guy, and soon there is a crowd in my little area discussing it.

Ten minutes later I have the root password for the machine that is doing the scanning, and I am going through the device. I am able to quickly see the process that is doing the work and kill it. Within a couple seconds a new one starts, and then a second. All of a sudden, I have an interesting job.

I quickly go through the system looking for what is starting these scans, and I notice a couple of things. I say, "It looks like some sort of exploit pack that runs a number of unique scans."

"What's an exploit pack?" Scott asks.

"An exploit pack is software that anyone can run that will figure out where the holes are in a system, allowing a hacker to break into a system and steal the data. Exploit packs can be bought, and there is nothing illegal about someone writing and selling the software, even if it's then used to do something illegal. There are a lot of them out there; some are expensive and some of them are free." I used to mess around with the free stuff, but I do not say that.

The crowd has become a little larger, and then Chet comes in. Chet starts peppering me with questions as well. As for David, well, he looks like a sheepdog in the corner. Tough to pretend you did the work on something when you can't even spell it.

My original inclination is to kill all processes and delete the software, but I am thinking out loud that it might be better to watch to see what they are after and not let them know we are onto them. I reason that if we stop them here quickly, we may not be able to stop them the next time. I would also like to know if this is a freeware program, something homegrown, or something bought. Finally, I want to see if we are being targeted for something specific, or if someone is randomly breaking into places looking for credit card numbers, Social Security numbers, and other personal information.

There are a lot of people in the room who are nervous about the competitive nature of the upcoming prototype, and in the end, they allow me to keep the software on the box, as long as I pull it off the main network. That will give me a little time to figure out what is on that device. They go down and pull the Ethernet wire from the device, unrack it, and walk it up to my office.

I now have a new toy, and people continue to stop by the rest of the day. The other cofounder and now CTO, Ashok Ready, stops in to talk. Ashok is tall and very skinny, is built like a long-distance runner, and has glasses that look like they are an inch thick. He speaks quietly and thoughtfully, with a light Indian accent. I like him instantly.

Ashok is the most nervous out of everyone I've spoken to, and he really wants to know if someone could have stolen plans and code from ART. Right now, the answer is a resounding "maybe," which doesn't make anyone feel good. His questions make it clear that he knows that the most important thing in this company is its intellectual property, which may have just been stolen by a competitor.

I end up working until ten that night and bring some stuff home as well to try to figure it out. That night I finally find something on one of the executables. It is not really out in the open but rather posted in some discussion groups. It is, indeed, part of an exploit pack, and it is expensive. From this, I deduce that either someone is really after something within ART, or they are just using their expensive tool on anyone they can find.

Chapter 5

Friday, March 27
Hodophi Headquarters

Ja Sin takes another puff on his cigarette and looks at Lan Su. "The information we have received from our friends has not helped. The designs, the plans—everything, they're all pieces of the puzzle we already knew. We need to figure out the heat dissipation methodology, nothing else. I thought you said the hackers that are working for us were good."

"They are! They broke in and got us a ton of data, just not what we need yet."

Ja sighs and says, "Not what we need yet?! We are running out of time. Don't forget that we still need to build and test this after we get it. Your budget is now unlimited. Get multiple groups involved. Get the best and pay them whatever."

He continues after a moment. "It's time to activate the people on the inside. I would introduce some changes in their code that will make their prototype fail, if they truly have a working design. In the meantime, anything about heat—get it. Our engineers should be able to reverse-engineer anything and finalize our design."

ART Headquarters

Scott wanders into my office, sits down in an extra chair, and puts his feet up on a box. He's dressed like he's about to go to the beach. He says, "Do you have five minutes to talk?"

"Sure."

"It seems to me that you know quite a bit more about computer security than from just taking a few courses. I don't need to know what you know, where you learned it from, or any details at all, honestly, but can you tell me other things we should be thinking about?"

I say, "There is a lot to worry about. For example, you not only have to think about your intellectual property going out to your competitors, but you also have to think about the integrity of the data you had there. What if critical parts in a design were changed? How would you know? You can check on file sizes and save dates and compare them to backups, but can't all that also be manipulated?"

I let that sink in for a second and then continue, "You can change a file, maybe just one item in it, save it to a file of the same size, trick the operating system into believing it had the same time and date as was originally saved, then delete all logs and references that you were on the system. Once they have full root access, they can do anything."

"Understood," he says. "What else?"

I answer, "This was not random, not just some kid just looking for credit card info. They were looking for everything, spreading from one device to the next...copying all data and then moving it off premises to service providers or hosting companies."

He responds, "Between us, make stopping these attacks your top priority. People were mad when you shut down that production server while code was compiling, but you do what you need to do and I'll get your back if you need it."

"Alright. And thanks," I say. With that, Scott gets up and walks out.

I think for a second. Why is he telling me that? Sounds like he is telling me to ignore what my boss tells me to do and to do this instead. Interesting. Maybe he knows David's an idiot or that he wanted to fire me. I need to watch out for David, with or without Scott having my back.

Five minutes later, Ashok walks into my office with a dark-skinned man who looks to be in his thirties and says, "Robert, I would like you to meet Jacob Collins. He came highly recommended by a friend of mine to help us part-time as a consultant with some of the computer security issues we have. Don't worry; this is from a very trusted source, and Jacob has already signed a non-disclosure agreement, so you can be upfront with him."

I stand up and shake hands with Jacob. He has a nice smile and a firm, confident handshake.

Ashok says, "Do you mind spending about thirty minutes with Jacob? Sorry, I should have asked you to check your calendar earlier to see if you could interview Jacob, but he just came off another job, so we were able to get him in at the last minute."

Interview? It sounds like Ashok has already made his decision. I reply, "Sure, have a seat. Do you need coffee or anything?"

Jacob replies easily, adjusting the wire-rim glasses on his nose. "No, I'm all set. I have had too much today already."

Ashok walks out and closes my storage room door. I say, "I bet you never interviewed in an office like this."

Jacob laughs, "No, can't say that I have."

I am not sure where to start, having never interviewed anyone before, but I want to cut right to the chase and see if he knows anything. "So, Ashok told you what is going on here. Where would you start?"

"I think I would start analyzing the attacks that have been going on in your network at the most basic level. In computer security, we call them indicators of compromise, or IOCs. Stop me if I'm going technically too high or too low with this stuff, but an IOC can be an IP address of the device the command-and-control channel is trying to communicate with, a web link that they are trying to get your employees to click on, or a hash value of a piece of malware."

I play dumb. "What is a hash value?"

He replies, "It's simply a mathematical computation on the bits of a file that acts as a unique fingerprint of that file. There are many different algorithms that do this."

I know all this and my mind starts to wander, but then he brings me back with his next statement.

"I would then take the IOCs and try to figure out what group is attacking us, and then find any other IOCs that are known to that group. This would take your security from simply being defensive, reacting to each and every attack they send us, to offensive, looking for the next potential weapon that our adversary possesses. We could look for them on our network, as well as proactively block them at the firewall and any other security infrastructure that you are using."

This is interesting to me; I haven't thought about this at all. As we continue to talk, I find myself learning a lot from Jacob, who had been working for a large consulting firm before starting a small business himself. When Ashok comes back to get him, I ask them how much time he can work a week, and Ashok replies that we're talking to Jacob about a two-month contract for twenty hours a week. I really like Jacob, and I tell him I am looking forward to working with him.

• • •

Meanwhile, the real project seems to be going well. The security breach has been very disruptive, but the developers keep working on the prototype and there is an increasing amount of excitement in the hallways. People are working long hours, but everyone seems committed. New people are continuing to come in at crazy pace for a small company. They expanded the office down one more floor, and from popping my head into a new-hire training, it looks as though we hired fifteen new people. I am getting to be an old-timer.

My job is still building servers, but I also have become the de facto computer security guy, as Scott had talked about. That is kind of neat, and although I want to do programming, this is really interesting and exciting. I also am involved in decisions about where to put things, and I work with the consultants, especially Jacob, to determine best practices.

We do a couple of things to improve the overall security. I ask Development where the critical data lies. We put that on its own network, and since I am still trying to get a feel for what is going on, we completely separate that from the rest of the organization and don't give them access to the internet.

We then physically move the servers to a separate room next to some offices on one end of the third floor. I would have liked to create another secure key-badged area, but being a startup, there is not a ton of money to go around building separate areas. The most we could do is post an access list, and only the folks on the list can work in there.

We call that area "Dev 2," and all the source code is moved there, along with anything that is critical to the software design and operation. The developers hate the fact that we did not give them internet access in Dev 2, but we wanted to make sure that hackers could not get to the code in that area.

We also spend a lot of time building some network defenses. We add a couple of firewalls to restrict access going from one part of the network to another, and we add open-source network intrusion detection and scanning tools.

One of Jacob's first tasks is to give a two-hour seminar for all our employees on computer security. It's just about the no-brainer stuff like how to craft a strong password and locking your computer, but I think every little bit will help us. The biggest thing I think he teaches them is not to click on links that are emailed to you, even if you think you know who they are from.

I had thought things were looking better, but in my mind, I know that whoever is attacking us will not stop. They seem very motivated to get our information, so why wouldn't they keep trying new attacks until they find something that works?

Sinh Lee's Estate
Shichahai, Beijing

Khan is tired, but he enjoys coming to his brother's house and especially sitting by the fire and looking through the massive windows at Qianhai Lake. This is not Sinh's summer house, but the house he lives in throughout the year, only about a ten-minute drive from Hodophi headquarters. He is shown into the room by Sinh's new butler, who seems to do everything around the house. Khan laughs to himself that his brother goes through more butlers than he does t-shirts.

Khan walks over and pours himself a glass of Glengoyne single malt scotch, one of his brother's favorites and another reason that Kahn enjoys coming here. He sits down by the fire and looks out at the glistening lake. Khan also enjoys spending time with Sinh's family—his ten-year-old son and his wife—as he does not have a family of his own. Khan remembers that Sinh's wife and son are at their getaway spot in Sanya, a coastal town on Hainan Island about a four-hour flight away.

Sinh's teasing voice rings out behind him, "You only poured one drink?"

Khan chuckles and replies, "I was going to pour you one when I started my second. I know you are a lightweight, and with the family out of town I don't want you to be sleeping early. We have some clubs to get out to tonight."

Sinh laughs and pours himself a double and closes all three doors to the room. "Any news?"

Khan smiles and replies, "Good news on a couple of fronts. First, it looks like Zamtech is lining up orders. We talked to our people there, as well as other friends in the industry. If we capture 10% of what they sell, this could be another $4 billion to $5 billion business for us in three years. Second, we have a couple people now on the inside of ART and a potential third that would be in a very good position for us come prototype time if required. And lastly, Hans Tsugilva has agreed to our price and will coordinate efforts both in Baltimore and Palo Alto. He is also involving other people he knows to work on surveillance and adding additional hacking resources. Hans will have a direct team of his trusted employees with him for the more personal requirements and will be traveling to Baltimore soon. He is also planning to be in Palo Alto for the testing. As you know, he was extremely effective the last time we used him."

Khan goes silent and waits for his brother to comment. His brother always thinks through everything thoroughly, which is surely part of why he has been such a successful CEO. Finally, Sinh smiles and says, "It's not over by any means, but this is all very positive. Thank you. I'm very happy we don't have to rely on our engineering team to do things that are out of their line of expertise. They can concentrate on the prototype and delivering product after we win."

Chapter 6

Monday, March 30
ART Headquarters

I am sitting at my desk enjoying my first cup of free company java of the day when I hear Scott's flip-flops slapping the floor around the corner. He steps into my office and says, "Yo, I logged in over the VPN last night and saw some weirdness on one of our QA machines. I don't think the stuff you found two weeks ago is all cleaned up."

"Show me."

He runs his hands through his hair and motions for me to get out of my seat. Within two seconds, his hands are flying across the keyboard, and he remotely logs into the QA machine he is talking about. I watch him type his Linux commands:

```
ps–ea | more
```

The screen immediately fills with all the processes on that computer and allows him to page through slowly. "See this one," he says, pointing to a file in the user directory called "timex.r."

He then runs the sudo command to be able to run commands as root and shows that the file is communicating with other devices on a little-used port. He opens up three more virtual terminals and remotely logs into other devices. He says, "A program

I was working on was taking forever to compile, and then the file name drew my suspicion, because I have been working on Linux machines since I was four, and I have never seen it."

He deletes it on the first server, and the process starts again a minute later. He checks in the crontab, which is used to schedule processes in UNIX, and sees that the process didn't start there, but he notices another filename that seems off. In a second he is opening up a VI editor to look in that file, and he sees a command to start timex.r.

He says, "I think you know what you are seeing, but basically they are scheduling a script to run that starts that timex.r process every minute if it is not already started. Not sure what that process does, but ten to one it's sending our data somewhere and looking to spread to other devices."

I agree. "Can you check those other servers you are logged into?"

He flies into the other terminals and finds the same file on one of the three devices he is logged into.

He starts logging into every server we have, looking for the file. When he finds it he deletes it, the script that started it, and the entry into the crontab scheduler. I like working with this dude, not only because he is very good, but also because he seems to know every password for every computer in the place. That is more than a little helpful.

I walk over to a new server I am building and ask if he can remotely copy the script and the executable over to that server so I can work on it. I gave him the IP address and root password.

Scott lets Chet know over the Slack messaging tool that he is shutting off all connections in and out of the firewall. No one questions him. We end up finding malware on seven servers and three different subnets. We do not find anything on two of our small subnets, so some of our new segmentation and firewalls must have worked. QA and some of Manufacturing are completely owned. QA is mainly testing compiled code, so that would not do them much good. Marketing is also compromised, but who cares.

A couple of the servers in Dev 2 are compromised as well, and that worries us. Yes, "us." Now that I'm a big man on campus, I actually care about this stuff. Remember the stock options conversation?

Scott also sends Ashok an instant message over Slack about what is happening, and two minutes later Ashok is in with us. As always, Ashok is dressed nicely and has a look of concern on his face. He questions Scott, who is cleaning up the systems, and me as I try to figure out what the malware is trying to do.

I disconnect the server I am working on from the network and play with the malware, trying to figure out what it is doing. It is easier on this machine because it is a fresh build and I know every process that should be on this server.

I show Ashok how the malware tries to open up a command-and-control channel to the internet. The malware is trying to get out using any port. I then turn on my phone's wi-fi hot spot and allow the server to get to the internet through it to try to see where it is going.

I explain to Ashok, "I am using my phone because this malware is trying to connect to other servers and spread, and I don't want to mess up what Scott is doing. Do you see that?" I point to my screen. "The software just connected to a server."

I copy down the IP address and then do a reverse IP lookup and find out that it is going to a legitimate service provider in San Antonio, Texas. I explain to Ashok, "Our investigation will no doubt end there. Whoever is attacking us buys computer time from cloud providers, steals data, and moves it to a server at the provider as a temporary stop. They will then move the data again, maybe to another provider, to make it hard to follow and then delete the data and shut down their connection with the provider—just like moving money through multiple banks and closing accounts."

I think for a second and then run an idea by Scott and Ashok. "Hey, can you guys buy me two extra servers? I want to build a honeypot to see if they can break into it and what they are trying to do once they're in. We can fake a new connection with a partner and firewall it into its own network."

Scott replies, "Yes, do what you have to do. And what the heck is a honeypot?"

I reply, "It's a system that we can put some fake data in for them to download. We'll make it look as real as possible, like it's a partner portal. We can then baseline it and watch it closely for any new processes to see what attacks they are trying on the rest of our network. The point is, we can steal the data that is on it and even try to send them in the wrong direction away from what we are trying to do. Ashok, if you have some things that you tried before with the technology that you know will not work, we can let them have it and waste some time. Make sense?"

Ashok says, "Yes, order the servers or use any that we have in stock and replace them. I do have some stuff that may work pretty well in sending them in the wrong direction."

I say, "Good, maybe I'll create some malware of our own as well and let them copy it back through their service providers and then back to their home base, and then we can collect some information from them and maybe find out who they are. If I don't have time to build something, maybe I'll just find a nasty piece of malware that exists already that destroys their machines, zip it up, and see if they are dumb enough to run it after they steal it."

Chapter 7

Tuesday, March 31
ART Headquarters

I am running a little late and pull into the office at nine fifteen in the morning, but I have a good excuse. I actually stayed until ten o'clock last night trying to understand everything I am seeing. It also helps that Sarah was working late, and I would think of an excuse or two to stop by her cube throughout the evening. I cannot seem to get her out of my mind.

When I walk into reception on the fourth floor, I notice a bowl of what I originally think is candy sitting at the reception desk with a sign saying "Take one." Upon closer examination, I see it is actually full of eight-gigabyte USB sticks with some marketing verbiage on them.

Seriously?!

I say, "Brenda, who gave these to us and when?"

Brenda, who looks younger than me with her short dark hair and freckles everywhere, looks at the USB storage devices and then holds one up so I can see a name printed on it. "Someone from this marketing company, Sky Marketing. They want our business, I guess. He was waiting here right when I unlocked the doors at eight thirty. He was very nice...why do you ask?"

I don't answer and instead ask, "Who has them?"

She laughs. "Everyone coming in has taken one today. Free stuff always goes fast!"

I grab the basket and tell her to take hers out if she put it in. I run straight to our IT team; Scott is there. I tell him what I suspect and ask him to send out an email immediately to the entire company telling them to take the USB sticks out of their computers and hand them in immediately in the boardroom.

I then grab one of the sticks and run to my test computer, which does not have access to the internet. I start it up. As it's booting, I go to grab a cup of coffee and run smack into our CEO. He asks what's happening, and I tell him I believe we have been targeted with some sort of malware on those USB sticks.

Joe is dressed in jeans and a collared golf shirt, and he has an air about him of pure confidence. He starts following me to my desk and asks, "What's malware, and are you sure?"

I reply, "I'm not sure, I'm guessing right now, but we are under attack from other angles. Malware is basically software designed specifically to target and exploit someone's network. It could be designed to go after an industry, like financial services or something, but I think at this point that we're being specifically targeted for our intellectual property. It's different than a virus. A virus's main activity would be to replicate itself and spread, chewing up resources. "

We walk along towards my office and I add, "There's a fifty-fifty shot as well that I don't know what I'm talking about."

As I sit down, I wonder to myself why I can't let a conversation go without saying something stupid. I like this job and want to keep it. Why can't I get a better filter?

I put in the USB port and I hear Scott's flip-flops slap in. He says he has someone walking around the office to tell people not to use the USB ports. I look at the USB port and at the same time bring up a process monitor screen to watch what is occurring.

As the computer light fills my darkish closet, my heart is in my throat. I am actually hoping that it will be malware and that I am right. Otherwise, I look like an alarmist, or like I don't know what I'm doing.

Nothing is happening.

We sit there for a minute, and the CEO shuffles his feet and says, "Could this be a false alarm?"

I take a chance, my heart pounding, and say, "No. I think there will be something here."

Washington Dulles International Airport
Dulles, Virginia

The man is not nervous at all as he hands his paperwork to the customs officer; everything is in order, and he has done this many times before. Hans Tsugilva has a passport that says he is Andrew Buchanan. He is tall and walks with the confidence and air of a high-powered CEO. He adjusts his glasses as the customs officer asks if he is traveling for business or pleasure. He responds "business," saying that he is in sales. He takes his passport back without any more questions and slowly walks to baggage collection. He received the instructions and a down payment just last week, and preparation is everything in his line of work.

In a couple of days, he would be meeting with his right-hand man and childhood friend, Dima Benko, and a third person that they have worked with before. Hans and Dima grew up together on the mainland of Russia, and both had worked for years as part of discrete part of the KGB that was often called upon to do the dirtier work for the security agency.

Hans is extremely intelligent and thorough, and as things changed in Russia, he realized his talents could be used to make a lot of money and earn him considerably more freedom. Hans' reputation and skill have enabled him to have five houses, passports, identification, and money in seven countries. He works about two to three months a year, but he does it because he enjoys the work and the thrill. His reputation and abilities have soared. He also enjoys the time with Dima.

He will meet his partners in two days in Baltimore and start executing the plans he has worked on. He understands the engineering team may have people electronically trying to stop this small company, but his contract comes from higher up, and he will be working on a different angle.

He will head to his hotel and then to the warehouse that has been rented for him to make sure the weapons and other supplies are exactly what he ordered.

ART Headquarters

I can feel the sweat dripping down my back as people look at my screen. There is nothing happening. We wait and watch.

I hear David's voice calling out as he walks past and pokes his head in. "What's going on in here?"

Scott replies, "Robert believes there is malware on that USBs that were given away this morning."

Finally, one small process starts that is new, and the screen that lists the processes moves.

The process that has started immediately starts another three processes. One of these processes tries to establish a connection to the internet through a high port.

I explain to them, "The processes are started by creating a command-and-control channel. This will be used to communicate, if need be, with the outside servers or transfer our data out."

I jump to another screen and bring up the log file for the device I am working on. I also lean over and double-check that it is not connected to the network.

"One of the processes is copying everything from my computer and trying to get it through the command-and-control channel. Another process is looking for other computers to move to on different ports. If people have plugged this in to their computers, it will be all over our network by now."

All of a sudden, my syslog file is deleted, and a new one shows up with nothing in it from a copy that must have been taken when it first started working.

I say, "Did you guys see that? This program is very good—it slept for a while before it even started to make sure we didn't have anything to pick it up. Anyone mind if I shut down the firewalls and all external communication before we figure this one out?"

Joe says, "Please do."

I turn and see David's face, which is an interesting shade of red. I guess this doesn't look good for his career here, considering he was trying to have me canned a couple of weeks before.

I write down the name of the processes and give them to Scott. "We need to find out how many people have plugged these USB sticks in."

Everyone files out of my office, and I sit back and take a deep breath. Wow, what if I had been wrong? Everyone would have thought I was an idiot!

We are able to get the network guy to help, and together we end up deleting and killing the malware from about seventeen different desktops and five different servers. It was moving quickly throughout the company.

One of the problems we have is there is no way to just find the malware and delete it off every device. We have to take down the network and essentially have all computers taken off it. This had spread fast, but it will not be able to communicate out, as we shut down the internet immediately.

One bonehead had even brought the USB stick into Dev 2, but there is no internet access there, so we are okay. We're actually very lucky, because one server in Dev 2 is using the internet through someone's telephone, but the USB was not plugged into that computer. Developers will always find a way around restrictions.

Chapter 8

Wednesday, April 1
ART Headquarters

Joe calls an emergency board meeting, and amazingly, I am invited as the guest speaker.

It's eight in the morning, and I'm feeling like the man. I didn't go out the night before, even though there were good happy hours around town (earning me some brutal verbal attacks from my friends). I have two cups of coffee in me, and I figure I can deal with these board guys because I know what I am talking about.

I'm smart enough to know that the people who have invested in a company generally make up the board of directors for a startup. In ART's case, they are all people from venture firms; some of them seem to understand what we do, and some seem to have no clue. I guess that mimics life a little.

Joe introduces me to the board and says that I have stopped several attacks already. He goes on to say that it looks like the number of attacks are increasing. After that, he indicates that it would be good to let me answer any questions they may have.

The first question comes from a guy in a jacket, no tie, sitting in the back. His eyes show a combination of intelligence and impatience. He asks simply, "Robert, what is your view of what is going on?"

Where should I start, I think to myself. I should stand up to answer the question, but I instead I sit there. I'm not up front; I'm sitting in the guest chairs, and David is in the back of the room. I say, "We are under a cyberattack from someone who knows what they are doing. They will not stop until they get what they want, which I suspect is our intellectual property and all of the information that has to do with how we are working on our prototype."

I think I sound pretty intelligent, but who knows?

"Should we call the police or the FBI? Are they are better trained to deal with this? What's your background?"

I suddenly feel like it's getting hot in here. I reply, "Well, the FBI would be the one to call since we are under a cyberattack, potentially by foreign nationals working to steal our innovations. That would be a great idea."

I wait for a second. "If we did that, I don't think we would get the prototype done in time, though, because an investigation takes time and resources away from a company. As for my background, I am a recent college grad with some real-world computer security experience and a computer science degree. The FBI would be much more trained and experienced than I am, for sure."

How is that for being humble?

"Wait, wait, wait," a guy in a long-sleeved Under Armour shirt sitting in the front speaks up. "What do you mean when you say we won't get the prototype done in time and that an investigation would take time and resources away from us?"

I think he sees dollar signs swirling down the drain. I reply, "Well, the FBI would probably come in here with a team of people, do forensics on all our machines, figure out what exactly the code is doing, probably take some of them to their labs, and analyze everything. That's what I would do if I was them." I really do not know what I am talking about here, but that scenario seems reasonable to me.

Another guy from the front speaks up—balding, wearing a jacket, no tie—and says, "Robert, if you were in our shoes, what would you do?"

This is one I have to think about for a second. I stand up and walk over to the blackboard like I am going to write something down. I think I am starting to get a feel for this. It helps that I really don't care too much what these board people think, but I do like my stock options, which makes me behave.

"Well, if this was my company and we had a month and a half to prove that our innovation is the best, and once we did, we were going to market with our technology connected to a big company, and we were going to make a ton of money... well, the first thing I would do is spend a lot of money to protect the potential we have here. Because to do nothing risks everything."

I pause and look around the room.

"I would put a real security door in to protect our Dev 2 area. Build it, if you have to, with key badge access, only allowing people in on a need-to-know basis." I have heard "need-to-know" from watching movies. Government spy-type stuff.

"Next, I would do background checks on all new employees, and don't let any of them into Dev 2. The attack from yesterday was a new front; they were not going after us remotely anymore. Our attackers had to pay some guy to deliver that neat little package or do it themselves. I would choose a date back before this stuff got serious and not give anyone access that was hired after that date."

David pipes up. "Do you think we need all this?"

Really? Did he just say that? I think he just wanted to say something. Maybe I'm still not over that Ivy league thing, or maybe it's the fact that he always looks like he wants to kill me, but I simply do not like my boss.

"I haven't even finished describing what I would do yet," is the best attempt at a response I can muster. I try to be nice, but I can't keep an annoyed edge from my voice.

"I would back up everything from Dev 2, if we are not doing that already, and I would store it in a locked safe—not online anywhere. I would do a daily backup and lock it away at a safe spot other than here. I would keep that very confidential and allow very few people to know where it is."

I keep talking as I pace in front of the room. "I would invest in a security guard for the company and security cameras in Dev 2. That is just physical security. On the more important cyber security side, I would hire folks to do on-site security monitoring of our firewalls twenty-four seven. I would have them do some log collection and install intrusion prevention devices. I would then add some sort of malware protection product to the network and all endpoints."

Joe asks, "Given all this, what would you recommend starting today?"

A good question. I reply, "I would lock up Dev 2 and do a complete backup and get it off site and secure—today. And if I can add another action item, I would hire one or two real computer security geeks. Go after NSA or federal consultants, not ones that show up at our door. They need to be people that we approach."

The first questioner chimes in again with, "Why that approach?"

Hmm. I said this guy seemed smart. I reply, "If you were trying to steal someone's data, how would you get people on the inside? What would be better than to get someone on the inside with a computer security title?"

They thank me and then kick me out. David is kicked out, too, which makes me feel better. He does not say a word to me as he walks down the hallway, so I just head to my office.

Chapter 9

Friday, April 10
ART Headquarters

Friday. Weekend. Spring weather. Awesome. This weekend, I am going to catch up on some much-needed shut-eye and then maybe drink a few beers. I should plan on going see my brother, William, in prison.

My brother was a highfalutin finance guy when he first started his career. He and his friend got a little greedy, however. They broke a couple of rules and made some money at it. He is now in the big house, as we jokingly call it. It isn't so bad, though. It's minimum security, and he is actually lucky to be near his family.

The whole thing broke my parents' hearts. His wedding was cancelled, his arrest and conviction played out in the papers, and all that. Funny; William was always such a goody-goody, but I think he got caught up in something beyond his control and didn't really think about the implications. I don't ask him about it much. He has a couple years left on his sentence, but he could get out early based on good behavior

Actually, I will make visiting him a priority this weekend. I promise myself. This is what I am thinking about as I cruise into the office to start my Friday.

There are a handful of new people who have come on board to work with the final testing. I have been asked to give some of the orientation information about computer security and security in general. The board has even hired a security guard for the main entrance on my advice—pretty fast movement by the board. They also actually put a door on the Dev 2 area that you need a key badge to access. That's definitely something. They have a physical security company out adding all this stuff, and that makes me feel better. They're actually listening to me, or at least whoever else they are asking.

While I am giving the security orientation to the new hires this morning, a pretty boy named Josh starts to ask a lot of questions. He is dressed better than everyone in the room and looks like a Ken doll. His arrogance shows in the way he asks his questions, and he is sitting next to another dude who seems to be writing down my answers.

The other guy is small and wiry. Josh seems to have an understanding of computer security, but the way he is asking me questions sounds like he is asking questions just to be heard. By the time I walk out of there, I want to give him some parking-lot justice.

I get back to my desk and the security consultant, Jacob, is sitting there looking at logs. I am happy to have Jacob to work with, as he works hard and is always willing to share what he finds.

We have put in place some anomaly detection tools that are looking for any behavior that's different. He tells me that something is happening on the network: nothing he can see from the logs that said specifically we were under attack, but network bandwidth had spiked up over the norm.

I take a walk down to Scott's office. "Scott, are you guys doing anything different on the network today? "

Scott looks up. "Oh boy, here we go again."

"Nothing to be alarmed about yet. The new security consultant, Jacob, just saw some increase in bandwidth utilization."

"We're not doing anything, just trying to hold on until we get through the prototype. Check with Chet."

I walk through the halls, feeling important, and reach Chet's office.

"Chet, sorry to interrupt, but are you guys doing anything strange on the network today? We noticed a little higher activity."

"Hey! Are you guys doing anything on the network?" Chet screams.

All of a sudden, five guys lean out of their cubicles. A chorus of "Nothing here," "Nope," and "Not my guys" rings out.

Chet looks at me. "There is your answer. Let me know if it turns out to be something."

The fact that neither Scott's people nor Chet's people are doing anything out of the ordinary makes me pretty nervous. I run up to the top floor. I don't even swing by to see if Sarah is at her cube.

Jacob is typing away on the computer. I look at him nervously. "Anything?"

"Nope, just continuation of a little heavier traffic then we see normally."

I say to him, "A while back I had downloaded a free tool that basically looks at the network and network bandwidth between computers and tells you who is talking to whom. Do you think that will help?"

Jacob looks up. "Absolutely. I was just looking for something like that myself."

I fire it up and see that most of the traffic seems to be coming from one computer, with limited traffic from a second and a third.

The map on my screen looks like bicycle tires: there are three wheels, and the primary wheel has many more spokes. All the wheels are connected.

To me, it looks like the first wheel is the one where it started, and then it talked to the second and third wheels. I wish I could see a timeline of this map I'm looking at, but the software is not that good.

Jacob wrote down the three IP addresses that are the centers of the spokes and circles the one with the most spokes: 192.148.165.24. He says, "In the old days, we would just be able to look this up, but now we have to figure out who has the lease on this."

I grab the paper and start running back down to IT. People must be getting tired of seeing me running around the building. I know I am tired of doing it.

I see Scott walking in the hallway. I hand him the list of IP addresses and say we need to know whose computers or servers they are.

He walks to a cube, gives a young lady wearing a white t-shirt and jeans the list of IP addresses, and tells her to find who has the lease on them—and quickly. She grabs the list, and I try to make out what her t-shirt says before she turns to head down the hall. I manage to read it before she walks away: "Beer is proof God loves us and wants us to be happy." Nice. She looks like she is about eighteen, and her red hair is pulled back in a bun. We walk back to Scott's office and wait.

Three minutes later, she's back with two names I do not know, but the circled IP address belongs to Wendy McBride, the head of Marketing. I tell Scott he needs to get the other two devices off the network and that I am going to Wendy's office.

I had met Wendy about three weeks before when she stopped by to introduce herself. She's really nice. She's also a native Baltimorean who grew up in the Towson area, had gone out west to school, and then returned. She is definitely older than me, around forty, I think. She has two boys if I remember right; she's into sports, and it sounds like she runs around all weekend, every weekend. She has a laid-back style to her, which makes her easy to talk to. All of this now makes me bummed that I am going to have to confiscate her machine for a while.

I grab Jacob, and into Wendy's office we go. She is on the phone, so I write on her whiteboard that her computer is doing some strange things and I need to get it off the network and try to figure it out. She excuses herself from the phone. "What is happening?"

"Not sure. Your computer is generating a lot of traffic; it may be okay, but we think it has been compromised. We really have to get you off the network quickly."

When she stands up, she is a couple of inches taller than I am. I look at her high heels, which have added to her already considerable height. I sense an athleticism that makes me think she probably played some volleyball or basketball during her day. She moves out of the way to let me jump on her computer and mentions that her machine has been going a little slow.

I quickly turn off her wireless and start searching through the processes that run on her machine. The personal computers on our network are running a mixture of Windows and Mac operating systems, but luckily for me, this is a Mac.

I go into the Utility folder and pull up the Activity Monitor. Jacob starts writing notes and says, "Most of these I know: calendar, mail, and other ones that I have seen before, but check these out. Kill PIDs 201, 714, and 851."

I do what he says, and about a minute later they are all back:

PID	Process Name	User	% CPU	Threads	Real Mem
201	ZX	wmcbride	2%	7	101MB
714	9_____5P	wmcbride	5%	5	141MB
851	T	wmcbride	3%	3	8MB

Jacob loads some software from a USB stick to analyze the processes, and we see that ZX is actually started by 9_____5P. ZX is trying to open up a high port to talk to another computer outside of the internal network. I write down the IP address for that, but I feel it will not do me any good, because it's probably a service provider that has been hacked.

I tell Wendy that it is going to take a while to clean up her computer and ask if she has a recent backup. On the way out her door, I think of something else. "You didn't click on any links you were sent in the last day or two, did you?"

She laughs. "No—I went through that computer training and wouldn't do that, although early this morning I did book my hotel from the conference I'm going to at National Harbor next week."

I stop cold. "Can you show me?"

I hand her back her laptop, and she sits back down to her desk and brings up an email. It starts with your standard boilerplate reservation language: "Thank you for registering your hotel stay with us..." But at the bottom of the email, there is a link: "Please confirm your attendance and select the days you will be attending." I ask her if she clicked on the link, and she confirms that she did.

I ask, "Did anyone know that you were going to this conference?"

And I get the answer that I know I am going to get: "Yes, I posted it on Facebook and the company's LinkedIn page."

We go back and do some reverse lookups on the link that she has gone to and, sure enough, the website has already disappeared—we just get an error message. We look up the real conference link, and it is just a few characters off from the link she was given.

Jacob leans back in his chair and says to me, "Someone placed a very specific piece of malware, directed at Wendy's computer, to get in here. They were probably targeting all the execs or anyone in the company listed in LinkedIn."

I reply, "This was done by people who knew what they are doing. They created a fake registration site for her to go out and enter information on. They were also probably able to get a password that she likes to use at the same time as they were dropping malware onto her machine."

"Exactly, and the malware went slowly, so it would not be identified. It barely generated any traffic. We were lucky that the small increase in load tipped us off."

I feel like I am in over my head. "Once again, it's time to take down the company's access to the internet and go through all the devices on the network searching for infected devices."

After cleaning the mess up all day, I realize I have not eaten any lunch, and I am exhausted. I figure it's Friday afternoon, so why not see if Sarah wants to grab a beer. I go by her desk, but the pretty boy, Josh, and his sidekick are talking to her. Pretty boy is actually sitting on her side desk! I wave to her and smile and then just wander back to my desk.

Jacob is back there, looking through logs. I feel we were really lucky to get him; he knows what he is doing and is clearly smart and working hard. I have no idea what we are paying him by the hour, but he is worth it.

"Jacob, you need to take a break. What are you doing this weekend?"

"No plans. I would actually like to come in here, if that is okay, to a get a handle on some of these recent attacks."

"Yeah, absolutely. I may stop in myself. You've been going at it hard in here."

He smiles. "I have been doing computer security for a while now, and I have not learned as much in all that time as I have here in the last week. The security work that I do is more policy-based stuff generally, and when companies get hit like this I am part of a forensic team, with just small pieces to the puzzle. This is a great opportunity for me."

Sarah pokes her head into my storage room. "Did you need to talk to me? And when is the last time you combed that mop?"

Nice. Giving me crap. My hair is always unruly. I could comb it all day and it wouldn't matter. I am trying to remain cool, so I quickly introduce her to Jacob and then say, "I wanted to see if you felt like a Friday-night beer. There is a place about a block and a half away that's small but looks pretty good."

She takes a second to reply. "Sure. Just one, though. I have to get some stuff done tonight."

I try to be casual and look at Jacob. "Jacob, are you up for it?"

He smiles and defers. "No, I'm all good. I am going to stay here for a while, then head home to see my family."

"You have children?" I ask, surprised.

"Yes, three. Ten, eight, and three—boy, girl, girl."

I think I should have asked that before now, but it's too late for that. I answer him lamely, "I am sure they keep you busy. We'll catch you later!"

I walk with Sarah down to her desk, and she gets her bag to throw in the car. Then we wander down to the bar.

She ends up staying for a second beer, and I really enjoy talking to her. She is sweet, unassuming, funny, really cute, and gives me garbage every step of the way. She is the second of four sisters and really misses her family, and I get the impression she will not be here long if she can help it.

The beers taste good. The place is kind of neat: one long bar with about fifteen beers on tap. I can see myself coming back here.

While we are walking back to the office parking lot, she asks, "Is there anything fun to do in town?"

"Are you kidding me? this is Baltimore! We have the Orioles and the Ravens! We'll need to play hooky and go to a baseball game one day, or at least one at night."

She looks pleased and says, "That would be fun. Do you ever hit the museums or head into DC? Or do you just lay around your parents' house and watch Netflix and baseball?"

"Hey, I never said I lived with my parents! And besides, I'm moving into a new place soon. Have you ever been to Federal Hill?"

She starts laughing good-naturedly. "Really sounds exciting," she says as she slips into her car.

And that's it: no opportunity to ask her about weekend plans, no hug goodbye. She does give me a big grin and wave as she drives away, though. If I were smooth, I would have found out something else to do that weekend, and then I could have asked her to do it. But I, unfortunately, am not that smooth.

I notice there are still a bunch of cars in the parking lot. The real programmers are going at it pretty hard to make the deadlines.

I stop back in the office to hit the bathroom, and I see the pretty boy's friend walking down the hall.

I try to be nice and make conversation. "Hey, it's Friday night, what are you still doing here?"

"Just finishing up, you?"

"Same. Have a great weekend."

Finishing up what? You are one week into to it! What is his name...the pretty boy is named Josh, I remember that... his sidekick was much quieter. Trent? Roy? Troy! That's it. I remember now. What is he doing here when barely anyone besides programmers are still working, and him only one week into work? Oh well...I guess part of being a security guy is you begin to suspect everyone.

Josh was the one asking all those security questions. This guy just got stuck with him as a new hire.

Chapter 10

Saturday, April 11
Towson, Maryland

Well, I sleep in a little too much today. At ten in the morning, I finally manage to get out of bed. I didn't even go out last night, but it's been so crazy at work—maybe that is wearing on me. My parents are still home, and I talk to them while my mom fixes me some eggs and coffee. Say what you want—living at home ain't all bad.

I grew up in this three-bedroom, split-level house in a nice, working-class neighborhood with sidewalks and good people all around. My parents' neighbors do everything from teaching in the local public schools to working construction and landscaping and everything in between. They now have retired people on two sides of them, some new neighbors across the street, and some large additions going in a couple doors down.

No, there's not much wrong with hanging at my parent's house; I'm not sure I'm going to have it so good when I move in with my high school buddy George. Our move-in date is the first weekend of May, pretty close to when the prototype will be presented.

It seems like they are trying to finish up all the testing by the middle of May and then they'll schlep it out to Silicon

Valley for the prototype, or "bake-off," with our competitors. I want to get involved in the actual products more than I currently am. I like what they are building and am really interested to see the solar capture systems of other competing companies.

Oh, man. Once again, I'm thinking about work on a weekend. Am I that much a geek?

I go by to see my brother, William, in prison and hang with him for about an hour. I tell him what company I am with and what I am doing there, and he listens and asks good questions.

He seems like he's in good shape; he's always happy to see me, and I think he genuinely cares about what is going on in my life. Maybe he is just bored, but he really is a good guy. He looks the same, which is funny given everything he's been through. He has a calm, quiet, easy way about him that always attracted people to him. Not that I ever try to compare myself to him, but he is taller than me by about an inch, and his dark, neat hair looks very different from my mop of sandy brownish-blond hair. He has always done everything better than me, but at least I am not in the big house, so I have that going for me. He is always very good to me, and I wonder why I am always trying to compete with his accomplishments.

I would describe William as definitely a "glass half full" type of person. Always cheerful, always looking at the bright side of things. As he gives me a hug when I'm leaving, he says, "Make us proud, Robert; I know you will. Love you, man."

I respond, "Back at you," all the time thinking to myself that he must be all kinds of lonely and bored.

I text George on the way home from the prison and ask him if he wants to grab a beer later so we can talk about our apartment in Federal Hill. I suggest the place I went to yesterday with Sarah because I want to stop by work first and just take a look around.

It's hard being under attack and not having a twenty-four seven staff to watch over things.

One thing I manage to do, though, is to have them power down unneeded servers on the weekends. There are some software jobs that they need to compile over the weekend, but other than that we shut everything down. Most of Dev 2 will be inactive, with only a handful of computers on. Plus, there's the additional security measure of it being under key badge. I walk up, use my key badge to get into the office, and go back to my office, which I just can't stop referring to as a storage room.

Jacob is not there. He must be playing Soccer Dad today or something. I told George I would meet him at three, so I have about an hour. I fire up my intrusion detection monitor and do not see any new events. I go to our network tool and see the utilized bandwidth is normal for the weekend. Next to nothing. Had our boys given up?

I wander around the office, say hey to two guys that are back in Development and John, who is testing all the new code. He says things are looking good. I do not have access to the Dev 2 area, because I insisted that only people that need to work on the source code should be allowed in. Kudos to them for sticking to that. The developers would not like it if I had access, anyway. I am not one of them yet, and they can get proprietary. There is a little window that I look in, and all is dark...looks like all the servers and all the monitors are off. Good to be a small company, where you can tell everyone to actually turn stuff off and see that they do.

Back upstairs I run into the CEO walking down the hallway. He is wearing a t-shirt, shorts, and a baseball cap, and it looks like he has come from a gym.

He looks surprised to see me and says, "Robert! Nothing scary going on, is there?"

"No, but I just wanted to check. It's nice having most of the servers down, and I appreciate everyone's focus on security."

He asks, "What do you think this is all about?"

Does he care what I think? I reply, "I think about all of the stuff you said in the all-hands meeting: the competitive nature of this upcoming prototype, that the winner of this will do extremely well, and all that. It's not hard to see our competitors are coming after us to destroy our stuff or steal our designs. They are playing hardball to win, and they are trying everything. It's funny; I've never even asked who our competitors actually are."

"Well, there are a handful, but there is one that is a true competitor: a company called Hodophi out of China. It seems that the two of us are further along than everyone else. We are the only two being asked to come in to do the prototype."

We are silent for a second, and then he continues with a thoughtful look on his face. "A third company will be invited to participate if we cannot do what we say we can do. They went through a paper evaluation to start, which a lot of companies participated in, but I think it's really down to us and Hodophi. We have some unique technology that is really cutting edge, but Hodophi is much bigger than us."

I reply, "Well, I either think they are scared of you doing better than them, or they are missing a key ingredient."

Joe turns and starts to walk away. "That is tough to argue. Have a great rest of the weekend."

Hmm, Hodophi. I wonder if I should target them? I would love to, but my parents may go over the edge if they have both boys in the big house.

I'm fifteen minutes late to meet George at my new favorite bar. Bless him; he has a beer waiting for me, a nice IPA of some sort. He also has his standard barrage of expletives and name-calling ready for me.

George was a decent athlete back in the day and is extremely intelligent. He is in incredible shape, but you would describe him as "big boned." His shoulders are about twice as wide as mine, and he is solid muscle, even though I have never seen him lift a single weight.

When we were growing up and throughout high school, he was always better than most people in everything, but he was and still is very low-key. He ended up joining the army after high school in an ROTC program at the University of Delaware because he could not afford college, and he served some time overseas. He then moved into Special Forces and went back overseas multiple times, never telling us where he was going.

He is now working full-time and had started working on his master's degree at night, but I think he has paused that, at least for now. He still has time to go out about every night of the week. He likes to have fun but is always able to deal with work the next day. Right now, he is working at a company that contracts part-time IT consultants to other companies that need the extra help.

After we talk about our new place, move-in plans, and all that, I tell him what I have been up to. I detail the attacks on the company, what I hear we are competing for, and how aggressive the computer attacks are.

At the end of it, he shakes his head, "You are as dumb as you look; while the company was lucky, and I mean very lucky, that they hired your lame butt and that you were able to catch someone sneaking around your networks, you are missing the big picture."

"And what would that be, you boneheaded gorilla?"

"If you were trying to get some data, really, really badly... what would you do? Yes, you would do everything that you have already caught them doing, but if that did not work, what would you do?"

I sit for a second, then hesitantly say, "Get someone of my own on the inside."

"Exactly—especially once they realized that you were on to them, and that things were changing on the inside...and that their channels were no longer sending them data."

"I told the board the exact same thing and that we should be nervous of new employees, and we tightened physical security."

"Yes, but there are many ways to get someone on the inside... a bribe, a threat, or blackmail. Soviets used to be great at that; they would hang out at bars known to be CIA hangouts and find people to bribe or get dirt on people to blackmail them with."

He takes a mouthful of beer and swishes it around like he is drinking fine wine. Then he continues, "You said they are good at what they do as far as stealing data, and don't you think they hit all your employees at home by now? Blackmail or bribes are probably better than getting someone hired, because the new person would not have great access. You have to think about this from the attacker's point of view."

Now there is a pit in my stomach, and George has just ruined my beer. I see it now: the other company wins using our technology, and the default security guy is to blame. Maybe someone I know is already selling them or giving them what they need.

I need to think about this more. Not much I can do right now, though, so I'll just have another beer.

Sinh Lee's Estate
Shichahai, Beijing

Khan Lee wakes with a start. His head is pounding. Sinh's wife is out of town again with the kids; this is becoming a weekly event. Maybe the stress on Sinh is causing problems at home? As Khan lays there, he tries to remember what happened last night. He was in a couple of clubs...the last thing he remembers is doing shots with his brother and a number of folks. He cannot remember going back to the limousine, which is strange for him, as he rarely blacks out.

Khan keeps trying to remember what happened and drifts back to sleep. He wakes up when his brother walks into the guest room. Sinh, who never seemed to get hungover, says, "Do you remember what happened last night?"

Khan replies, "Not after we were down by the Houhai bars. You?"

Sinh says, "Same. I wish we hadn't done the late-night shots, but that is how I always feel. Did we ever talk about the prototype?"

Khan says, "We planned on it. If we did, I hope we did not say too much, but I think we were having too much fun."

Sinh asks, "Any updates?"

"Is this room safe?"

Sinh replies, "I have the same audio jammers used in the main room surrounding the entire house, and I also added soundproof glass about two years ago."

Khan sits up. "I didn't know you did that. Can you get me some painkillers and a scotch?"

Sinh laughs. "Sure. The things I do for you." He shakes his head. "Be right back."

Khan lays there and is thinking about what he had talked to Hans about when his brother comes in and hands him a glass of scotch and water and two small pills. Sinh also has a glass and says, "This should take care of any hangover. Cheers."

Khan takes his pills with a hard swallow and says, "I talked to Hans on Wednesday over our encrypted phones. He has two guys on the inside and a third that we potentially can use if they get as far as the prototype. I think we have all the information out of their networks that we can get; unfortunately, what we need must have been programmed in early, and we only have the compiled code, which is virtually worthless."

Sinh nods and waits.

Khan continues, "The very positive news is we believe we are able win the deal right now because we have cut our heat losses considerably. We are not where we want to be, and we don't specifically meet Zamtech's requirements yet, but they need to go with someone, so unless ART can match the requirements, we will win. We have inside information that Zamtech needs to make a decision or lose valuable time trying to build themselves what we have already done."

Khan takes another sip of his scotch and looks at his brother, who intimidates everyone else in the world except for him, and says, "This reduces our problem set considerably, as we no longer need their information. It would be great if we get it, and we are still working heavily on this angle, but we know the number one priority is making sure their prototype fails."

Sinh nods again and paces the room, thinking. This time, Khan waits for Sinh to make a comment.

Sinh finally says, "The two people on the inside of ART, is there any other way that they can help us?"

Khan replies, "No, we have everything we need from the company networks. The third person may be critical if we have to sabotage their prototype, but the other two are low-level. I spoke with Hans about cleaning up any loose ends, and he says that process has already been started."

Chapter 11

Monday, April 13
ART Headquarters

I thought that I would end up at work on Sunday, but I decide not to go in, which is good. I want to clear my head a little. I get up late, do my churching with my parents, eat a big breakfast, take a nap—you get the picture. I am thinking about my lazy day when I pull into the office.

What is going on here? There are police cars, an ambulance, and people standing outside and crowding the parking lot.

I park as far away as I possibly can and try to walk up as nonchalantly as possible. I see my buddy John standing a little away from everyone having a cigarette, so I walk up to where he is standing.

"What is going on?"

"A dude killed himself in our offices, I guess?"

"Seriously? What the heck?!" I now notice police tape at the entrance of the building and police standing around right inside the tape.

"Yeah, a new guy; Brandon in Development came in around six and saw him, and then he called the cops."

"Oh my god. Who was it?"

John throws his cigarette on the ground. "Don't know him. Joshua something?"

It irks me when people throw their cigarette butts on the ground. Have you ever had to clean that up? Brooms don't pick them up. You literally have to bend down and pick them up by hand. If these guys ever had a job where they had to clean up something like a parking lot or building, which I have had, they wouldn't toss their butts. What's wrong with people?

Amazing how my mind switches like that. Wait. Joshua. Josh? The pretty boy asking security questions? He's the one who killed himself? What the heck is going on?!

This day turns out to be a total wash. We do not get back into our offices until around three, and then everyone is just standing around talking to each other. I am pretty much a professional at standing around and doing nothing, but I have that sinking feeling again in my stomach. Something bad is going on here.

For starters, Josh was found in the Dev 2 area. He had no access there, but the police are not answering questions as to why he might have been in that area. Everyone is saying that it was a suicide, that he must have come by the office last night with the intent of killing himself and shot himself in the head in Dev 2. They found a note and everything.

The police still have our Dev 2 area blocked off when the CEO calls a meeting at four. Sarah is sitting up to the left, and I gave her a "Hey" as I walk in. She smiles, so at least I have that going for me. I sit in the back of the meeting, as I am a back-of-the-class type of guy. There is light chatter in the room as the CEO came in.

"I am sure everyone has heard about what has occurred within our ART family. We are saddened and distressed about the loss of this promising young life..."

My mind, of course, phases out after the first minute of the talk, but I learn some things. Josh was a Baltimore native, new to ART but in Dev 2 and did not have access. Joe says that someone probably accidentally left the door ajar. I do not believe that, so

I'm not sure what is going on. The police say he did not have key badge access. I'm thinking he stole someone's key badge, and my mind is racing now:

Is he the insider?

If so, why would he kill himself before he was paid?

How did he get in? Had anyone contacted the security group for our physical security to find out who accessed the room last?

Did we ever hook up the security cameras (as I had recommended)?

Did he really kill himself?

This is all crazy. It seems way, way too suspicious to be coincidental. How much money is this crap that we are building worth?

Joe finishes up saying that Josh's family is in our prayers and that if anyone wanted to talk to come by his office. He lets us know that they are going to give everyone information as they get it. He also suggests everyone shut down systems and go home. He looks like someone has punched him in the face.

When he leaves, I brush off conversations and walk straight to his office. The CTO is in there with him. What George had said is pounding in my mind.

"You guys don't think this is unconnected, do you?"

Joe looks up, his expression showing annoyance that I just barged into his office. He has been CEO of large companies before, where that would probably be unheard of, but then his face softens. "I'm not sure. What do you think?"

"Absolutely, it's connected! Dude was either an insider and working with someone else or doing it alone. My biggest question is why he would then kill himself? Or did someone set it up to look like that? I also don't buy the fact that the Dev 2 door was left open. He got in somehow; either he stole a key badge or someone let him in. Have you talked to the security company about the last access badge used?"

Ashok jumps in and speaks softly, "The police are looking into all that right now."

"When will we hear back on that? Why can't we call them? Who set up that contract?"

Joe breaks in, "I set it up with them, and they are a local company."

I am actually getting annoyed with these guys, even though they're at the top of the company food chain, and it probably shows. "Joe, you need to call them. We need to understand if data was taken before he killed himself; we probably need to assume it was. Ashok, is everything in Dev 2 what our competitors would need to steal everything? Do they have enough time before the bake-off to use it effectively? Do we have backups, and can we compare it to see if they changed or corrupted data?"

Finally, I see some anger and fire in their eyes. Ashok grabs his cell and calls Chet, and Joe goes to his desk and starts looking for the security company's phone number.

Chet is in the office one minute later. Yes, the backup was done and driven to another third-party site. Full backups were done on Saturday morning, and partial backups were done on Sunday morning, so at least there is that.

Ashok is now pounding Chet with questions, which is great. He looks fired up. Only the board and the folks in the room when I presented know that we are running backups and moving them off site.

Joe jumps back into the conversation after giving a bunch of passwords to the folks on the phone. The security company tells Joe that Frank Moskowitz was the last person to access the room on Sunday night at seven.

Chet calls Frank while explaining to me that he is new on the Development team and that Chet knows Frank from his previous company. My mind is racing. Was Frank blackmailed? Is he in on this?

Frank is in the office two minutes later with a blank stare on his face and looking like someone ate his Cheerios. "No, I did not come in this weekend. No, I did not lend my key badge to anyone."

Chet asks, "Where is your key badge?"

"I keep it locked in my desk drawer."

I break in, my temper rising. "You really leave it here in a desk drawer with all that we have been talking about security? While you know that we are under attack?"

Frank replies, "But I thought all the attacks are through the network."

"But we just put in all the physical security, too, so don't you think we were worried about that?"

Chet interrupts. "Please show us where your key badge is."

Frank walks us back to the desk, and to my astonishment, he opens his overhead bookshelf, pulls a key out of a coffee mug, opens his filing cabinet drawer, and pulls out his key badge.

I tell him he ought to put it down on the desk and not to touch the area. If he is not responsible for opening Dev 2, then the police may want to fingerprint his area. I am thinking that if he is not involved, then someone put the key badge back. And obviously it wasn't Josh.

Most of the folks are gone, and Joe calls the investigators, who are still in the building, to tell them what Frank said. I am sure they are going to want to talk to him, but my gut feeling is that he is too stupid to be an insider trying to steal information.

A minute later a tall, serious-looking guy comes in, and Joe says, "This is Detective John McGrath," and starts to explain what we just found out. I looked at Detective McGrath, who has a stern face and a military-cropped haircut. He is not happy.

Detective McGrath just nods through most of Joe's background, and then he says he will need to talk to Frank and look at his area and his key badge. It makes me laugh that Joe actually asks the police to start watching our building and some key employees for us.

Detective McGrath says, "You guys just had an apparent suicide, but it is not confirmed. We don't know if it will be an active crime scene. There are a lot of other murders in this city, and unfortunately, we do not have the manpower to watch an office building. Would you walk me to this Frank guy?"

Joe looks annoyed and walks Detective McGrath out of the office. Ashok and I just stand there looking at each other. I ask him if he wants to walk down and grab a beer in about thirty minutes. I don't think he's going to say yes, but he does. Bummer—I was hoping he'd say no so I could ask Sarah, but a beer is a beer and this dude will probably be interesting. Good to know the CTO anyway, since I am in technology.

We get to the bar, and there is just one old guy sitting at a table in the back. Not too surprising that it's so empty; it is before five on a Monday.

I start asking Ashok questions, and he is really interesting. He was born in India but has been in the United States since he was nine. He went to school at Stanford and, to my surprise, follows college and pro sports. We talk about the NCAA basketball run Stanford had, and we talk about college and pro football.

His degree is in electrical engineering, and he is pretty passionate about the company and our particular function. He is really, really excited about the overall solar project that we are a part of and believes this will bring a change as big and influential as the internet or cell phones.

He wipes his glasses and looks thoughtfully at me. "Tiny solar panels that have the ability to get sufficient sun even on cloudy days will change the world, all for the better. Think about it: everything we require energy for can be powered by the sun.

The biggest problems are storing the energy and transporting the energy, and ART is working on the solution for transporting the energy. Zamtech already has the technology for capturing it."

I am thinking about another round, which I order before I say, "How do the solar panels work on cloudy days?"

"It's really cool. We will have to bring you out during the prototype; in fact, we'll probably need to for this security mess. Instead of being a one-dimensional collector, the panels have a series of mirrors. The actual collectors do not sit on boards, they are just strung through the air, which allows the limited light to actually bounce around inside this maze of mathematically spaced collectors to gain optimal energy. It's such cool stuff."

He takes a big swallow as he continues to get fired up about the project. "Then the problem becomes you catch too much energy on any day with real sun, so you need to transport it out as quickly as it comes in. We break it into parallel communication paths immediately when we get it and use magnetic fields at different powers to keep the energy moving quickly through our channels, and then we use software to load balance the entire process."

I look at him and ask, "What do you think the folks targeting us are looking for?"

"It could be any of it, but the complex part is using magnetism with different wavelengths based on the mathematical optimization techniques to ensure nothing overheats. We combine it with load-balancing techniques that are often used in computers; when any of the parallel lines go over a threshold of heat or energy, we automatically move it to another track."

He goes on, "The really neat thing is if we are locked out of an entire track to send energy down based on too much heat, we can spin up an entire new track. This uses cloud computing techniques, where basically cloud computing companies use elasticity to spin up new computers virtually. We are doing the same thing with actual hardware communications channels... it's revolutionary, and it all works. We are just finalizing and fixing some bugs in software."

I look at him in awe. "Wow, so could the other companies be missing potentially more than one part?"

He finishes his second beer before answering. "I would like to think that. It's all very complex, but all these companies have smart engineers as well, and we all have been heads down on this problem for a while. We got lucky figuring some things out that others may not have yet."

We decide to call it an evening after two beers. It has been a strange day, and we are both driving, so we don't want to get too buzzed. I like Ashok. He's a little older than me, but he's a regular guy in many ways, even though he is off-the-charts smart and really believes in what he is doing. I wish I had passion like that about something.

Chapter 12

Tuesday, April 14
ART Headquarters

I am in the office by seven thirty. I walk by Dev 2 and there is police tape on the door. It sure makes it hard for our guys working on code when they cannot get into the area where their code is. I walk by Sarah's cube, and see she is not in yet, so I have another cup of coffee and start looking through our security systems.

There is nothing really going on that I can see. I want to look through the logs and the network monitors in Dev 2, but I don't think I can with police walking in and out. I do have a list of servers that I have to build, but I really don't feel like doing that with all the action going on lately. It seems strange going back into my storage room and doing regular work.

The good news is when I bring up the servers, they are not being scanned. We have made it hard for hackers to get in, but I have no doubt that the people we are working against are too motivated to stop. They are obviously also very talented, given what they have done lately. Rats! I would love to start probing some of those companies myself.

Time goes by slowly because I am unpacking servers, installing the Red Hat operating system on them, and then testing them. Boring. I uninstall all applications that we don't need to reduce our attack service, giving hackers fewer applications to hack into. I am thinking more about Josh; what was going on with him, and why would he kill himself in Dev 2?

I take a walk and, as usual, bring some papers to make it look like I have something going on. Walking papers places is also a good excuse to walk by Sarah's cube. She is in, so I start with my best line: "Hey."

This gets a big smile from her. She looks dressy without being dressy, as always. She has on a pink long-sleeved shirt and a skirt. She responds, "Hey, how are you doing?"

I sit down on her guest chair, trying to be smooth, and say, "Okay, you?"

"Same. Just...this is all really weird. Josh seemed nice. He didn't seem like anything was bothering him. He was just really curious and excited to be working here...but I guess you never know."

I never liked that guy, myself, and thought he was a cocky pretty boy. I don't say that, though.

"What are you doing for lunch? Feel like walking to the bar and seeing if their burgers are any good?"

"I would like to, but I made a sandwich, and I have a lot of work to catch up on."

I laugh. "Come on, we can be quick. And the reason God made fridges is so you can save the sandwich."

She smiles and glances at her screen. She responds slowly while thinking, "Okay, but let me get done with this first. Meet you downstairs at twelve thirty?"

"Done."

Did I tell you I am smooth? As I am walking down the hall, I wonder why I had to meet her downstairs? Maybe I'm not so smooth after all if she doesn't want to be seen hanging with me.

Time crawls until twelve thirty. Jacob is banging away on his keyboard. He has done assessments of every device and is constantly updating patches to fix security problems. He is also constantly monitoring firewall logs and intrusion detection alerts. We could use seven more of him to keep this up twenty-four seven.

Twelve thirty finally comes, and I decide I'll show Sarah by waiting outside instead of downstairs. It is a perfect spring day: a little cool with white clouds sporadically breaking up a light-blue sky.

There is a baseball game today; the Orioles are playing the Blue Jays. About a month ago, I would have tried to talk Sarah into guzzling some beers and jumping on the light rail to the stadium. The problem is the new me is worried about whoever is trying to steal our company's invention.

At the bar, it is very easy to talk to Sarah, and I continuously fight myself not to get head over heels too quickly. I love the fact that she has a bacon cheeseburger and throws some jalapenos on it. I let her know that I should have been trying to talk her into throwing down some beers and playing hooky for some day baseball. I also tell her that I don't believe Josh killed himself because he loved himself too much to do that.

All is great until I try to pay the bill. I tell her she can take the next one. My credit card is rejected, however—which is unexpected—so I pull out my AMEX. Also rejected. How stupid do I look? I want to tell the bartender I'm a regular and this is a load of garbage, but Sarah ends up paying with cash.

We head back to work. Now I have to call my stinking credit card companies on top of everything else. I buy so much stuff online that someone probably stole them. What a hassle. When I start calling the customer service lines, though, I find out I have bigger problems. This isn't just my credit cards. All my bank accounts are closed, too. I end up having to go to my main bank to talk to people for the rest of the afternoon.

At the bank I found that apparently "I" had set up another account and tried to transfer all my money into it. I had also run up bills on all my credit cards. Crazy. The entire rest of my day is wasted. My personal email has also been compromised, as someone had actually changed the password to my account.

As I go to sleep that night, I can't help thinking that my credit cards and banking problems are related to what is happening at work. I am going to have to spend considerable time over the next several days getting my life back in order. Identity theft is no small thing, I think to myself as I drift off to sleep.

I wake with a start and hear someone yelling over a loudspeaker. Red and blue lights flash against my wall. What are they yelling over the speaker?

"You have one minute to drop your weapons and come out with your hands up. The house is surrounded."

I hear my mom calling and running down the hallway. "Robert! Robert, what is going on?"

"Mom, stay calm. I don't know, but we need to do as they say." I see her in the hallway, her white nightgown flowing and her face panicked. My dad is following her in his white t-shirt and boxer shorts and the same look on his face. They may have just aged another three years.

The loudspeaker breaks through my thoughts as I looked at the time on my iPhone: 11:27 p.m. "I repeat: drop your weapons and come out with your hands up. The house is surrounded."

"Please Mom, Dad, this is a mistake, but we need to walk out now like they say."

My dad says, "Are you okay? I'm going to grab some shorts."

"Dad, no. We need to go out now, or this is going to get worse."

He shakes his head as he walks to his room. "The hell if I'm going out there dressed like this. Linda, do you need anything?"

"Can you get me my slippers?"

I say, "Please, let's just walk out, they're going to be coming through the windows any minute."

After the all-important shorts and slippers are found and we gather in the foyer, I push open the door wearing my boxers and a t-shirt. There are spotlights in my eyes, and I can't see anything as I lead my parents out. I shiver—whether because of nerves or the cool breeze that runs through my shirt, I can't tell.

"Raise your hands higher and keep walking slowly down the driveway."

As we walk forward, I realize exactly what is happening.

The officer on the loudspeaker yells again; I note that he's standing next to a sharpshooter. "Is there anyone else in the house?"

My dad responds quicker than I can think in a clear, concise voice: "Not that we know of, but we don't know why you are here. We were all sleeping. What is going on?"

A second later, black-uniformed officers move through the night and enter the house. I hear the back door splinter.

We are moved behind a big white van and frisked with guns trained on us.

I say loudly to a guy who looks like he may be in charge, "This is the work of hackers. It's called being swatted. Someone probably hacked in to your computer system and sent you a fake armed hostage situation—or worse."

A look of puzzlement hits his wrinkled face as he starts getting reports from his team that the house is clear.

Chapter 13

Thursday, April 16
ART Headquarters

I pull into the parking lot of ART at 6:25 a.m. thinking about how much of a geek I am becoming. The days are getting longer, but the pounding of rain on the roof woke me up at five, and I could not get back to sleep. I don't even know if the Orioles won yesterday. I also hadn't slept at all on Tuesday night after we were swatted. The police did not leave until three in the morning, leaving us only with lame promises to fix our back door.

As I pull into the parking lot, I see two regular police cars and what looks like a third unmarked car next to our CEO and CTO's cars.

I probably won't barge into our CEO's office again, but since we are the only people in the office, I poke my head in quietly. Ashok is in there, too. "What's happening?"

Joe looks flustered. "The police are treating this as a crime scene, because they no longer believe the suicide note. They think Josh's death was a homicide."

Ashok turns away from the large bay window where he seems to be watching the rain and says, "The door to Dev 2 was only open for five-second intervals; it was never propped open, which means Josh could not have returned the key badge to Frank's drawer. They are up in Dev 2 now fingerprinting everything."

I look at Ashok. "If you consider all the data from Dev 2 stolen, do they have everything of ours?"

Ashok thinks for a while. "I would have to talk to Chet. We kept most of the source code in there, but I did some early development that would not be there—I guess you could call it some of the secret sauce."

I ask, "What does the secret sauce do?"

"The early development had many of the load-balancing algorithms that we have not needed to change. Most load-balancing techniques would use a finite series of channels that they are load balancing. Basically, if Channel 1 is being used, use another channel in the series."

He continues, "We can spin up thousands of channels that are lateral to each other and put them in what we are calling 'energy tubes' to dissipate the heat. We don't fill any of them, but they continuously spin up in a matrix. The algorithms that do that were written into the code during the early days, compiled into subroutines at my house on old computers, and have always just worked. We have not needed to do anything with them since we've been here. Dev 2 just has the subroutines."

I look at Joe and say, "We may still have a chance, then. They may be missing one piece. Not only that, they need time to put together all that stolen data and build and test it."

Joe looks at Ashok. "Are we done with everything? I know it's not perfect or where it should be from your standpoint to win this thing, but can we start building the prototype somewhere else, where no one can see what we are doing?"

Thinking about what my buddy George has said about an insider getting paid or blackmailed, I jump in. "Listen, I have not told you this yet, but my parents and I were swatted on Tuesday night, which means hackers called in an armed hostage situation on my parents and me. That happened the same day as all my bank accounts and credit cards were closed. I have not been able to do any work this week because of these distractions. Not to mention what happened to Josh. These guys are playing hardball." I paused, thinking. "Let's do something a little different. Only a handful of people should know about it. Let's build a backup prototype that everyone knows about, but build a third prototype that maybe just the three of us know about and use code from about a month ago so we know it's not altered."

It's clear from the looks on their faces that this is a good plan.

Ashok and Joe then barrage me with questions about getting swatted, but they agree in theory to my proposal. I make plans to meet Ashok the next morning to move all of the original code from his house. I'm feeling like a champion, and I haven't even had a cup of coffee or gone for my morning bathroom break yet.

Friday, April 17
ART Headquarters

This morning, I have chatted with Sarah multiple times over Slack, asking her how she is doing and trying to make her laugh.

I also stop by her cubicle once to see if she wants to sneak out for happy hour at my favorite bar around five, and I tell her that I want to introduce her to my bud George. She says she's in, and I text George, who is always up for a beer.

It's crazy—two months into my career and I'm spending all my time thinking about coworker and my job. I hope George doesn't scare Sarah away.

At ten, we all head to a company meeting that Joe has called. The place is abuzz with people walking the halls and talking to each other. I can't imagine much work has been getting done this morning. When we all assemble and Joe walks into the room, the place goes dead quiet. The room is hot. There are probably forty people in here, and it was only made for twenty-five.

Joe stands there for a second without saying anything. Ashok is next to him. "We are all very sorry for what has happened here this week. I am not sure if you know, but funeral services for Josh will be tomorrow morning at ten. We will be getting the details out in a separate email for anyone who knew Josh and would like to go."

I wonder if there a traitor in the room or if Josh was in it by himself, allowing an external person to walk in with him and giving that guy data downloaded from those servers. Leaving Josh's body in Dev 2 was probably intentional as well to stop us from accessing our code base while the police investigated.

My attention cuts back to Joe. "Also, as you have probably heard and figured out, the police suspect that this is not a suicide, as was first thought. Please be careful; do not come into the office alone, and do not come in at night unless you call our security company to come in with you. And always bring a coworker. Do not leave your key badge anywhere, give it to anyone, or let anyone else in anywhere or at any time.

"We have known for a while that we are under attack, but the attacks had been contained to the networks. Now things have changed. I mentioned before that this contract is an industry game-changer, netting not millions of dollars, but potentially billions of dollars for the winning team. People will do a lot of different things for that kind of money, and they will also hire people that will do anything for that kind of money."

He pauses and looks around the room. "Zamtech's stock and size could easily triple the industry giants of today, and we could be a core piece of their technology. Ashok, can you say a few words about where we are on the technology side?"

"Yes, thanks Joe. I also would like to say that I am sorry for the tragedy here this week. I did not know Joshua, but he was part of our family, and I am sorry for those of you who did know him.

"On the technology side, as many of you know, we are very close to where we want to be for the prototype. We have the technology; now it's a matter of putting it together. I would like another month to figure out all bugs, but we have been slowed down.

"We will spend time now documenting all known bugs and how we are going to fix them rather than actually fixing them now and doing another release. We will not hide anything from Zamtech; that is not who we are."

Ashok paces the front of the packed room. He is dressed like a banker today, with nice slacks and a button-down shirt and jacket minus the tie. He continues, "We are looking at renting some office space in the San Jose area, starting in May, to stage our prototype. There will be a number of members asked to go to that office, while the rest will work on documentation and fixing the bugs for a later release."

He pauses like he is waiting for questions, then starts again. "We are going to do a code freeze today and then start working on the next release, which will not be released until after the bake-off in Palo Alto. I thank everyone for your continued hard work. We are onto something huge here that not only can change the face of industry and start a new one but also can change the environment and everything about the way we use energy today."

Joe steps back up. "The date of the bake-off has been set for the Tuesday after Memorial Day. I'm sorry that some of us will have to miss that weekend with our families, but it is what it is. We will make it up to you. We plan on shipping all materials needed for the prototype early in May. I would like everyone to be diligent about their duties and the security of what we are doing. Again, I am sorry at the loss of Josh, and I will see many of you tomorrow at the funeral."

Happy hour with Sarah and George is fun, but they seem to bond by making fun of me. It is short, though. I'm not sure why, but Sarah is going to the funeral the next day, and I end up bailing on going out to bars in Fells Point with George because I'm exhausted.

Chapter 14

Saturday, April 18
Towson, Maryland

I meet Ashok at his townhouse early Saturday morning. Ashok is going to the funeral and is already in a suit. I decide to bag the man's funeral because I did not know him well or like him much. I have asked Ashok if I can take any computers that he had used in the early days, when he was working on the algorithms by himself, and move them to a safe place. Ashok feels I am being paranoid but has finally agreed.

Downtown Towson is a nice little town with many bars, restaurants, and more bars. It is close to the university. His town-house is in the middle of a stretch of townhouses, and we walk out on the back deck, which overlooks a wooded area. We drink coffee and talk about baseball.

He lives by himself, and it shows. There are no decorations in the house and only a scattering of unmatched furniture. There is one big recliner close to a flat-screen TV in his living room. He takes me down to his basement, which is loaded with computers, computer parts, old stereos, and tons of electronics parts lying around.

"I love what you've done with the place."

Ashok looks up, a little surprised. He probably isn't used to anyone giving him garbage, but then he laughs. "Thank you, it took a lot of planning."

"Will you show me the computers where the source code is for the heat dissipation algorithms?"

"Most of the work was on these two computers: one for coding and one for compiling and testing."

I look over and see two large computers outside of most of the mess in the room. We walk over to them, and he asks me what I want to do.

"I would like to grab the hard drives and any backup and drop them at a friend's house or, if you feel better about it, lock them up in a safe deposit box."

"Really? Are you that paranoid?"

"Absolutely I am. You are about to go to a funeral for a guy involved somehow in this stuff. They may have used him and then decided they did not need him anymore, or whatever."

He frowns and shuffles his feet, looking at the ground as though he is responsible for Josh. "Okay. I don't think we need to open a safe deposit box, but it's your call."

I think for a second. "I'll decide later."

He picks up a screwdriver and pops out the hard drives, then puts them in a small purple bag that must have been from a trade show. He looks me in the eyes like he is going to say something, but then he walks around a big desk to a drawer and pulls out a backup drive and places it carefully in the bag. Then he hands the bag to me.

He takes a deep breath and finally speaks. "Please don't lose this. I may be able to recreate it, but this is a lot of the original IP behind the company."

I say, "And more importantly, it's probably the only thing that your primary competitor does not have. If they replicate this, they will win the prototype with more bells and whistles created by people with a lot more money, and we will all have wasted our time."

I leave his townhouse and think about what to do with the bag. Putting it in a safe deposit box would be the smart thing to do, but that takes money and time, and I need to do some things quickly.

I call George on his cell and take a barrage of curse words for waking him up on a Saturday morning. Then I swing by his parent's house with my bag. His mom gives me a big hug and brings me in for some breakfast.

When George finally emerges, he looks and smells like garbage. After breakfast, we walk out into the backyard and I give him the bag, saying that there are some serious people after these hard drives and he needs to do me a huge favor and hide them—not at his house, but somewhere else that they will be safe.

I also tell him not to tell anyone about the drives. I think he understands this better after I give him an update on what's happening.

I roll out of George's parents' house and over to the office. There are no cars in the parking lot. I've found out from Sarah that Josh's buddy's full name was Troy Beale. He's the squirrely looking dude that followed Josh around like a puppy dog. I first go to his cube and check in and around it. He has two servers under his desk; both are turned off as we have instructed every-one to do on the weekends.

He has no pictures anywhere in his cube, no decorations, nothing. Strange, I think, but I really know nothing about him. My phone reads nine thirty; no one will be here for a while. My heart is pounding as I turn on his servers. I am sure I can get fired for this, even if I think I am in the right. Standard login screens pop up, and I have no access and there's nothing on his desk that can even help me guess at his password. I will have to come in from the network.

I walk back to my desk and boot up my secondary computer. This will not be hard, as I have set up a trusted relationship with the computers that I build. Probably not the best security, but I have done it anyway. Because of this trusted relationship, I am able to remotely log into both his computers as root. I open two windows, one with each of Beale's computers.

I spend the next hour going through everything on his computer—mainly just looking at the stuff he is working on. It looks like he is building subroutines that will be called by main programs to do something. I would love to do the same thing with Josh's computers, but the police took them. I should have done that when I first met him.

I cannot get into Troy's email application, but I'm able to see all files saved to the computer. If he is involved in this, I doubt he would use email, but you never know. A friend's dad used to tell him, "People are stupid." I would like that to be the case here so I might find some low-hanging fruit.

After I have completed that useless exercise, I install some open-source software to copy every keystroke he makes. I copy it to a file and create a channel to send it to another server that is more of a testing server I have. I also install some software that will show me exactly what his screens look like and what he is seeing and typing. Lastly, I install another free program that basically will carve out any web login information through a web browser and send it to me in a special file. I plan on finding out where he has been.

I then spend the next forty-five minutes deleting my activities from syslog in case he is paranoid and looks at this. I also wipe out all traces of my remote login. My programs are in a hidden directory, but they can be found if he knows what he is looking for. He may suspect something if he finds my software, but maybe he will think that they are part of a standard build.

I am almost done when I hear a familiar voice behind me. "Robert, what are you doing?"

I smell his heavy cologne as I turn slowly, resisting the urge to exit my terminal windows and trying not to look too guilty. David is there in a blue suit with a red tie. What, is he running for president? "Hey David, just looking at some logs. Did you go to the funeral?"

He does not answer, and I can tell he is trying to see what is on the emulation screens. He turns and walks quickly down the hallway towards the steps without saying anything.

I remotely shut down Troy's servers and exit the emulation screens. Will the server be shut down before he walks by his cube? I bring up two new emulation screens on a server that I am allowed to be on in case he comes back.

I will have a tough time explaining stealing an employee's data without asking about it or anything, even to Ashok and Joe. They will probably think that I am involved. I sit there for a while wondering if David will come back, but he does not. I shut down my servers and casually walk out.

I then go to do some highly important activities. I get an oil change and a car wash and then whack some golf balls at the driving range. It is a low-key afternoon and really a low-key rest of the weekend, besides my feeling that David has gotten HR involved and is trying to fire me as soon as possible.

Chapter 15

Tuesday, April 21
ART Headquarters

Well, I survived the dreaded Monday yesterday with no ill effects from the weekend; HR and David were not waiting in my storage area office to fire me, so David must not have walked by Troy's computer as it was shutting down. The bonehead was probably checking management computers.

The work atmosphere has changed now as there are internal meetings on moving. With a building full of engineers, of course there are timelines established, working groups convened, dependencies outlined on what devices should be shut down, and lists of who should be going and who should be staying back.

On the computer security side, there is not a lot going on. I don't believe for a second that this is because I have stopped the attacks. For the time being, though, I feel like I am a rock star computer security guy. But at the end of the day, they had used one means or another to compromise basically every system in the place. I may have slowed them down some, but even the room that I had taken offline is compromised.

The only real defense we have is the bit of code, compiled before Ashok even started the company, which may be what they needed. I am not sure if the folks that had been stealing all our information could figure out what that compiled code did and take its outputs without knowing what is in the code itself.

The software I installed on Troy's computer is working, and I have a list of most of his logins that I have sent to a test server. I have passwords to a Yahoo email account, a Gmail account, and a bank account that I can start investigating. The passwords are similar to each other but not the same. I do not want to risk messing around with his stuff during work or emailing it to my own Gmail account, so I download the data to a USB drive.

I know Scott is coming before he gets to my office by the clicking of his flip-flops in the hallway. He asks if I would like to join him in a meeting at ten to talk about the timeline for the prototype.

The meeting is interesting. I sit in the back and do not say a word. Tom McAndrews, who is on the business side of the company and reports to Joe, walks through a PowerPoint presentation with ease and confidence. He is dressed in jeans, a sports jacket, and a collared shirt, and all of a sudden, I feel more confident in our chances with Zamtech.

"Zamtech is going to be delivering a final draft of the testing requirements for the Pilot on Monday, May 2. The basic testing will be a real-world scenario of what the end project is. Zamtech is going to hook up our circuit boards to two energy sources simulating actual solar panel output."

He picks up circuit boards that do not look like normal computer circuit boards because they are long and thin—about two inches by eight inches. He walks to the windows and glances out at the spring day, and then he hands the boards to someone in the front of the room to pass around.

Another guy stands up, and Tom introduces him as a sales engineer, Bill something. He is wearing jeans and a polo shirt; he's a standard-sized guy with short, dark hair and a receding hairline, even though he looks to be about thirty. He has a full goatee, which really makes him look like a tech guy. He also speaks with confidence and ease, and he gives you the feeling that this is a good team in front of customers. He walks assuredly to the front of the room. "All of the software that ART had been developing and testing will be embedded into these circuit boards. Zamtech plans on layering ten of our boards together to create a block of them."

He continues, "As many of you know, each of these boards has a controller that works with the controllers on the other boards to help move the energy through the matrix of channels. On the main board, there is a master controller, which load balances all the boards in the block."

The circuit board is passed to me, and I look intently at it. The energy channels look like small tubes, and there are eight of them on each of the boards. I have heard the tubes contain a matrix of thousands of high-end fiber-like channels. The load-balancing techniques Ashok has talked about are embedded in the controllers.

Ashok has built algorithms that will tell him if any of the channels are becoming overloaded, and the tube controller will send down energy to another channel. The entire time, the tube controller is reporting to the controller on the board the energy level of every channel, which allows the master controller to load balance across the boards.

Bill interrupts my thoughts when he says, "The output of these energy tubes will be directed to a source on the following end that is specified by Zamtech. Zamtech has the technology to convert the energy that they have received from their high-end solar panels to work on the other side, sort of like a drive shaft."

He continues, "Our entire product basically takes one energy source and separates it into many channels that can be used for specific purposes without overloading any one. Zamtech's receiving technology cannot handle a large load and needs it in smaller chunks. Different applications will need different numbers of blocks: for example, two circuit boards could be used for a car, several blocks could be used for a house, and about ninety blocks could be used for a hotel."

He walks over to the window again and looks out. He does not seem to care that there are a bunch of people in the room. "This is all really cool stuff, but to be a part of this, we need to win the prototype. ART will have to supply computers to monitor the transfer of energy at every stage of the design."

He smiles as he talks. "Monitors will be hooked to overhead projectors so scientists from Zamtech can understand how we are doing each step of our process, and Ashok will give them a description of what is actually occurring at each stage. We will need about twelve different computers to show all the different functions at each stage of the process."

Tom gets up again as though they all have practiced this routine. "ART will stage the entire process, and we will do everything the week of May 18 in a hotel close to Zamtech headquarters. We will move it all into the actual testing area at Zamtech the week before Memorial Day. This will give us plenty of time to recover if anything gets damaged in the shipping."

He sits down on a small table at the front of the room and continues, "We will stage the entire test before shipping it out, and we are going to be taking over the boardroom for this task. See Bill for action items for your group."

Scott walks over after the meeting and hands me a piece of paper. On it is my name and my tasks, which are networking the computers together in the boardroom and then helping pack and ship computers. No excitement there.

He also hands me a list of people that are going to be going out to Silicon Valley. I am not on the list, which bums me out.

Chapter 16

Wednesday, April 22
ART Headquarters

When I get in this morning, there is a yellow sticky note on my computer and a new list of the people that will be going to California:

> Robert,
> I want you to be in the group in CA to help from a computer security standpoint.
> Thanks.
> Ashok

My name is now on the list. The hotel shows "TBD." Boss man David is not on the list, so that's one less thing for me to worry about. I had hoped there was another change that would put Sarah on the list, but it's not my lucky day.

I text George and ask if he wants to help me with some computer security stuff tonight. No reply, so I text, "The computer security stuff we do will be on the offensive side." Immediately he responds and says he's in.

I am messing around, sending Sarah instant messages, trying to make her laugh, and then I make a decision to involve her in tonight's meeting with George. I message:

rdulaney:	Hey, George and I have some special computer security work to do tonight...do you want to help? ☺
sdonnelly:	Hmmm, sure you do. What type of computer security work?
rdulaney:	Top secret. Tell you later...
sdonnelly:	OK, I will help. But I really want to go for a run right after work...how about 6:30?
rdulaney:	Works for me. I'll tell George. Oh yeah, we need to do this at your apartment.
sdonnelly:	Ugh, it's a mess. Why?
rdulaney:	That's top secret, too.
sdonnelly:	OK, how about 7 then? You buying dinner?
rdulaney:	Sure, pizza or Chinese it is. See you then.
sdonnelly:	Pizza over Chinese. I'll text you my address.

I pick up George at six thirty and tell him we are heading to Sarah's.

"You really like her, don't you?"

I did not really want to go there, but I answer, "What's not to like?"

He puts the seat back as far as it can go and says, "True. So, what are we doing tonight?"

"Breaking into someone's personal accounts from work."

He looks at me and smiles; "Now that's what I'm talking about! By the way, my temp position is ending at the end of April. Got to find me some other gig."

"Is this going to affect us getting the apartment?"

"Heck no little man, I have plenty of bread from my years in the army. No place to spend it while I was on tour. I'll find something. I'm actually talking to a couple of companies already."

Sarah lives in downtown Towson, which is pretty close to the office and about fifteen minutes from Federal Hill and downtown Baltimore. It is a couple of miles away from Ashok's townhouse. We find a spot to park right around the corner from her place.

She lives on the fourth floor, and George and I knock on her door a little before seven. She answers with a smile and looks awesome in jeans and a white long-sleeved shirt. Her hair is wet and combed back over her shoulders.

We take a quick look around the place, and I really like it. She is able to give the entire tour standing in the living room: small dining room, small kitchen, two bedrooms to the back, and a deck overlooking a busy street.

Laughing, she says, "So, what's the top-secret operation?"

I pulled out my Mac and announce, "We are going to see what Josh's friend Troy has been up to." I then explain what I did on Troy's computer at the office while everyone was at Josh's funeral.

George has a big old smile on his face. He opens Sarah's refrigerator and helps himself to a Corona. "I have never been prouder of you!"

Sarah laughs nervously and asks me if I would also like to help myself to a beer, which I do.

She then asks, "Is this legal? I don't think we should be doing this if it's not."

I respond confidently, "I'm now the computer security guy, I just can't do this at work because there is probably an insider for the attackers and it may tip them off if they catch me."

Sarah looks at me intently as she seems to be making a decision. She does not say anything.

We order pizza, and then I want to get started with the files I had downloaded from Troy's computer. I start up my Mac and Sarah moves her flat-screen monitor to the table so we can all see what I am doing.

I plug in the USB port and move the files to my hard drive. First, I tell them what each file is. Scraps of passwords from anywhere he has gone on the web, his actual activities starting

Saturday, every website he visited, and every search that he did—I have it all.

I log into his Gmail account without issues. Sarah laughs nervously and mentions her parents will kill her if she goes to jail. George is opening cupboards looking for chips and then cracks a second beer. He yells in to Sarah asking where she keeps her junk food. She doesn't have any, so George will have to wait for the pizza.

"I thought looking at my own email was boring," I say, sort of to myself. "Looking at other people's is much worse." Most of it is marketing information, and there is nothing that would make me say this dude is bad. It is just my gut telling me he is.

Sarah says, "He is nice, just quiet."

I reply, "Josh had to be working with someone, and Troy was closest to him. The police have all Josh's machines, so we can't break into them."

Troy had forwarded an email to a second Yahoo email address. I copy down that address and navigate to it.

George is back munching on some crackers and starts commenting, sarcastically, about how fun this is. I had envisioned the three of us working in a war room scenario, all on computers—not me sitting here getting heckled.

I tell him he's worthless, which he already knows, and the two of them sit there talking as I go through all the emails. I try the same password on the Yahoo email account, which does not work, so I decide to start looking at his banking accounts.

The pizza guy comes, and I throw some cash at George and keep looking at my computer.

The first bank account is a credit union. He has a credit card, a car loan, a savings account, and a checking account with them. Nothing very exciting. I do find out his car loan is for $17,495, payable over four years.

Sarah says this really feels a little wrong if he is not involved in the attacks. I start feeling guilty, too, as they pass out the pizza and work on emptying her beer supply. I have a piece of pizza and crack another beer as I jump into his Citibank account.

Whoa. Finally, I find something.

"Check this out, guys! Our boy Troy got a $48,000 deposit exactly one month ago...it's an ACH transaction that he then transferred three $15,000 payments to other banks—or to someone else."

Sarah walks up behind me and looks at the screen; she smells lightly of a perfume that reminds me of a beautiful fall day, for some reason. She says, "Do you think it could be some sort of gift from someone, a parent, or something?"

George finishes another beer, throws it in recycling, and says, "He has to have some legitimate business behind it, I think. The IRS would be all over that otherwise, but I don't know the rules."

I wonder if Sarah will allow George in her apartment again. Next time we will need to bring our own beer.

I say, "Maybe he does, but maybe folks are giving him money for information. They disguise it as developing software or something for them, he pays taxes on it, no big deal. They could even set up a fake company and send a W-2 to him."

I go further down the screen. "Check this out. Another $17,000 about two months ago. Where is a simple test engineer getting that sort of cash in those sorts of chunks?"

I click to show earlier data and said say, "Another $17,000 earlier that month. This has to be before he even started at ART. This little bastard is involved."

Sarah laughs, "You don't like that guy, do you?"

"No, can't say I do. I didn't like Josh, either. Something about them both bugged me, even before finding out any of this."

We go through the rest of his files but do not see anything exciting. I want to get into that Yahoo email address, but it is getting late, so we decide to bail. I may try some other things later tonight.

George hits the bathroom to get rid of some the five beers he put away during our visit, and I have a quick second to be alone with Sarah.

I get up and throw away some of our trash and start towards the door. Sarah follows me down her little hallway and we just smile at each other, a little awkwardly, and then she squeezes my hand and looks seriously into my eyes. My heart is pounding in my ears.

Then George is there. "Sorry to interrupt you two. I should have hung in the bathroom the whole night—I promise I will next time if you two will feed me beers and pizza again."

"Thanks for nothing, as usual," is my only reply as I turn toward the door, the moment lost.

We say goodnight and walk down Sarah's stairs to the street. It's dark, and George tries to convince me to walk to a bar for one more beer, but I am driving and have had my limit, so I put up with the insults that always accompany saying no to George.

As we turn the corner to walk to our cars, I hear a quick sound behind me and George yells something before I feel a blow to the back of my head and pain like I have never felt before. Then I slip out of consciousness.

Chapter 17

Thursday, April 23
St. Joseph Medical Center
Towson, Maryland

I wake up sometime in the middle of the night with a huge headache and see my mom and dad in the room. The smell of disinfectant is heavy, and I know I am in a hospital. It hurts my eyes to open them, so I close them again and call out to my parents, "What happened?"

My mom and dad seem to be talking at the same time, but I slowly start to understand my dad's words.

"You and George were mugged in Towson. It sounds like they came up behind you and hit you hard in the head and took your computer bag. The police have a witness from inside a store who said it was three guys wearing dark clothing and baseball hats pulled down who ran to a car down the street."

"Ugh. How's George?"

"Same as you. A concussion and some swelling. The doctors think you both will be fine, but they need to do CAT scans every couple of hours to make sure the swelling around your head goes down."

"Where is my computer?"

My mom speaks up, "Sweetie, we just told you: they mugged you and took it, but they did not take your wallet or phone. You need to close your eyes and get some more rest."

Oh no, my computer bag...my head hurts, I am so tired...

I wake again sometime in the morning, and my head still feels like there is a train going through it. It feels like it is early, but there is light coming through the shades. I lay there in bed trying to put together what happened the night before.

I remember beers with George and Sarah while hacking into Troy's email and bank accounts. We found good info on Troy, George wanted to go for one more beer, George yelled something loud, and then there was a sharp pain in my head. I guess that's all.

I try to sit up, but then there is more pain going up the back of my neck through my head. I feel like I am going to get sick, so I lay back down. I reach for the little button to push for a nurse and wait for a minute.

A tall, thin nurse sticks her head in the door, peering over her wire-rimmed glasses. "Can I help you, honey?"

"Yes please. Can I get some pain medication, and am I able to see my friend George, who is here as well?"

She walks in quickly and runs her fingers through her short, gray hair as she looks at a chart at the end of the bed. "Sorry honey, we can give you some more medication in another hour. What is your friend's last name so I can check where he is?"

"McCarthy, thanks. Also, are my parents still around, or is my cell phone anywhere?"

She smiled and says, "I'll check, honey."

I think to myself that I have been called honey about five times in the last five minutes, so I've got that going for me.

I switch on the TV and turn the volume down as low as possible. There is someone next to me through a screen of some sort, and my head is still pounding. The local news tells me it's 6:50 a.m.

The nurse comes back in and says George is down the hall and I can visit later. Then she opens the drawer next to the bed and pulls out a little bag with my belongings and hands me my cell phone. I wonder why the muggers didn't take my iPhone? I know they can be tracked, but they could have turned that ability off pretty quickly...and why didn't they take my wallet, for that matter?

I turn off the news and figure I will wait an hour or so before calling work. Time for a nap, as my noggin is pounding.

I am not sure how long I slept, but I wake to the sounds of my TV and see George is sitting in a chair next to my bed with his feet up.

"What's up, little man?"

"Nothing, just hanging out, you?"

"Same."

I close my eyes and am trying to get a feel for how badly my head still hurts. "Feels like we went out very, very hard last night. How's your head?"

"Hurts, but it's getting better. I had a CAT scan this morning and they think I am good. You?"

"I have not had one that I remember, but I probably had one last night."

"They will probably bring you in for one again soon. They are going to release me this afternoon. You probably need to get tested again before they'll let you go."

I think for a second with my eyes closed. "Do you remember anything from last night?"

George remains quiet for a minute. "No, not really. I saw something moving quickly behind you and started to say something, and then I got whacked. I was not expecting that at all; that's not a bad neighborhood, and it was not that late."

I ask him to hand me my cell phone. I call the main office at work and ask for David and am happy to be able to just leave him a voicemail.

I then call back to the main number and ask to speak to Ashok. He picks up on the second ring with an, "ART, Ashok speaking."

"Ashok, this is Robert Dulaney, do you have a minute?"

"For you, absolutely," he said, laughing. "Nothing crazy is happening on the network, is there?"

"No, not on the network, but I was walking with a friend last night and was whacked on my head. My laptop was stolen, too. I am at St. Joseph Medical Center in Towson, but I should be released today at some point."

"Man, sorry to hear that. Are you going to be okay?"

"Yes, just a concussion. My head feels like there is a concert going on in there, but I will be fine. Same with my friend."

"Anything on that computer we need to worry about?"

"Nothing they were looking for, but yes, some stuff that I will explain later."

He is quiet for second. "Were you mugged, or were they after that laptop?"

I answer, "Well, they left my wallet and my cell phone, and they didn't take a thing from my friend George."

He is silent for a second, and I can see him in my mind adjusting his glasses while he thinks. Finally, he says, "Okay, are you going to be in tomorrow?"

"I hope to be; I'll let you know if I can't. I left a message for David too, so I should be good, but if anyone is asking, please let them know what's up."

We say goodbye, and George sits there not saying anything, so I shoot a text to Sarah saying we were mugged and we are at St. Joseph Medical Center, but all is okay.

She calls right away, and I explain the entire story again. The concern in her voice makes me feel good. She asks if she can come by. I tell her she does not need to, but I will give her a play-by-play at work.

This girl is all right. I am psyched after hanging up the phone. George just sat there, not saying anything.

Finally, the gorilla stands up, towering over me, and says, "Police are going to come by in a little and take statements, do you need anything? I'm going to try to get out of here."

"All good, thanks."

My parents come by shortly after George leaves, and the entire rest of the day is filled with a CAT scan, a police statement, and organizing my release. The police statement I give is worthless because I have zero information, and they will not give me any either. My parents drive me to my car, and my dad drives it home. When we get there, I take another nap.

Chapter 18

Friday, April 24
ART Headquarters

I never make it into the office on Thursday. I basically sleep on and off all day and talk to a few folks. George has recovered more quickly than I have and stops by the house.

It is a crisp, clear spring day as I walk into to the office Friday. It's on the early side. I go through email and our security logs, but there is nothing exciting. There is a little information on the move and a couple requests for new servers. I have a number of new ones in my office, so I unbox them and start installing Linux.

While they are loading up, I log into my server that is getting Troy's files to see what he has been up to. I go to the directory and find that all the files have disappeared. I can't believe they are all gone; I haven't deleted the ones from the other day. I go and check the syslog files for anyone who would have logged in, but there is nothing there. Everything is deleted.

I check on the progress of my servers' installations and then decide to take a walk. I cruise by Sarah's cube, but there are a couple of folks talking to her, so I wave and keep going. I walk into the Ashok's office; he is on the phone but waves at me to sit down, which I do. I start mucking with the trinkets on his desk.

When he hangs up, he asks, "How are you feeling? What happened?"

"Can I close your door?"

"Sure, by all means."

I close the door, then start. "So, I decided that Josh's friend Troy may be involved with whatever has happened. Do you know who he is? A smaller guy that hung out with Josh?"

"No, I'm not sure, but go on."

"Well, I had the inkling that he is involved if Josh was. By the way, have you heard anything from the police?" Oops, my ADD is coming through.

"Nothing yet, just a bunch of questions from them."

I continue, "So anyway, I created a little program to send me what he was up to. You don't need to know too much, but I was getting the information sent to me on a test computer. I think I had read somewhere that the company has the right to monitor anything that employees are doing, so I figured that would include me, since I am in security. The other night I had put Troy's information on a USB storage device and was checking out what he was up to on my personal Mac. My Mac and computer bag were stolen when we were mugged. Nothing else—no wallets, nothing."

He looks at me like I just ate his cat. "Is Troy involved in something we need to watch out for?"

"I would say that's a definite yes. He got a number of direct deposits over the last several months of $48,000 and then two deposits for $17,000, all of which he moved to three other bank accounts."

He puts his head back and looks at the ceiling. "You're kidding. How did you get his banking information?"

I respond, "He had logged into one of the bank accounts during work. The worst part of all this, though, is I checked this morning and all the files and everything I had set up are gone. He or someone else is onto me. I was the only one that had access to that server. My guess is they found out I was watching him, broke into the server, and cleaned out all the evidence quickly."

Ashok thinks for a couple seconds and then says, "I would like Joe to hear all this stuff. Hopefully he won't be angry that you were spying on one of our own guys."

He picks up the phone and asks if we can go down to talk to Joe, then hangs up and we wander down the hall. Walking down the hall with the CTO heading to the CEO's office, I feel pretty important—especially when I walk past Sarah's cube and she notices me and smiles.

We walk into the big corner office and Joe says, "Hey guys, have a seat. What's up?"

Ashok closes the door and says, "Go ahead, Robert."

I explain everything again to Joe without giving too many details. He gets the story. He asks how I am feeling and then sits there thinking.

Finally, Joe grimaces and says, "So you think he is involved?"

"Doesn't seem coincidental. His best friend here is probably involved and is killed. He gets a bunch of money over the last several months. I have some evidence on my laptop, which is taken, and then someone breaks into my server and clears it out."

Joe says, "Yes, I get it. Ashok, do you think the competition knows everything now?"

Ashok replies, "They know a lot, but I don't think they know the original load-balancing algorithms—our secret sauce."

"Where is that source code?"

Ashok speaks slowly, "Well, it was at my house, but Robert thought it would be good to get it out, and he took a couple of my hard drives and put them at an undisclosed location. We do not need them for the prototype because the algorithms were in compiled subroutines that worked from when we started. Our software just calls those subroutines, which are executables and therefore cannot be read to understand how it is working."

I start thinking that he is going to ask me where it all is, and I am hoping George put them someplace safe. Joe stands up and looks out his window. "Robert, you seem to know what you are doing in this type of world."

I reply with a smirk, "I have a criminal mind." Somehow, I can never stop myself from making dumb comments, no matter what the situation.

"Well then, Robert, what do you think we should do now?"

"Well, it seems to me that our competition is desperate. Either they don't have what they need, or they think we are sufficiently ahead of them. They have been banging around in our networks since before I even got here. They also have at least two people on the inside, probably more, and they were willing to kill someone. How big is this contract again?"

Joe smiles. "It really could be off the charts; if Zamtech can do what they think they can do, it will change the world."

"So, say they are missing a part of what they need, or they think we are ahead of them. They have two options: steal what we have and replicate it, which they have clearly tried to do, or sabotage what we have and hope that the rest of what they have is close enough. They would then get the contract and work out the rest once we are out of the picture."

I think for a moment. "If I was them, I would wait until the night before our pilot to destroy our prototype or introduce malware into what we are doing so everything blows up right in front of Zamtech."

Ashok laughs nervously. "You really do have a criminal mind."

I continue, "The third set of servers that I talked about, the one that just the three of us know about, may be our only shot. We have the second set of everything that becomes our backup for show, but then the third set is code from a month or two ago, before they would have thought to sabotage what we are doing."

Ashok chimes in: "We can actually build everything out in the Valley for the third. Don't ship anything, just build it all there in a hotel room."

I chime in and say, "I have been thinking about this. We need to buy the computers from a different source, not using work computers to even order them. We set the third one up in a hotel room that's not linked to us. We then show up with the third set the day of the prototype. We can't tell anyone about it. We need to assume they may even have someone on the inside at Zamtech."

We bat the idea around a little more, and Ashok is really getting excited. Joe seems intrigued, but he also looks tired— like he'd be willing to let us go with our plans if it meant getting closer to the end of all this.

We are about to wrap up the meeting when I have another idea. "I have a friend that can help. He is an ex-Army Ranger. We would need to pay him, but maybe we could do that with stock after the event so he is off the books. He can stay at the other hotel. I am willing to run with all of this if you guys can accept some big expense reports after the prototype, whether we win or we lose."

Joe looks at me with his eyes slightly narrowed. "Not too big, but yes, we trust you, and we probably would not be in this position without you."

I reply, "This position? All our data stolen and an employee dead?" I then say quickly, "Everything I'm going to buy and do will be needed, but I need to trust you to take care of my friend, who will also be putting himself at risk. Can you get back to me on how much stock we can get him if he agrees? His name is George McCarthy, and I'll get you all his information."

Joe says, "Yes, we will need someone to physically help with all those computers, and if you trust him, I'm good with that. I have to go to the board for any stock options, but I will bring it up on a conference call without sharing these plans."

I go back to my desk, check on the servers, and pull out a little notebook I carry. Nothing should be on computers for now. I write down a handful of ideas:

- Get with Ashok—need to get a complete list of software and hardware that is being set up for the second prototype to be used for the third prototype
- Purchase MacBook Pro
- Use a different internet connection and set up a new email address to start buying equipment
- Find out where Zamtech is headquartered and look into a hotel room suite
- Talk to George about being the guy in the hotel for a stock grant
- Figure out a timeline to order all equipment

I look at a calendar and think to myself that there's about six weeks until the prototype, and about five weeks until we will need to be setting up equipment. I keep writing:

- Have Ashok talk to David and tell him that I am going to be working on computer security and may be in and out of the office and that I will need to be reporting into Ashok for this project
- Get access to the backup tapes from a month or two earlier, whatever Ashok decides

Thinking about all this, I really need to figure out a company credit card or even something that is off the company records.

Everything we were going to do costs money, and a lot of it, and I have to move quickly.

A smell of cologne wafts into my office. "Am I interrupting anything?"

I turn around. Ugh. David Rogers, boss man, dork. I say, "Just getting my brain cells around my to-do items. How are you doing?"

I wonder how long has he been standing there watching me write. Oh well, he can't read my chicken scratch from a distance.

He replies, "I'm good, busy as everyone is. I am glad to see that you are going to California. Are you excited?"

"Yeah, sure. I can learn some and should be interesting."

He says, "Good stuff. Hey, how are you feeling? Thanks for getting me the message the other day, that mugging sounded crazy."

"Yes, it really was. I guess I was in the wrong place at the wrong time. I'm bummed about my computer, but I guess insurance should cover it, and I probably spend too much time on it anyway."

He says, "If there is anything you need from me, just let me know. Thanks for all the hard work; you really do well on this computer security stuff."

"Thanks David, let me know if there is anything you need."

"Will do, talk to you soon."

Hmm, that conversation was more pleasant than most. I look up Ashok's calendar and set a meeting with him for this afternoon at four. I book an out-of-the-way conference room.

Nothing really happens for the rest of the afternoon. I ask Sarah to grab lunch, but she has meetings, so I go to a Subway and get a sandwich and sit there with my sports page. Back at work I continue getting the servers ready and deliver two.

I ask Scott Williams if I can be part of the movement of the backups over to these set of servers, and he agrees. I need to learn everything that is going on these servers, and a great way to do it is to join the team that is building the second prototype.

My meeting with Ashok is good, as expected. I go through my notes, and he takes notes and comes up with action items to get back to me as soon as possible. He says he will grab Joe and talk to him about how we can do the expenses. He is also going to request that he brings the backup drives out himself so we will have them all, including the ones from two months back.

Sarah and I grab a cup of coffee after work at a small coffee shop that's two doors down from our bar. We sit outside on this perfect spring evening. Her parents are coming in town for the weekend, so she is going to be busy showing them around Baltimore. I ask her if she needs any help, and she says she will have to play it by ear.

She tells me she saw me with Ashok and asks what he thinks about the stuff they were finding involving Troy. I want to tell her everything, but I have to refrain. I told Ashok and Joe that it would just be the three of us in on the secret of the third prototype, and my word is my word. I also wonder if I can trust Sarah. I quickly push the thought away—of course I can.

She squeezes my hand again before she walks to her car. Are we going to get stuck in the dreaded "just friends" mode? I am really falling for her, but as I walk away I feel a strange pit in my stomach. I feel all alone. I decide to just go home and hang out with my parents and watch some TV.

Chapter 19

Saturday, April 25
Towson, Maryland

There is nothing like hanging out at home. I sleep in until ten and wake up to the sounds and smells of my mom making bacon, eggs, and toast. I drink two cups of coffee while I talk to my parents at the kitchen table. I'm not really talking about much, but they are interested in the science of what my company is doing. I have to admit, I am pretty proud of what we are doing too.

We also talk about the Orioles, who have just climbed back to .500 in this early part of the season. I decide I will stop by and see my brother. I had not been there for a while.

He is in the Baltimore City Correctional Center, which is really not a very nice place, but it is close to my folks' house—I think the judge felt sorry for my parents because they went to his trial every single day. It is not a white-collar criminal kind of place. There are drug dealers in with him, but I think they have him in a minimal security section. Still, he is not a free man. Visiting hours end at two. I better get moving.

I call ahead and go by after lunch. Will is waiting in the visiting room. He has a look of confidence and pride as he strolls across the plain room wearing his jailhouse greys. He is always happy to see me and has a big smile on his face. We hug.

I never really know what to say, so I just break in like a dumb younger brother would. "What have you been up to? How's the big house?"

Will laughs. "You know, it's awesome. I am working out every day, reading four newspapers cover to cover, making great friends. Seriously, it's not too bad, but I'm just ready to get out and start my life again. I don't have too much longer, if I keep behaving myself."

"What are you going to do when you get out?"

"Well, I have had some time to think about it." He laughs. "First, I'm going to move back in with Mom and Dad, spend a little time with them while I look to get started over. I will have exactly zero money, so that is where I will have to start, even if I don't want to. Twenty-nine years old and moving home with the parents!"

He frowns, "I still have some friends in finance, and there were a lot of people I actually helped in my short career. It's funny though; being in here really separates me from the people I knew. Most people I worked with don't want to talk to me, much less help me out. I get an hour a day to work on the internet; most stuff is blocked, but I have used LinkedIn and other tools to communicate a little. There are a couple of my college friends in good companies, but I think I need to do some startup work with people who still know that I'm not a bad person."

He seems to get a little energized. "I'm also going to figure out a couple of service trips to go on, get back to basics, spend time at church. The big house has a way of making you want to get back to your faith and give back and try to help people. It can also take people the other way, making you bitter and angry and making you feel like all you want to do is to take everything; I have seen a lot of that here, as well." He pauses for a minute, looking lost in thought. He shakes himself out of it shortly, though. "What about you, how is that job going? First job, good stuff!"

I decide at that moment that I will explain everything that is going on at work, and about Sarah, and about being mugged—with the exception of the details of the third prototype we are going to build. I talk for about fifteen minutes straight, and he sits there listening and asking questions.

He cannot not believe my parents have not told him about me being mugged, but I tell him it just happened and it is not a big deal. In the end, he asks specific questions about Zamtech, Hodophi, and the prototype.

He sits there thinking for a little, and then he says, "Can you create a new email for you and I to communicate with? Not the same Yahoo email address that we have been using. I have a new Gmail account that I have been using only for work-related stuff: william.dulaney8@gmail.com."

"Why the eight? And why do you think we will need a separate email?"

"It's Cal Ripkin's number. And I'm sure your personal email has been hacked—wouldn't they have started there if they are that good? I want to do some investigating for you and give you some help if I can. When are you going to California?"

"The pilot starts the day after Memorial Day, so probably a couple of weeks before then."

Just then there is a loud lock on the door and a guard yells through, "Visiting time is over. Wrap it up."

William smiles as he stands and says, "Hey, we never talked about when you move into your apartment. How is George doing?"

"Moving in next weekend, and George is standard-issue George. It should be good living with him, though, besides the fact that he will want to go out every night of the week."

He gives me a hug. "Email me with a new address, use my computer until you get a new one. It will need some updating, but it should be good. Be careful."

"See you, Will. And thanks."

As I walk out again, the feeling in the pit in my stomach hits again. Man, why don't I see him every weekend? He's a great guy. He made a really bad mistake when he was twenty-five, but he has been sitting in prison for two years, and how many times have I been over? Maybe ten. As I leave, I think about how he is done now talking to people from the outside for the rest of the weekend.

I make a vow to myself to create another email address and keep him up on what is happening in my life. It seems really important to him. Even though we are not the closest because of our age difference, I do have great memories of him playing football with me, wrestling, and all of that, and he always made it a point to see my sports events when I was in high school. I have been so focused on myself for so many years. Sometimes the real world can just hit you like a brick.

Sunday, April 26
Los Angeles International Airport
Los Angeles, California

The two men walk slowly through the airport after a very long flight and an hour in customs. They have two hours before their next flight up to San Francisco. Both men have false names and professionally done passports that are correct in every format, including backend information in all international databases.

They are not part of any company or part of the pilot program, but they have been requested by a friend of a friend and paid handsomely for their efforts. Their initial job is to do some preparation locally and then to meet up with some counterparts who have been working on the East Coast.

Their expertise is a mixture of high-tech counterintelligence, physical surveillance, and often the elimination of the subjects. They are both tired from their trip, but they are generally very happy about a new contract, which will have them working for almost two months and pay them more than what most people make in five years.

Towson, Maryland

I sleep in again today. Then I hit Mass with my parents and afterwards sit in my kitchen with them, just talking. Sarah did text me last night, but things were very busy with her parents, and I guess I am not going to be introduced.

I shoot George a text: "What's up, dog-faced boy? O's game today?" He ended up not being able to go out last night, so I had stopped by the bar for a beer and some wings by my lonesome and then gone home. I sat on the couch, watched some bad TV, and created another Gmail account using my brother's Mac. I told my parents that William had told me to use his old computer, as we were going through insurance to get a new one. Luckily my dad is going through the paperwork for the stolen computer, so I had that going for me.

Ten minutes later a text comes back from George: "Done, you foul-smelling semi-excuse for a mammal. Meet you at Pickles in an hour?"

"Yes," I reply.

It's 11:15 a.m. already, so I jump up and tell my mom and dad that I have to roll. My dad offers to drop me at the light rail;

my parents understand that a day baseball game with George definitely involves some day-drinking.

I take him up on it, and as we get in the car I notice a car at the end of the street pulling out at the same time we do. It is a standard-issue white four-door sedan. Am I getting paranoid?

My mind drifts as it normally does, and I bring it back to the conversation with Dad. He is asking about solar applications that can be used and is really interested in powering cars with solar.

I agree that would be off the charts and could change the way the world uses and consumes energy. My dad says he is tired of putting $45 in the tank every week.

When I get out of the car, I noticed a couple of similar white vehicles pulling into the parking lot. My so-called criminal mind had not picked up any distinguishing characteristics of what the first car really looked like, so I am not sure if I am being followed or not. I thank my dad and tell him I would grab a cab or Uber it home later on.

The Falls Road Light Rail Station is a little crowded for a day game, and I buy my ticket and make my way to the very end of the platform. I am trying to see if anyone is looking at me differently or following me down the platform. Most people are looking at their phones. I guess I need to stop my paranoid behavior at some point after getting bopped in the head.

I wander into Pickles at around twelve forty-five and there is George, sitting at a bar stool, drinking a beer, and looking at his phone.

"What's up, dogface?"

"Nada. What is your pleasure?"

I sneak a quick look at the bar taps and answer that I would like a Dogfish Head 60-Minute IPA. We talk for a little about the upcoming baseball game. He asks if I am ready to move in next week, and I tell him I am just going to throw my clothes in some garbage bags and run it down after we pick up the key. I am going to buy a bed and bring that over instead of trying to steal furniture from my parents.

I finally say, "I have something serious to tell you."

He replies, "What's up, little man?"

"Well, you know most of everything going on at my work, and you know that one of my coworkers turned up dead. I don't think it was a random mugging when you and I got jumped; I think they were after my computer."

"Yeah, I figured as much on us getting jumped when the hospital returned my wallet."

Keeping my voice a little lower and looking around, I say, "I think they are still at it. I think they don't have what they need, or they think we are going to win. I think they potentially have other people on the inside, and when we go out to California, they are going to sabotage all the work we have done."

The bar is getting a little more crowded now. The bartender comes up and we grab another round, since I still have more to tell him.

George says, "So what are you going to do?"

I do not like the fact that people are coming closer to us at the bar, so I say, "Not now, but we have some plans."

We finish our beer, and he takes the tab and pays. "You'll be getting the next rounds," he reminds me.

It is a perfect spring day: blue sky, clear, and about seventy-five degrees. There is a lot of activity with people walking towards the stadium, people selling tickets, and kids with baseball gloves and popcorn. I grab a couple of hot dogs and two waters from a street vendor.

As we walk, I look around and make sure there is no one in earshot before I say, "I asked our CEO if you can be involved, and he is going to get you some options and cover expenses."

"Stock options?"

"Yes, I'm not sure how many. I got twenty-five thousand as an employee. If we go public or get bought, we can make some legitimate money—potentially really legitimate money. Your job would just be to help us get through the prototype so we succeed. I figured you would be game because of your job situation?"

He says, "I am interested. Who do I have to kill?"

I reply, "Basically, you would be taking a clandestine trip, staying at a separate hotel, and helping us set up an entire network and prototype that only a couple of us know about in the company. We may even set it up in your room, but I'm not sure of that yet."

George replies, "I'm in, dude; let me know what I have to do."

"Also, just to let you know, someone may be following me today. I'm not sure, so we can't talk about this stuff near anyone."

"Why do you think you are being followed?"

"A car started and followed us out of our neighborhood when my dad was dropping me off at the Falls Road light rail. I believe I saw the same car at the station, but I may just be paranoid."

He smiles. "Interesting. Could be exciting. I am so in. Get me some good options, will you?"

"Cool beans."

With that agreed upon, my man George and I drink beer all day, watch our Birds pull one out over Toronto, and eat some sausages, and by the time I am back on the rail, I am a tired man.

I take an Uber from the light rail home and take a nap on the couch as my mom fixes dinner.

At dinner, my phone is buzzing. I don't know the caller. It rings back a couple of minutes later, but I leave it again. After dinner, I am still feeling the effects of the day, and I see I have a message. It's from Ashok, who sounds like he is a mess. I can barely tell what he is saying, but I finally make out from the message: "Robert, need your help...Something bad happened in my house...Call me."

I call Ashok back. He answers on the first ring and starts talking very fast.

"I was in New York this weekend seeing friends. I came home today and my house was ransacked. They went through everything; the computers are gone, and almost all the electronics are gone. I called the police right away, but then when I went down in my basement, my neighbor was there..." He stops for a minute, and I can hear him swallow hard. "He was there on the floor with blood all over his head...Robert, he's dead. The police are here, they have been interviewing me for the last hour. They say I have to go down to the station and give a formal statement, and then I'm free to go, but I can't come back to the house."

He starts talking fast, a nervous chatter. "I tried calling Joe a couple of times and he did not answer either, so I looked up your phone number from an email. I didn't know who else to call. I haven't met a lot of people here because I have been so busy."

I finally get what he is looking for. "Ashok, do you need a place to stay? You definitely can stay here; it's my parents' house, but they have a guest bedroom. Do you want us to come and get you?"

"No, I have my car. I'm going to head to the police station first, and then I'll come over. Where do you live?"

"I'll text you the address."

"Awesome. Thank you—thank you so much."

I hang up the phone and sit there for a couple of minutes. Wow—this isn't make-believe any longer; something really bad is going on here. I wonder if Ashok told the police it is probably connected to what we are doing at work.

I go up and talk to my parents and tell them what happened to Ashok—basically the short story. My parents are horrified, and then they jump up to prepare the guest bedroom, my mom wiping down the bathroom and everything else they do when we have guests. I am lucky that we actually have a guest room; I don't know what they would have said if I asked if he could sleep in William's room.

Ashok does not get to the house until about ten at night, so my mom fixes some snacks and the four of us sit around the table talking.

The police believe Ashok's neighbor was walking his dog in his backyard behind the row of townhouses on Saturday night and surprised the burglars. His neighbor lives alone, and his dog is now missing. The sliding glass door to Ashok's walk-out basement had been left open. Ashok says he mentioned to the police that the break-in could be about technological innovation, and he told them what happened at work a couple weeks back.

We sit there for a while talking, but finally everyone decides that we should go to bed. Ashok is very grateful, and I think again about the fact that he is a really good dude who may be in over his head, just like me.

I go to my room and fire up William's computer. I go into my new Gmail account and fire off a quick email to William about the day's events. I then think about Troy's other email addresses and potentially going to into work right now to see if I can break into those. I decide to bag it for tonight and hit the sack.

Chapter 20

Sunday, May 3
Fells Point, Maryland

I wake up very early and go to morning Mass with my parents. We then go out for a bagel and a cup of coffee. I am excited to get the day going. Today I am finally moving into the new apartment, and I am psyched.

This last week has been pretty low-key after last Sunday's craziness. Police are working both cases as though they are connected, and they have interviewed a lot of people at work. They also interviewed me about my computer robbery and asked if I had sensitive company information on the computer, which I told them I did not.

I did have sensitive data, but it is banking data from another employee I am spying on. I do not believe that it would be in my best interest to relay that fact.

Yesterday I went out to lunch and a movie with Sarah, which was fun. We had a great time. She continues to grow on me as she is a lot of fun, but she's still elusive when she says goodbye. I think she likes me as well, but maybe she does not want to get too involved with someone at work.

After I get home to my parents' house, I throw most of my clean clothes in a garbage bag. My dad helps me put an older chair in my trunk that they do not want. It's is hanging out the back, but he ties it up well enough that a small warhead would not dislodge it. My parents promise to stop by later this week to check out the place. I am thinking of inviting Sarah down to help me move in as well.

Happy days! Spring is in the air, and I am going to finally be an adult, or semi-adult, and live in my own place. I call George on my way down to the place, and he says he is just getting out of his parents' house and will be on his way shortly, so we agree that I will pick up the keys and meet him in at the apartment.

Federal Hill is, I think, one of the coolest places in Baltimore. It has shops, apartments, bars, and restaurants, and it is about five minutes away from the inner harbor. I find a parking place on the street and go into the business office that is connected to some of the other condos. I get the keys and our residential parking permits, which are going to be awesome, and jump back in my car to head to the place.

Our apartment is in a condo facility above a couple of restaurants and a little bakery, which is cool. I find parking on the street, put on my residential sticker, and take the folder of keys and head up to our place. We are on the third floor, and we have one of the apartments with a little outside patio, which we are both willing to pay extra for. I cannot deal with not being able to go outside, and neither can George.

I walk up into a totally bare apartment with fresh paint on some of the walls and a mixture of hardwood floors in the common areas and carpet in the bedrooms. The apartment is nicer than we both deserve. I text Sarah a quick picture of the new pad and ask if she wants to come down to check it out and help us get stuff together.

I then start bringing up my garbage bags of clothes. I have no dresser, so I just leave them in the bags in one of the bedrooms. George's brother has a pickup truck, and we are going to do some afternoon shopping—first for beds and then maybe some other stuff. I quickly come to the realization that we have absolutely nothing we need. No cups, no plates, no anything. Oh well.

Sarah texts back that she will drop by later this afternoon and to text her when we are on our way back from shopping. The day is looking good!

George is always late, so I use my hotspot on my iPhone to connect to the internet with William's computer and plop myself on the floor to play around a little. I continue to try to break into Troy's other email accounts and finally have luck with his Gmail.

He uses one of the passwords that I had stolen from my screen scrapes with a $ sign after it. This email account is almost empty: only a few messages in the inbox, and all of them are read, so I jump into them. There are a couple of bank notices, but no login information. Looks like my boy is working about four banks at the same time. Interesting.

I go into his sent folder and I see there are a few emails. There is one there to a funky address that I have not seen before—rk5b83@canwyn.net. There is no subject, and the message is simple:

> Pilot ship 5-8
> Setup 5-18
> Dest—unknown
> Team assigned—Y to question, he is going

George and his brother finally get here and enter the apartment noisily. George is carrying a twelve-pack of Samuel Adams and one gym bag. His brother is carrying a single wooden chair, potentially for a kitchen table if we had one. I shut down my computer and have a beer with the brothers.

George's older brother, Dave, is about an inch taller than George and has the same big-boned thickness to him that George does. He probably weighs about 240 pounds, but he does not seem to have any fat on him. You would think he is a quiet, serious guy, but then you get to know him. He is quiet, but he is also really funny and genuine. He is one of those people who you really do not get to know until you have a beer with him. He is an attorney in a small law firm in Baltimore and has a serious girlfriend—I wouldn't be surprised if they got married soon.

After our first beer and before George can crack another, I tell them that we have to get moving to get some furniture so we can get back and set up before we go to bed. We make a couple of runs from their truck and my car and throw stuff all over the place in every room. George has his bed from his house, which is good. We don't have to shop for that. After about thirty minutes, we are three across in the pickup truck heading to Towson to a furniture store.

There is not much to furniture shopping with a bunch of dudes. I pick a bed in about two minutes, and we tell the guy we can carry it and throw it in the back of the truck. We also pick up a table and some chairs from the same store. Nothing great, but they will do. We go to another store and grab some silverware, glasses, plates, and whatever else George is just piling in our cart. Not half bad.

Back at the place we have another beer while putting my bed together and assembling the table. Dave starts working on hanging George's TV in the living room. Things are coming together, and I am really liking it so far.

The rest of the day goes by quickly. Sarah and Dave's girlfriend come over, and we all sit out back on the porch on the few chairs we have. Sarah has brought us a housewarming gift of a small wine rack and a bottle of wine, which we display proudly on our kitchen countertop. We then walk around Fells Point and grab dinner at a sports bar. Life is good.

The night is another beautiful one, clear and crisp, and it is beginning to turn dark as I walk Sarah back to her car. We are laughing casually about the brothers and the furniture in the place. When we come to her car, she turns to me and smiles and I finally take a chance. I brush her hair from the side of her face, keeping my fingers in it as I move my hand back.

I feel my heart pounding and I wonder if she can hear it, and all of a sudden, my fingers are trembling. I step in and lean down a little, and she smiles and closes her eyes and leans in to a kiss. She pulls back after a couple of seconds and smiles at me, and then she takes my hands and steps up again for another little kiss as she lets go. She walks around the car and my heart leaps as I watch her get in and smile and wave as she drives away.

That night after everyone has gone home, I log back into the computer and shoot William a note about the information in Troy's email without telling him where I got it. I tell him I know two of the items—our ship date (May 8) and our setup date (May 18) for the prototype. "Dest—unknown" is easy. He does not know the destination of our setup area. The last one is a simple response to a question, and while I am not sure who the "he" is, I think it may be me, as I am the new one added to the list.

I do not spend any more time on it, but I want to keep William involved because he has asked me to. I then crash for the first time in my new place, very happy about the day.

Chapter 21

Monday, May 4
ART Headquarters

I have the windows down and the music blaring as I travel in
the opposite direction of most commuters. Spring and fall are
awesome in Maryland, and today is one of the great days. I get into
work early, but I am a little bummed to see several cars already in
the lot. There is just something I love about being in first.

I key-badge in and walk to my desk to boot up my computers. First, I check through a bunch of logs and some correlation
software that is supposed to be sending me a list of our firewall
and intrusion prevention logs. Not much is happening. There's
nothing really of interest, which scares me. I figured a while back
that they had stolen everything that was not locked down and
the so-called security dude (me) had been had, with the exception of the algorithms that had already been baked into the code
before Ashok brought everything here.

We have an early all-hands meeting where the business guy
who is working with Zamtech will go over the final pilot plan.
We then have two breakout meetings for the group that is going
to be on the ground there: one meeting for the overall logistics
and the second for the early planning of the overall presentation.
They are both in the afternoon.

Ashok stops by my storage space and says the CEO wants to talk to me after the all-hands meeting. He says Joe doesn't want to talk in his office but instead in a conference room that Ashok says is on the fourth floor. Ashok seems to be doing okay after everything that happened to him. He has actually stayed at hotel for the past week, and the police tell him he can be back in his place by Friday.

In the all-hands meeting, Joe introduces Tom McAndrews again, who is the interface with Zamtech and has spoken to us before. Tom is very even-keeled and says the schedule for the prototype has not changed. The prototype is to start June 1, the day after Memorial Day. We are allowed to be in their facilities and do the testing the entire week before. We have decided as a group we are going to stage the prototype out the week before that at a hotel.

I start inputting dates on my phone:

- Week of May 11 (next week): Ship everything
- Week of May 18: Pre-stage prototype in some hotel
- Week of May 27: We can be on site at Zamtech setting up the prototype

He says those on the team should plan on being at the hotel Sunday, May 17. I have not figured out my travel plans yet, but I am getting excited.

He says that Ashok will be the lead and will walk Zamtech through the high-level design for the first half of the first day. He then says we will give a complete demonstration of our offering by demonstrating how the energy is transferred on our test equipment. We will then show where and how everything is moving at each stage of the testing.

This will take us all day Tuesday and Wednesday. The Zamtech engineers will then bring in their test equipment and hook it into our systems and basically retest everything during Thursday and through lunch on Friday. The remaining afternoon will be a wrap-up session where we will need to talk about current bugs in our system and answer any questions on methodology. They will also bring up any outstanding questions that they have from our original RFP response.

Leaving the meeting, Sarah comes up beside me and grabs my arm and says, "I'm so jealous you get to go out there and have all that fun." She has a big smile on her face and adds, "But I bet you will be missing me."

I laugh and say, "You got that right! You should come out for a weekend."

"I wish! Unfortunately, there isn't that much free cash lying around when you have to pay all your bills plus college loans."

"Well, maybe we will both get rich if this hits big."

She laughs as she turns toward her desk. "Then just go make it happen."

I go to the fourth-floor conference room for my meeting with Ashok and Joe, and I wonder why we are not meeting in his office.

Joe seems to be fired up on coffee or Red Bull and he says, "Okay, Robert, here is what I have: the good news is that you and your friend George will get fifty thousand shares of restricted stock, or 'RSUs.' These are unlike options because you own them; you don't need to buy them. The current board-set price is sixty-five cents a share. The value at this price of your award is $32,500, but our aim is to make it much, much than that."

My mind is racing. He is giving me more shares as well as George?

He continues, "We are giving them to you for your ongoing activity and what you have done for this company so far. We are giving them to George for the risks associated with what he is doing and based on our faith that you have picked the right person for the job. These are unlike typical options in another way as well: half the value of them vests if we win the prototype, and the second half vests immediately if we go public or there is a change of control. You now have a very vested interest in making this successful."

"That is a huge show of faith, wow—thank you!" I am happy I actually did not make a dumb comment like I normally do in these situations.

"We will also be making your friend George a temporary employee of one of our venture firms, so he will be getting a salary and benefits. We will need George to reach out to HR at our venture capital firm, since technically he will be working for them. Here is a typed list of numbers that he can call. He will need to schedule a time to come in and verify his I-9 and sign this paperwork."

He pauses and then goes on. "You also need stop by our HR office and tell Jeannie that you need to sign some paperwork. She knows this is not to be discussed, and we are telling her you will get shares based on performance."

He then looks serious again. "You mentioned doing a third prototype to cover the risk that they will destroy the backup one either through malware or physical damage. Ashok and I have discussed this. We need you ordering all the equipment and taking the lead for the third prototype. The second prototype will be 100% a decoy, as there are already too many people that know about it. Ashok will tell you what you need to buy and where might be best to get it, but timing is crazy."

He continues, "We have opened a special bank account and have a credit card here for you for these purchases. This is outside anything that should show up under our company name, as our venture capital firm set this up under a separate name. There will be also a card for George for his hotel room and expenses. His paperwork will not be in any computers and will be kept separate with our investors. He will need to keep copies of all paperwork."

"Wow, you get stuff done! I guess this is why you got the CEO position."

He smiles and says, "The time frame is incredibly tight right now. You need to call in sick tomorrow and spend the day ordering equipment. The hotel for the third prototype will be where George is staying, and we are going to order the equipment to be delivered to our investors' offices in Palo Alto. George will need to rent a large car and pick up the equipment from there. Here is the name and location of our venture firm to ship the equipment to.

"We need you to pretend you are out there messing around and working on the second system, and then spend your evenings replicating everything into the third one. Ashok will come over to test and make sure things are going well, but this will be a lot of work.

"The second one of our venture investors are getting us cell phones. There will be four of them with numbers not associated with our names. We are to use them only in an emergency or to communicate critical information to one another. They also had a security expert come in and talk to me, and you are to turn off all GPS tracking and positioning apps on your phone and potentially leave your regular phone in your own hotel room when you are going out to George's room. Does this all make sense to you, Robert?"

"Absolutely, I love the paranoia. We needed this from the start."

"Good. Any questions?"

I reply, "When will I get the phones?"

"We should have the phones to you by the end of the week."

He continues, "I will be seeing you out there, but we actually have a dinner with Zamtech execs on Wednesday. They are having one the next night with our competitors too, so it's no real advantage. I probably won't be interacting with you about this from this point on, except via cell if either you or Ashok need it."

Ashok jumps in, "I will get you the equipment list in paper format by close of business today. It will be an exact replica of the second backup system. I already have backup drives from our code freeze two weeks ago that I have duplicated for this and will also give them to you today. Please protect them. Like Joe said, call in sick tomorrow and get a jump start buying equipment with rush orders. Please do not tell anyone anything, as you know."

They get up, and both shake of them hands with me. I feel like Joe's kid when he looks at me and says, "We are counting on you and your friend, Robert."

Wow. My heart is beating a thousand beats per second as I walk out of the room and head down the hall. I want to run and tell Sarah everything, but I figure I will go back to my desk and work on travel logistics while I calm my nerves and then text George to meet sometime this evening to discuss.

I pick a direct Southwest flight out of Baltimore heading into San Francisco on Sunday, May 17. My return flight is scheduled for Sunday, June 7. I figure after the prototype is completed, I will have to help pack and ship equipment, and it would be nice to actually see San Francisco if I have time, as I have never been there. It sounds like we are going to be incredibly busy the whole time, though.

Zamtech is based in Palo Alto; our hotel room where we are doing the second prototype is right across the street from the headquarters, and I believe it will be up to George where he wants the third prototype and hotel room to be. He and I will be the only two that know where that is, unless Ashok can get some time to help us.

I now have calmed my nerves and go down to talk to Sarah. She is banging away at her computer, as always. I ask her what she is working on, and she says her team has moved on to create more involved heat-testing code for the next release that is scheduled for the end of the summer.

I sit down in her cube and tell her about my trip and where I am staying.

She smiles and grabs my knee and says, "You mean I have to stay here and work on code while you get to be having fun in San Francisco?"

"I suppose so. Sorry about that. Should I tell them I don't want to go? That I want to stay here and continue to build Red Hat servers and unsuccessfully try to catch bad guys breaking into our network?"

"You did catch them though, that's why they love you around here."

"I did catch and stop some of their attacks, but other attacks worked perfectly, and I don't know if I actually accomplished keeping data out of their hands."

"I think you did stop the attacks. Isn't that why they bashed you on your noggin?"

"Well, maybe. Thanks Sarah. You rock."

As I am getting up, she says, "Hey, do you want to meet and go for a run or something tonight, something casual?"

Well, I have not exercised for a while, but I did run in high school, so I answer, "Sure, your place or mine?"

"I have a nice three-mile trail I know, or we could get to know your neighborhood?"

I answer, "I'll come by around six. I need to get my running stuff at my place, if I can find it, and then I'll come up. I'll leave here at five."

"Deal!"

As I am walking away, I think, this is really cool—too bad I am tremendously out of shape. Guess I will have to grab George later.

Sarah and I meet up after work as planned, and she takes my breath away in her pink running shorts and a plain, untucked white t-shirt. We run three miles around the Towson area, which also takes us around Towson University. I am having a little bit of a rough time, but I manage to keep up with her, as she does most of the talking. I am struggling for breath but am able to ask her a question every once in a while to keep her talking. We talk easily, and then she makes me a dinner of peanut butter-and-jelly sandwiches and Oreos for dessert. High-class living.

When I get home, George is not there. He is almost certainly out on the town as usual, so I send my brother an email checking in and then hit the sack early. I hear George banging around sometime in the middle of the night when he comes in, but that is all. I am sure he was getting to know some of our local bartenders.

Chapter 22

Tuesday, May 5
Fells Point
Baltimore, Maryland

I wake up at seven and call David Rogers and leave a voicemail that I am coming down with something and should probably stay home. I hate doing that, as honesty in everything I do is becoming one of my mantras, but this is a top-secret mission I am on, isn't it? Oh well; if he complains to HR, the CEO has my back.

I start going through the sheet of paper that Ashok gave me. I will be purchasing twelve servers, all very high-end. I also am purchasing a bunch of random equipment. There are specialty fiber communication online sites with very expensive tubes that have fiber-like channels enclosed. I am able to look them up by the specific part numbers that Ashok had provided me. I recall that this is what we are going to use to move the energy, but the secret sauce is in the load-balancing routines in the software on the circuit. Ashok also made a note that he will be handing me the circuit board and that several were developed during the manufacturing process.

I can't remember everything, so I start a Word doc of what I need to purchase and what I need to do:

- The circuit board and our algorithms to load balance heat are what ART has to offer that is unique, mainly the software controlling the balance of the energy transfer (Ashok to provide)

- The energy tubes also are unique because of the way that we are able to load balance the heat traffic going through them, but they appear as if they are built out of common, off-the-shelf components that I can get from the backup configuration

- Build the energy tubes with George, as well as prepare all the computers with the testing routines that are supposed to be simulated

- We will hook up the computers to screens to show at different times the energy flowing through the tubes, as well as how much energy is getting through and how much heat is being generated; this will show how well we are performing

- Zamtech will provide the solar energy systems or simulated devices that will connect directly to our tube mechanism and circuit board

- The computers purchased will be running some of Zamtech's testing software, as well as software we have developed to show what is happening

My train of thought is interrupted by George, who is finally getting out of bed at ten thirty. He scratches his belly as he walks out wearing a t-shirt and boxer shorts.

I say, "You are a sight for sore eyes. What did you do last night?"

"Met some of the neighborhood, you?"

"I went for a run with Sarah, and then I came back here and crashed."

George gives a thoughtful look and then says, "Went for a run? What are you trying to be, human?"

"I guess, if that's what humans do."

He looks at me a little perplexed, his hair sticking straight up, "Oh yeah, why are you here?"

I debate what to tell him, but decide paranoia should win out at all cost. "I called in sick, needed to get some stuff done."

"You, calling in sick? Who would have thunk." He walks into the kitchen and opens a Diet Coke and starts mumbling, "Going for a run with a girl, calling in sick, stuff to get done...what is happening to my boy?"

I do not answer his ramblings. "Let's go and grab something to eat, you up for it?"

"Yep. Give me two minutes."

He walks back to his room and gets dressed, and we walk out into our new neighborhood. A misty rain makes a pattering sound on the brick sidewalks as we walk around looking at the many different restaurants and bars. We pick a little deli and sit down towards the back in a booth with red seats after we're done ordering. The deli is nice and light and smells of bacon.

I say to him, "So, the real reason why I took some time off is to talk to you and order some stuff that we will be needing."

"For the apartment?"

I say, "No, for my work, which you are now becoming a part of. The CEO has agreed to give you roughly $32,000 worth of stock for helping me out in California. The stock will be worth much more than that if things go right. If we win the prototype, one half will vest immediately, and if we get sold or go public, the other half will vest immediately."

He laughs. "Are you messing with me?"

After we order, I go on to explain basically everything that we will be doing. I tell him that we need to be extra paranoid and not talk about things in our place or with anyone besides each other and that there are only four people total who know about this. He asks a couple questions about the process and where we are staying. His first activity is to go to one of our venture firms and sign papers. They are located in northern Virginia, and I give him everything he needs to schedule his meeting.

He sits there quietly and listens, and finally when I pause to take a breath he says, "Do you really think these bozos may be monitoring our place or that there could be actual danger here, or are they just a bunch of nerds trying to hack in and steal your loot?"

I reply, "Well, there are two people dead, if you count Ashok's neighbor. You and I could have been killed, but they just wanted my computer. I think this is big; I think we could use you not only for your help as a trusted person to set this up but also because of your Army Ranger experience. These guys seem desperate to me, but I am not sure."

George smiles and sits back. "So I actually have to earn this money?"

Our turkey club sandwiches are delivered along with potato chips, and as we eat, I give him his credit card for making hotel reservations and the dates he needs to be there.

I say, "Pick any hotel in one of the towns surrounding Mountain View and get a big room or a suite. That whole area is called Silicon Valley, and it is a collection of towns like San Jose, Palo Alto, and Sunnyvale. Everything in that general area is surrounded by mountains."

I continue, "I will be ordering equipment today using my new credit card to ship to a second venture capital firm, and you will need to pick it up."

He is generally excited when we walk out, and I am glad, too, to have him along. This whole thing is getting really serious, and I have to admit I'm a little nervous. It'll be good to have someone I really know there with me.

Instead of going back to the apartment, I decide I am going to test the resolve of our company and drive to the Mac store in Columbia Mall and buy a new Mac. I am tired of using William's, as it is a little dated and slow. I put it on my new company credit card. I then go back to my apartment and configure it.

I then go through and use two different resellers to purchase a total of twelve servers and ship them to Palo Alto. They are high-end devices, and I am using different resellers then our company purchases through. I think I am tricky that way. I order software as well, and I know at least how to get them loaded with Linux before we start using backup drives to transfer information to them.

I then go to a list of sites Ashok has given me to purchase some random scientific equipment that we will be using to transfer the energy. Ashok is not taking anything for granted and will configure everything new for the third prototype. Ashok has made a note that he will hand me the actual circuit boards loaded with software that was tested and worked a while ago that our integrator is building for him.

I text Sarah that I am taking a personal health day, and much to my enjoyment, she texts me throughout the day.

Chapter 23

Friday, May 8
ART Headquarters

I am thinking to myself that this week has been relatively tame. Our computer security consultant has seen traces of what he thinks is malware on our systems, so he cleaned it up. From a computer security point of view, I figure that we have already been owned, but we are lucky that potentially what they need is not here. We have also moved the backup drives to a safety deposit box in a bank, and that is what we are going to use to form the third prototype.

I read an email from my brother describing what Hodophi does. He has some pretty interesting information about their CEO and their other lines of business. Another Chinese competitor has accused them of unethical behaviors before, but nothing has been proven. They have made their billions in energy and high-tech parts that are embedded in other products. The company's technologies are household names.

A second email from him has reports on the Chinese and Russian hacking communities for hire. There is a big market out there, and reading through his message, it seems like nothing is safe.

I spend the afternoon trying to be involved in the setup of the second prototype. Everyone is nice but busy trying to replicate the setup for the first prototype, which will be shown to Zamtech.

I look in at the original prototype, and there are monitors everywhere, along with simulation equipment, and Ashok is pacing the room asking questions. He looks like one big stress ball. He says hello, but we really don't engage. An hour later he stops by my office holding a small box.

He says, "Do you have a minute?"

"Sure."

He closes my door and then slowly unpacks a box of the small tubes I have seen in the staging room. He then pulls out what looks like a block of small circuit boards and hands them to me.

He smiles and says, "I want to show you how these things fit together for when you build our double-secret prototype. It's not hard; this is just the circuitry that all our software tells what to do. The complexity is in the software."

He continues, "First, take one of the two end blocks and set it on the table, pushing all those little wire connectors to the side. See that larger chip in the middle? That is the controller that you have been hearing about. The tubes plug in all around it."

He hands me a tube. "Go ahead, right into those slots."

He hands me the tubes one by one, and they fit in easily. He then hands me the second square circuit board and says, "This fits in the top to stabilize the entire block, and it also carries the load-balanced energy across these tubes to multiple sources on the other side. You can basically program each output to go to different locations, but that is through software. Our software will eventually be embedded in these chips that are doing the work, but for purposes of the prototype, they will be on the computers we are bringing."

He then walks me through how testing is going to occur, which I have heard before but is more interesting coming from him.

After Ashok leaves, I finish up building my last server and I stop by Sarah's cube; she is working away. I ask if she is up for hanging out tonight, but she is going out with two friends for a girls' night out. They are going to dinner and then to some of the bars, and she asks if I want to meet up with her later on. I give her a "maybe" and she gives me some garbage, which is probably deserved. I just am not sure if I'm up for heading out by myself to the Towson area later, even if it is to see her. I tell her I will check in with George and shoot her a text later. I figure I will end up going, because she is always on my mind.

Fells Point
Baltimore, Maryland

I leave work around five thirty, and people have already cleared out by then. Friday night! I go home and tinker around the apartment for a bit. There is a note from George that he is out and to shoot him a text. A note? Why didn't he just text me?

There is not a bite of food in our bachelor pad. Feeling sorry for myself, I grab the book that I have not read for weeks and my laptop and head out. Walking through the streets of Fells Point, I decide I will first grab something to eat, maybe a beer or two, and then I will figure out what to do. Probably get in touch with George and see if I can convince him to Uber up to see Sarah and her friends.

I find a nice local bar and grab a table. There are people there, but it's not too crowded. My waitress comes over and I start with a Flying Dog IPA, which is a local brew—well, the brewery is from Frederick, but that's close enough. I check out the menu and decide on a bleu cheeseburger and fries. After all, it's Friday night, and I'm bored.

I decide to leave my computer alone and get out my book. It is a good book, and there is nothing like drinking a beer and having a read while waiting for a burger. Life is not that bad, after all, and I find it hard to continue feeling sorry for myself. I end up having one more Flying Dog and then schlep back to my apartment.

• • •

Hans enjoys this spot immensely. It reminds him of Paris, where the chairs sit facing outward at coffee shops and restaurants so the people eating can watch the crowd. It reminds him of Le Tournebievre on Quai de la Tournelle. He has a three-bedroom flat in the surrounding neighborhood that is off the beaten path but close to Notre-Dame. He never does work in the countries where he resides, and the Paris flat is one of his favorites.

Hans takes a long puff of his cigarette and runs his fingers through his cropped hair. He and Dima sit quietly drinking their coffee and occasionally looking up the street at Robert and his friend's apartment building. They see Robert wander out on his front porch once and stand there with a contemplative look on his face as he looks around. He does not stay long on his porch. Then he turns and wanders back into the apartment.

Finally, Robert walks out of the apartment building with his laptop bag directly towards them on the other side of the street. He seems very tall from this angle, but Hans knows he is only a little over six feet. Robert's hair seems to be getting longer since the last time Hans saw him, right before he knocked him out and took his computer.

Hans has received a message from his employers that it is time to step up all activities; this is good for Hans and his team, because this will involve much more money. Hans continues to look over at Robert out of the corner of his eye as he talks in a low voice with Dima. They have not seen Robert's roommate all afternoon. Robert stops and looks at the outside menu of a bar directly across the street and then moves on, walking confidently out of sight.

Dima and Hans pay their bill and then casually walk to their car to pick up supplies. They will be visiting the CTO of the small company right after this meeting with Robert. They have been to Ashok's house before to look for the hard drives and had been surprised by his neighbor. Hans figures they will know if they can get the hard drives one way or another by the end of the weekend, and they can change tactics from there if they have to.

• • •

The steps and hallway are dark as I walk up the stairs, and it looks like a bulb is burned out above my door. As I start to enter the apartment, I have a funny feeling that something is not right. Maybe it is going into an empty apartment by myself when darkness is just starting to fall.

I start to pull out my phone to text George when a dark figure appears out of my peripheral vision and I feel a sharp pain in the side of my head. As I am falling, I have the fleeting thought he must have been standing behind the slight wall that separates our kitchen from the living room.

The good news is I do not black out like last time, but the bad news is my head hurts and my vision is blurred. I try to swing a kick at the dude who attacked me while I am lying on the floor, but someone else from behind kicks me in the ribs. I feel like I am going to throw up as another kick crunches my stomach.

"Don't worry, you little asshole, we aren't going to kill you or even mess up that nasty-looking face of yours if you give us some information."

I am trying to figure out which person is talking and what his accent is, but everything is still fuzzy. I can tell they are both wearing ski masks. My mind races, and from watching movies and reading books I figure it's a good thing I don't know what they look like. That's usually a sign they aren't going to kill you. I respond, "That is nice of you. I'll try not to puke on you."

There's a hard kick to my back from behind and I suddenly feel I may, in fact, throw up for real. I struggled to sit up, and again the harsh low voice speaks: "Look, dumbass, we are looking for something you may have. It is connected with the project, but it is nowhere to be found. Do you know what I am talking about?"

"I'm the friggin' new guy, I don't know what the hell you are talking about."

I am leaning on one arm, and I feel the kick again coming from behind me, but this time it hits my ribs and I lose my dinner and beer. This guy is not very nice.

"We searched this dump, and you don't own much of anything, so the question is where is it?"

I reply, "Where is what?"

As I say it, I know I should not have said anything, and suddenly there is a blow to the side of my face. I think it is from a fist, but it could have been from a boot again. Either way, my head hits the floor. My vision is obscured, and I think there is blood coming from my head and dripping into my eyes.

Keys rattle and there's laughter in the hallway. I smell sour nicotine breath as one of them leans in close to whisper, "Say anything, and you die today."

The door starts opening and I see one of the goons slip behind it as it opens.

"George, watch out!" I manage to scream fairly loud, surprising myself, as I feel movement again to my left and hear a sharp sound, which turns out to be the cracking of my head.

I am not sure how long it takes me to come to, but I am moving and I am surprised to wake up remembering everything. I am in an ambulance, and George is talking to the medic in the back.

"Yo." My voice sounds like a whisper, as I am trying to be cool.

"Hey little man. You need to stop getting tuned up like this."

"How did it end?"

"I was walking in with Dave and some of his girlfriend's friends when I heard your yell and raised my hand enough to block a shot coming at my head. Dude had some force, though, and he knocked me down. He had something like a crowbar on him. He was off balance and Dave wrestled for the crowbar, and the dude just let him have it and then pulled a gun and pointed it in his face."

George pauses thoughtfully and then continues slowly, "I think that dude was just going to shoot him, but the guy working on you told him to walk, and the two of them kept guns pointed on us as they left the apartment. They even closed the door behind them. I checked your pulse and your breathing and called 911. Dave went out on the front porch and looked to see if he could see them getting into a car or which way they were running, but they had totally disappeared."

He stops again. Through my mental fog I am trying to think, but my head is screaming in pain, I think worse than last time— maybe because I was out longer last time.

He then goes on. "The entire thing lasted about sixty seconds from when I heard your yell to when they left. I think we are lucky to be alive. There were silencers on both their guns."

My mind races. Ashok.

Adrenaline starts pumping. "George, do you have my phone? They will go after Ashok!"

George shakes his head no, and the medic who is silently working on my IV says, "There was nothing in your pockets when we loaded you in here."

"I had it out to text you before I got jacked at the place. It must have hit the floor when I did."

George says, "The police are in the place, and my brother and his friends are probably still there. I'll call."

I close my eyes and let my head pound as I hear George leave a message for his brother. If they think I know something, they have to know that Ashok, who wrote the algorithms, can give them all the information they want. They must have noticed the missing hard drives when they went to his place and connected it all to me.

We pull into a hospital, and I am on a stretcher moving fast. I must be okay, because George is not putting up a fight when they will not let him go back with me. He says he will find and warn Ashok. I yell at him my cell phone password and tell him Ashok's number is in there.

Chapter 24

Saturday, May 9
University of Maryland Hospital
Baltimore, Maryland

I am in and out of sleep for a while. I hear my parents in the room and then George, too, so I figure everything is okay with me. My head is pounding, but I finally open my eyes.

"We have to stop meeting like this."

My mom is first to talk. She is visibly shaking and tears are in her eyes. "Robert, is this something that you are connected to at work? You need to quit that job. There are plenty of normal places to work where someone is not attacking you. This is simply not okay."

Before I can say anything, she continues, "No, Robert, this is one thing after another. I know you like the work, but this is not worth it. You are in physical danger. I will talk to your CEO for you or whoever I have to so you can get out of this."

I do not dare interrupt now, but then she softens for a second and asks, "How are you feeling?"

"I'm good, Mom, my head just hurts a little."

My dad walks up and puts his hand on my shoulder and says that the doctor says that everything is going to be alright but that I need my rest.

I look at George. He says, "I talked to Ashok and Sarah, and your cell phone is on your night stand."

"Great, thanks George." That is all I want to hear, and now I shut my eyes. I think to myself that I'm glad we were able to warn Ashok, because I don't know a lot, and he knows everything about the systems we are building—he'd be in even more danger than I was.

Courtyard Marriott
Hunt Valley, Maryland

Ashok has done everything that George recommended after getting the news last night. He turns off his phone completely. He has gotten cash out of an ATM near his house and checks into the hotel about fifteen minutes north of Towson, and he tells the front desk someone had stolen his wallet so he has no credit cards for incidentals. They tell him to pay an extra $100 deposit that he can get back in lieu of using a card.

He is beginning to feel now that this is not worth it. The early computer attacks are one thing, and he thinks that they have stolen all his work, but he is lucky that they are not able to get his original work. Now all these physical attacks are out of hand. He is not sure if Robert knows, but the police had told them that Josh's murder was apparently a professional job.

He went out to eat Chipotle for lunch, but he's back in his hotel room bed and bored out of his mind. There's nothing to work on, and he is beginning to get angry again about the people that are attacking them. He wonders if Robert might be paranoid and that he might just have been mugged randomly. He watches the nightly news and sees this kind of stuff happen all the time.

As he is pacing the room, he picks up his phone and absent-mindedly hits the on button. He is about to turn it immediately off, but he is thinking about the project, and he still has the feeling that Robert is being paranoid, so instead he calls his lead engineer, Sam Jennings, who runs integration between software and hardware and leaves a message to remind him to get together during the week to schedule a dry run of everything before packing up. He listens to a message from his brother checking in, and then he decides after all that he should listen to Robert. He holds the power button down, turning it off.

Kiev, Ukraine

There are four of them packed in a small room with computers scattered all around. The newest member of the group, who is the cousin of the leader, Tapac, looks up and smiles. "I have something here."

He shows his counterparts the raw transmissions he is seeing from the cell tower communications of the U.S. telco company they are monitoring.

Tapac, who is gigantic in stature, smiles. "Send me the coordinates."

A second later, a beep alerts him to an IM, and he cuts and pastes an address in an email to a friend in Russia. He then shoots his good friend Hans a text message to let him know an address is being sent to him in email.

Tapac is not sure what the information he provides is used for; most of his work is looking for vulnerabilities in applications using homegrown methods and selling them to the highest bidder. There has been major money coming in recently from his friend in St. Petersburg, who has connections worldwide. This address will earn his group €20,000, which is equal to breaking into about fifty small European or U.S. business bank accounts or stealing about 10,000 credit card numbers. This is good work and only getting better.

Loch Raven Reservoir
Baltimore, Maryland

Ashok sits in his room for another thirty minutes trying to figure out something to do that doesn't require turning on his computer or using his phone. He flips through the stations on the TV and then decides to go to Loch Raven Reservoir for a run.

Loch Raven Reservoir is a large lake with plenty of trails. He parks his car on the side road where a couple of fishers or hikers have parked, and he walks down to the lake. It is a beautiful spring day, clear and warm, and there are a couple of hikers out. It looks like someone is down off of a trail fishing. He stretches and starts running.

As he runs along the path, he thinks of all the things going well in the project and everything that needs to get done for a successful pilot in California. He wishes he could turn on his phone to use the app that tracks his distance and speed, but he knows he should not. After about twenty minutes, he turns and goes back the way he came, as he does not think he can actually make it all the way around the lake.

Ashok looks for the entrance that he came down and the area where he thinks he saw the fisherman, but everything starts looking the same. He slows and starts walking and looks around as a hiker walks toward him.

The hiker breaks the silence in heavily accented English, "Beautiful day."

"Yes, it is. You don't know where the road is, do you?"

The hiker comes a little closer and says, "It is just up about 100 feet, and there is a trail that leads straight up. I am actually going to walk you there." With that, he shows Ashok a gun just inside his coat.

Ashok's heart skips a beat, but he starts walking. "What do you want from me?"

The man steps in behind him and says, "Just be quiet, and this will work out for you fine."

As he walks, Ashok wonders if he should just run. They need him for something, and he doubts they would shoot him in the back if they need him. He then looks ahead and sees that there is someone else on the trail that appears to be waiting for them. He thinks that the good news is that they had jumped Robert twice and had not killed him; they are just after the algorithms, and it will be almost too late to program anything if he just gives the algorithms to them.

The second man is with the guy behind him, and they guide him up the trail. Ashok looks down the street and sees an SUV another 100 yards down the road with two other men standing by it. Both men get into the car as they approach, and Ashok is guided into the middle seat. The SUV appears to be a rental of some sort, clean and new-smelling.

One of the men next to him grabs his head brusquely and holds a wet cloth over his mouth and nose, and then everything goes black.

Chapter 25

Sunday, May 10
Towson, Maryland

I was released from the hospital last night, and my parents had insisted that I come home over George's insistence that he would keep me safe. Sarah had come by, and my parents loved her, of course. She was cool and able to sit in the hospital room with me and make fun of me a little while everyone got a good laugh.

My head still hurts badly, and I guess I have had my second concussion in less than a month. They should pay me like I am in the NFL. I finally figure I should get up out of bed and get moving. It is only eight in the morning when I go downstairs, and for some strange reason I remember it is Mother's Day. I wish my mom a happy one and tell her I am sorry I didn't get her anything but had decided to spend it in the hospital instead. She laughs and makes me a big breakfast of turkey bacon and eggs. Nothing like home.

Sarah and George both check in over text. My parents and I go to Mass at ten thirty. We then go by and have a group visit with William, which is nice. He is intrigued by my story and hangs on every word. Man, I have been out of the house for a week, and it already feels good to have the routines and comforts of house and family back. My head still hurts, but it is more of a nagging pain that anything. My ribs and jaw also hurt from the punches and kicks, but I am okay.

I start thinking about work the next day and the collection of equipment that needs to go out to Silicon Valley. I know I should be really excited, but right now I am very worried we are in over our heads. I don't want anyone else to get hurt.

Warehouse near Baltimore Washington Airport Linthicum, Maryland

Ashok sits on the ground in a room with no furniture and shivers. The room has no windows or light, but he had felt around the room sometime in the night and there is basically nothing. It has a cement floor, and he slept some, but his body is hurting in different areas.

He feels he has been there for some time and remembers nothing about how he got there except for when the man next to him had held the wet cloth to his face.

Hours seem to go by, and he feels angry and scared and cold. There's a dampness in the room that sends a chill through his bones. He thinks the shivers might be a reaction to whatever they had given him, as well.

Finally, light comes into the room, and he is almost glad.

In a soft voice, someone says, "Ashok, I am sure you want to get out of here quickly. We do not want to hurt you, but we need some information."

Ashok is silent.

"We just need you to tell us where you moved the hard drives from your computers at home. It is as simple as that."

The room is dark again as the door closes. A pin flashlight shines on him, maybe from a cell phone, and a second person grabs him from behind. Someone wrenches his arm, and he feels a needle piercing it. Almost instantly a warm sensation fills his body—it feels good. A second later the door opens, and he can see three people walk out.

Again, silence. Ashok tries to understand what is going on. He feels a bit giddy, and he tries to step away from his feelings and analyze the situation as he has been taught his whole life during meditation training from his parents that started at a young age.

He concentrates and says out loud, "They are trying to get information from me. They need me, and they want something from me."

He then thinks to himself that the information he gives could endanger other people, and he cannot do that. He forces his mind over and over to repeat that. Hard drives from the computer, heat dissipation algorithms.

He tells himself, I threw the hard drives away. I drove them to the dump. Where is the dump? I threw them in the dumpster behind Mt. Washington Tavern. He has to make himself believe this.

He keeps going back to his meditation training and continually forcing his mind to believe that he threw the hard drives from his basement away.

He then says out loud to no one, "I did not need them anymore; I threw them in the dumpster behind Mt. Washington Tavern. I can recreate the algorithms, so I did not need them. It would take time, but I could recreate them if I needed them. I did not need them. I did not need them. Dumpster, Mt. Washington Tavern.

He wakes up with a start. He sees the penlight again. Hears the questions again about the hard drives. Does not answer. Feels fluid and warmth going into his arm and closes his eyes.

Silently he thinks of his meditation instructions. He wants to tell the truth, disassociate, and watch himself do that from far away. His mind races and his heart pounds. Why would I save the drives? I can recreate all that. I threw them all away; that makes sense, why wouldn't I throw them away? I should have thrown them away. People are getting hurt from this. I did throw them away.

Again he wakes up to the light and people talking to him.

Again the voice asks, "Where are the hard drives?"

"I don't know why you think I would keep the hard drives," he heard his voice yell.

"I don't need them. I can always rewrite the algorithms, I know the answer. Why save them, who's asking? Who cares?"

Another needle, this time in his neck. Some pain, more warmth.

Ashok hears voices, someone talking on the phone. Another language, but he's not sure what. He feels he is going to get sick; his arms are shaking.

The voice comes again: "Where are the hard drives?"

He hears his voice in a whisper say, "Dumpster...the dumpster behind Mt. Washington Tavern."

There's the sound of someone on the phone again, and he feels himself throwing up on his lap and then on the ground. He concentrates on his meditation and drifts outside of himself.

The voice asks, "How hard is it to rewrite the algorithms?"

"Easy. I know the answers."

"How long?"

For some reason, Ashok is laughing and shaking. "I don't know, a couple of weeks."

The voice on the phone speaks again to the person on the other end.

Ashok thinks there is another shot going into his neck, but what he is actually feeling is a blade severing his artery.

Ellicott City, Maryland

Troy has nothing to do all Sunday. He had called his mom, who lives in Chicago, to wish her a happy Mother's Day earlier, but he has basically been bored all day since then.

He is nervous as well. He sits around his new condo thinking about everything that has gone on. His friend Josh had talked him into a "win/win" situation, telling him that they would simply get some guys some information and they would get some money. Some friends of Josh's were looking for people on the inside of this nothing company in Baltimore, and Josh said they could make a bunch of money to "start us off in our careers and pay off some student loans."

Troy knew Josh from their shared computer science classes at Purdue. Josh was very smart, but he generally took the easy path. Troy knew Josh had cheated in school and should not have taken his advice, but based on his skills, the headhunter had really wanted him for this job. He should have left it at that and not searched and sent information as requested, or set up the bank accounts, or any of that. But Josh had seemed so sure of himself, and now he's gone, and Troy is scared.

His email contacts are no longer valid; he gets return emails saying that the address is incorrect. He has not been contacted after the last time he sent them information, and he knows that folks at ART are on to him as well. They have no proof though, and he has put his resume up looking for another position. He wants out quickly, but he is really nervous that the people he was passing information to are no longer contacting him, even on the secure email they had set up.

He cannot stop thinking about it. Why don't they need him anymore? Did they kill Josh? Why?

He decides to go out to Panera Bread to get something to eat to break up the monotony and to hopefully make himself less anxious.

• • •

Gordie sits on a park bench that looks across the street at the condos and watches Troy walk outside. This would be easy right now, but he decides to wait. Gordie has worked for Hans Tsugilva before and was trained up with him and Dima in the elite section of the KGB.

He always receives his assignments from Hans in a simple unencrypted, encoded email. Nothing too sophisticated— basically he takes the tenth letter of the email and writes it down and then counts out nine characters, then eight and so on down to one. From one he takes two letters from there, writes it down, and then climbs back up to ten. Very simple, but very effective. Hans always continues a story about his sick mom as a cover text. It is very remedial, and they both knew it, but no one ever suspects it in the millions of emails that people and foreign agencies are always trying to monitor.

From a simple email he is able to get the name, address, date it needs to be done, amount for the job, and where to pick up any weapons.

Gordie is not wanted in any country, and he intends to keep it that way. He has been in the military as a sniper and also has done hand-to-hand combat. His superiors recognized his skill and used him for a couple of side projects, which started his professional career. His only problem is his lifestyle. He spends too much money.

Hans approached him for a side job after Gordie had left the military, and their working relationship continues to this day.

Hans has categorized Troy as a low-value and low-risk target in the encoded email, but he still needs to be cleaned up.

Gordie takes every job seriously, and he is not going to make simple mistakes on this one. He will approach this job the same as if is a high-risk target. He will wait and take his time.

He walks back to his car and drives to a spot on the top of the hill. He wears a professional disguise and has a license plate magnet on his rental car. He will return it and make an 11:10 p.m. redeye back over the Atlantic from Washington Dulles International Airport. If he cannot make it on time tonight, he will simply rebook his flight for tomorrow. No need to rush. He has watched Troy off and on for the last three days and knows his routine. The guy seems like a loner; he will go somewhere to eat and come back right at dusk. He figures he will be on the road by eight thirty, tops, to northern Virginia.

The park has an easy exit area and close proximity to get onto Route 32 and then 95 South. He opens his trunk and pulls out his guitar case and wanders up the trail. This is a nice little park; the condo owners and Gordie are lucky to have it here. He then walks up into the tree line to a spot he hiked to earlier in the weekend disguised as someone else. He hopes no one will be unlucky enough to hike down this trail over the next hour or so.

He carefully sets up in his spot and lines the rifle and sight to where Troy will be coming back. Unluckily for Troy, his designated parking spot is towards the end of the parking lot. With the amount Troy had paid for the condo, Gordie thought he could have done better. Gordie wants to drop him right when he gets out of his car so the parked cars will hide him for a while. He had thought about waiting in his condo or just walking up to the car, but this would allow him to move quickly when he finishes.

It is now 7:50 p.m., and he watches Troy's car come back into the parking lot. He takes a number of deep breaths and follows the car with his gun sight. The spot he picks is next to a tree and off the trail about ten feet, allowing him to rest his arms on a low-hanging branch to stabilize his shot. He lines the sight up with the driver's side window and waits. Troy grabs something from the passenger seat—maybe leftovers. Gordie wants to wait until Troy shuts the door. That will possibly buy him more time to get away, as it will be more difficult to notice the person lying next to the car if the door is shut. An open door arouses suspicion. Troy's head pops into view in the sight, and Gordie waits for the door to close as he slowly exhales.

There is no wind. The weather is perfect, and he is about 500 yards away. He eases the trigger back and shoots. Immediately Troy's head snaps back and then he slumps down between the cars.

Gordie packs up the rifle in the guitar case and slowly eases back onto the trail. He will be throwing this guitar away at a dumpster at a rest stop right after Route 32 on 95. He does not care if it is found, but it will not make it easy on anyone if it is. He will deposit his disguises in another garbage can at the same location along with the empty McDonalds boxes and drink containers he collected earlier.

As he walks out of the park toward his car, he thinks to himself: another day, another €50,000.

Chapter 26

Monday, May 11
ART Headquarters

I stayed at my parent's house again last night. They surprised me by inviting Sarah over to dinner, which was awesome. She must really like me, right? She came over and we really enjoyed ourselves at dinner, and then Sarah and I took a walk around the neighborhood. As we walked, Sarah reached out and took my hand, and we strolled and talked easily that way for quite a while.

My mind raced, though. It seemed like there would be attackers around every corner during the walk. I told myself that the attackers had looked all through my apartment before I got there and had not found the hard drives. When they threatened to kill me at gunpoint and I simply did not know where they were, they seemed convinced. The could have killed us all already if they wanted to.

Sarah is also really concerned about me and George, and I guess there is reason to be. I have a cut above my eye around two inches long that the hospital had stitched up. And to top it off, my head still hurts. She and my mom wondered out loud during dinner if this work is really worth it. I tried to calm them both down and said that it was, in fact, worth it if we are actually successful. It will mean a lot of money and job security for me, but my mom simply wanted me to be safe.

I also told them all it was more than that now and what we were doing was important, and if we just backed down, what would we do? Plus, I thought that it was exciting stuff, but I assured them it would not be worth it in the end if someone decides to shoot us next time. I was just trying to make light of the situation. I told them I am going to be extra careful from now on. Sarah stayed around for a while and watched a little TV with my parents and I, and then she had to head home.

I walk by her cubicle this morning but she's not in yet, so I head to the main staging and packing area. There are already people working on packing devices. I start asking a bunch of questions, and I just jump in and start helping like I belong here. I learned early on that the people who constantly ask how they can help are never really able to help. Just find something that needs to be done and start doing it. If someone stops you, well, move on.

Chet Hartley comes in walks over to me. "Robert, how is it going? You have been crazy busy since getting here."

"Yeah, it's been fun. Well, sorta."

Chet laughs and adjusts his glasses, his flannel shirt hanging over his large belly. "When are you heading out to Silicon Valley? Wait, what happened to you?"

"I'm going out next week." I put my hand up to the cut above my eye. "Oh, this. I got jumped on Friday night."

"Again?"

"Yep, they must think I'm an easy target."

"Is it connected to what we are doing?"

"Who knows. It was in my new apartment, and it may have been a robbery I walked in on."

"Wow. Are you okay?"

"Yep, just a mild headache again."

I finish up a box and say, "Have you seen Ashok yet today?"

"No, I haven't. Let me know if you need anything from me at any point, okay?"

I think about Ashok. I need to talk to him. And Joe, too, if he has not heard that I got attacked again Friday night.

A dude walks up behind me. I turn around quickly because I'm beginning to get jumpy when people walk up behind me.

"Hey, I'm Bill Milano."

"Robert Dulaney, nice to meet you."

"Wow, I've been traveling for a while, and then I come back and there are a bunch of folks I don't know. What do you do here?"

I think to myself, I'm doing something, so move along dude. But he has an easy way about him, and he's talking to me with a smile. "Well, I was hired to do software engineering, but then I ended up building servers, and then I guess I added computer security when we started getting attacked. You?"

"I think I'm the company's only SE, but who knows. I have been out so much on the West Coast that they may have hired some more."

"SE?" I ask, even though I saw him explain the product earlier in the boardroom and knew what he did.

"Sales engineer. Basically, I explain stuff technically to the people who are purchasing our equipment. I also worked a lot on the RFP. I kind of bridge the gap between our engineers, our salespeople, and our customers."

"Sounds like a pretty cool gig."

"Yes, it really is. I get to know a ton of folks in our company, as well as different customers. I spend most of my time with the folks at Zamtech, but there are other prospects too. We need another play if we don't get that, and it's a hot area. Figuring out how to move stored energy is big, and our boy Ashok is a rock star."

"Have you seen him today?" I ask. There's a pang of worry in my stomach.

"No, but I was looking for him though. I have not seen him for a while. I was employee number five about eight months ago, so I spent a ton time with him then."

I say, "I'm going to take a walk down to his office. I need to talk to him."

"Cool, I'll join you."

I like this guy. He's straightforward and easygoing, and he seems to always be smiling, which is cool to me. He is a little taller than me, and as we walk down the hallway, he riddles me with questions, smiling all the while. He constantly grooms his goatee with his fingers like he is not used to it.

I can see that Ashok's light is out, and it does not appear that anyone has been in his office today. I walk in and look around. I check my watch. It's about ten after ten. I feel that worry pain again. Bill is saying something, which I am really not paying attention to, but it's something to the effect of Ashok always being in first at the office.

He then says, "I'm going to be around for the next week, and then I'm going back out to Zamtech."

I respond completely distracted, "I'm heading there as well."

"Good deal, I'll see you around. Great to meet you."

He leaves quickly and heads back the way we came. I stand there for a second. I decide I should talk to Joe Benfield and walk down to his office.

I knock and he looks up from his computer. "Hey, good morning, Robert."

"Do you have a quick second?"

"Absolutely, what's up?"

I walk in and shut the door.

He asks, "Have you talked to Ashok today?"

I respond slowly and thoughtfully, "No, but I was attacked again Friday night, and the guys attacking me wanted to know where the hard drives were. I was beaten up, but my friend George and some other people walked in and they bailed. George said there were silencers on their guns, and he felt they might have planned to kill me. On the way to the hospital, I had George call and warn Ashok to basically turn off his cell phone and hide. George talked to him, and Ashok said he was doing it, but it seems strange that he's not here."

Joe gets up from his seat, and pulls out his cell phone. He dials Ashok and it goes right into voicemail. He looks at me and says, "Are you okay? I just noticed the cut and bruises on your face."

"Yes, fine, but now I am really worried about Ashok."

He says, "I'm sure he's fine. Maybe his cell is just off because you guys told him to, but let's take a drive."

We walk downstairs and he tells Brenda, the receptionist, that we are heading out for a bit and if Ashok calls or comes in to have him call Joe immediately on his cell phone.

We jump into a hybrid Porsche SUV and he flies out of the parking lot. I am thinking about the attackers from Friday night; the police had questioned me again on Sunday, but over the phone. I wonder if they got to Ashok right after George called him. I am scared about what we might find.

Joe had been to Ashok's place before and we get there in no time. The townhomes are built into a cul-de-sac that is basically a big square with homes on every side. There are only a few cars in the parking lot since it is a Monday during work hours, and Ashok's is not one of them. We go and knock on the front door, neither of us expecting an answer.

I look at Joe and say, "George had told him specifically to turn off his cell phone, get cash from an ATM, and go stay somewhere not near where he got the cash."

Joe has a scared look on his face. "He is probably still there, laying low. Let's go around back."

We walk around and look into the back of his townhouse on the bottom floor where his neighbor was killed. The condo is dark, but we can see some of the computers and boxes.

Joe is clearly nervous and mumbles, "Let's get back."

We are quiet on the way back and he is flying. I am actually nervous we are going to get in an accident on the way.

We rush through the front doors and Joe asks Brenda if Ashok has come in or called. She says no. We walk straight to his office and he closes the door.

He says, "I'm going to send an email to the entire company and give it five minutes, and then I'm calling the police."

I walk around his desk and watch as he types:

Has anyone seen or heard from Ashok this weekend or this morning? If so, please just reply to me or stop by my office immediately and let me know when you talked to him, where he was, and what he said.
Thanks, Joe

He marks the message urgent and sends it.

We sit there in silence, and then there is a knock on the door. Sam Jennings comes in. Sam is as scruffy a dude as you will ever see. He has hair everywhere—some coming out of his shirt, a ton on his head in a bun on top, and a thick, full beard.

Joe says, "Hi Sam. Is this about the email I just sent?"

Sam speaks quietly and confidentially. "Yes, I heard from Ashok this weekend."

"Can you close the door?"

I stand there silently by the window with my arms folded and my heart pounding.

"When did you hear from him?" Joe asked.

"He left me a message on Saturday afternoon about doing a dry run before boxing up the equipment. I tried calling him back, but his phone went straight to voicemail. We actually had started packing this morning, but I had everyone start to set up the network again so we can walk through it with Ashok."

I jump in. "Joe, that means he gave away his position when he turned the phone back on Saturday."

Joe says, "Really, just like that?"

I know the capabilities of the hackers that are attacking us probably better than anyone. "Yes, really."

Sam quickly asks, "What's going on?"

Joe quietly replies, "We think Ashok may be in danger."

He picks up the phone and dials a number from a piece of paper he has on his desk. "I would like to talk to Detective McGrath. It's urgent."

I give Joe a nod and walk out of his office, my heart pumping and my mind racing.

Sam follows me out and closes the door behind him. "What's going on?"

"We think Ashok's in danger from the people trying to get our intellectual property."

"Anything I can do to help?"

"Not right now. But I bet you Joe will call you in to talk about the voicemail you got, so just don't delete it."

My heart continues to race, and I go and grab a cup of coffee, which is probably the last thing I need. I walk back to my storage area and turn on a new server and start to boot it up. I guess I want normalcy, and building a server will give me something.

A minute later, Sarah pops in and just walks up and gives me a big hug. "What's going on?"

"We think the people that got to me on Friday night got to Ashok, too. We can't find him."

She slumps into my guest chair. "Oh no...I thought he hid?"

My mind wanders to how pretty she is, but then it comes back and I respond quietly, "Maybe not well enough. I think he made a mistake. I think this is my fault. I should have had George stress to him the importance of keeping his cell phone off, or had George go pick Ashok up."

Sarah also looks scared. "We'll find him. Maybe he's just sick or something."

I just shake my head. "I don't think so, Sarah. My gut is telling me that this is really bad."

Sarah gets up and gives my shoulder a squeeze and then turns and walks back to her desk.

Ten minutes later my desk phone rings, and it's Joe asking me to walk down to his office.

When I get there I see a man and woman in suits. Joe reintroduces me to Detective John McGrath, who has an angry, mean look about him. Detective Susan Winchester looks much more pleasant.

Susan starts. "Robert, can you tell us about the robbery on Friday night and why you feel Ashok is in danger?"

I hear myself saying, "Can you tell me how much you know about what is going on around here, so I can put that in context?"

Detective McGrath says, "We have been working on the staged suicide and the shooting at Ashok's house as related to the work that you are doing here. We also know that there have been consistent cyberattacks against your company."

"Okay, that's good. Did you know about my previous robbery, and did the police inform you of the attack on me Friday night?"

Detective Winchester responds, looking down at her notes, "We did know that you and a George McCarthy were attacked in Towson and that your laptop was stolen. We added that in with the cyberattacks, but unfortunately the police that responded on Friday night had not flagged your attack as relevant to our investigation and they were investigating that on its own."

I say, "So, on Friday night, the attackers specifically asked me about hard drives. These are the same hard drives that they were looking for in Ashok's house. The information on them is the only thing that they were unable to steal from our network, and they are after them because they contain the original code Ashok wrote. I was lucky because George and some friends came home and the attackers decided to leave. For some reason they thought that Ashok may have given me the hard drives."

"Why did they think that?" Winchester asks.

"Maybe because he did."

The room goes silent.

McGrath finally says, "Do they know that for sure? Where are the drives now?"

I respond, "They are safe; they're not with me any longer, and no, I don't think they knew that for sure; they probably assumed I knew because I am the computer security guy that may have told Ashok to get them out of his apartment."

I continue. "On the way to the hospital, I told George to warn Ashok and for Ashok to get some cash, get out of his apartment, and not to use his cell phone."

"Don't you think you should have called us at that point?" McGrath said.

"Hindsight is twenty-twenty, and I was at the hospital and pretty shaken up. Don't you think your own team should have called you after I was jumped?" I snap.

McGrath, to his credit, says calmly, "Fair enough. What else can you tell us?"

"It looks like Ashok used his phone sometime Saturday when he called Sam, which means that they may have been able to figure out where he was. Hopefully he just told them I have the hard drives and they beat him up a little bit like they did me."

There's silence again in the room. McGrath changes the subject. "What can you tell me about Troy Beale?"

Joe jumps back into the conversation. "Why do you want to know about him?"

Winchester replies, "We originally found out from our investigation into Josh that Troy was close with him and they went to school together, but we had no reason to suspect Troy in Josh's death."

Joe says, "Why are you asking about him now? Do you suspect him now?"

Winchester thinks for a couple seconds and then replies, "Troy was found dead by a jogger early this morning, right next to his car. Preliminary investigation suggests a long-range shot, which tells us it was done by a professional."

Joe and I sit there for what feels like a long time looking at our shoes. I am dumbfounded and really nervous for Ashok. Joe finally says, "Robert has always believed that Troy was involved in giving away information to our competitors."

McGrath stands up and looks hot, "Mr. Benfield, when are you going to start giving us information that is relevant to our investigation? You have two employees who are dead, one that continues to show up in the hospital, and now one that is missing!"

Joe replies, "When are you going to share any information with us? You have barely come in here to talk to us about the investigation. We separated our computer security issues from these other issues, just like you did."

Winchester interjects, "Okay, we are not getting anywhere. We need to be a team going forward. Your company is under attack, and we need to figure it out."

Joe replies, "What can we do to help?"

Winchester says, "Just share with us anything at all that you think is relevant."

She walks over and gives me two business cards. "You both now have all our information. Call us anytime. We are going to head up to talk to the investigators working on Troy's shooting, and we will give you information as we get it. Joe, can you call Sam in here so we can listen to the voicemail and get a timestamp?"

I wander back to my desk and just sit there. Five minutes later the phone rings again, and it is Joe asking if I can stop back by. Two months ago, I would have never believed I would be in and out of the CEO's office at my first real job—now I am wishing he would leave me alone for a while.

The detectives are not there, and Joe asks me to close the door. He says, "Thoughts?"

I plop down on a chair in front of his desk. "Ashok is in real trouble; I should have alerted the police."

Joe replies, "You were knocked out and going to the hospital. You would think they could have tied it together themselves."

I say, "I also think whoever is after us is out of the stealing-information phase and into the destruction of our pilot. If we are lucky, maybe they are just holding Ashok until after our pilot, knowing our presentation won't be as good and Zamtech will not want to pick us if we don't have our visionary and CTO."

Joe says, "Holding him is not in their playbook, Robert."

I look down. "True."

Joe says, "Since you are the only other person besides Ashok and myself to know our backup plan, what would you do if you were me?"

I say, "Well, as you know my friend George is also aware of the situation. I think we need to push forward, hard. They have not found what they are looking for. My gut tells me that our prototype's results are better than theirs, period. They first tried to catch up by stealing our information, and they got everything except a key ingredient. We were lucky there, but maybe if they got that, Ashok would be standing here with us. As I mentioned, they have changed tactics. I'm sure now that they want to destroy our prototype. First, we lose credibility if Ashok is not there. I don't think the rest of us are in any danger as we are not necessary for the actual prototype."

I continue, "What is now in danger is the prototype itself. They need to destroy it. They probably will figure out a way to destroy the prototype and the backup, and then they think they have won. We walk in with a working prototype they don't know about at all and let our results do the talking."

He sits up straighter. "Agreed on that. I am going to tell everyone what is going on with the exception of the third prototype. You need to be very careful."

I walk back to my desk, and within five minutes there is an email from Joe to the entire company saying we will be meeting in the boardroom at eleven thirty. I kill some time working on my servers and then walk down to the boardroom. I give Sarah a smile across the room. She's talking to some software engineers.

Joe walks in and the place goes silent. He looks around the room and speaks in a low, even tone.

"I'm sure everyone was surprised to see an email from me this morning asking if you have heard from or seen Ashok. Unfortunately, he is missing. Everyone knows we as a company have been under a computer attack, we believe by a competitor, for the last several months. On Friday night, Robert was attacked at gunpoint in his apartment by masked men looking for hard drives of Ashok's that they did not find when his apartment was robbed. We believe those same people went after Ashok, but we are hoping we are wrong.

"I also have some more sad news to tell you. Troy Beale was found dead this morning. He had been shot. I don't know how many of you knew Troy, but he was a close friend of Josh's. I just got off the phone with the chairman of our board. I would like everyone to take the day off today. If you have any information related to any of this, come in and talk to me, and I will get it to the detectives working on our case. We will have HR set you up with counselors at no charge if you would like to talk to anyone about this. If you no longer believe you can work in this environment, please let HR know, and we will do the best that we possibly can as a small company to get you severance and back on your feet with another company."

He then raises his voice and speaks with passion.

"If you want to stay, it's game on tomorrow. We are going forward to win this pilot, which has the potential to completely transform the way the world consumes energy. Not only will this project make energy more affordable and usable, but it will also have a positive environmental impact on the world by reducing carbon emissions and eliminating the need for strip mining for coal. If anyone is not familiar with strip mining, that is where they literally blow the tops off of mountains and strip them to the ground, destroying everything for the coal. We are only scratching the surface with this technology.

"This project also has a major humanitarian impact. Developing nations that do not have access to electricity will be able to by using more efficient solar paneling. Think of the effect in countries like Haiti, a ninety-minute flight from Miami, which is one of the poorest countries in the world and also has the least amount of electricity."

He stands there a second looking fired up and then continues, "We are going to go through with the test as Ashok has requested. Hopefully Ashok is back in time to help us win this, but if he is not, we are going to win it for him. Tomorrow, we will have another company meeting in this room at ten, and we will get more information and put our game plan together. Thanks for your time, and I am sorry to give you this much bad news at once. Anything you think of that is relevant, please call my cell, which is listed in the company directory and on all the time."

I should be excited for an unexpected afternoon off, but instead I am fired up and want to get cranking on the work to get the third secret prototype going. I also am scared for Ashok. A couple people say they are going to lunch, and Sarah and I join them. Everyone is shaken up and asking me a lot of questions, so I bail pretty quickly. I tell Sarah I will give her a ring later and go home to check into all the equipment we are ordering.

George is in the apartment when I get home, so I ask him to go for a walk and I explain everything. He tells me he has brought his guns down to our apartment, which quite frankly scares the heck out of me, but the day passes without incident and we ate in: mac and cheese and hot dogs.

I try calling Ashok for the heck of it, but it goes straight to voicemail. I then shoot him a text to call me. I call Sarah and we talk for a bit, I email William with the developments, and then I hit the sack early.

Chapter 27

Tuesday, May 12
ART Headquarters

I am able to get to work early and have a cup of coffee at my desk where I am building a server like everything is normal. Everyone is in early, and there is a lot of chatter before the ten o'clock meeting.

Joe comes into the boardroom at ten on the dot with Chet Hartley, head of Software Development, and the room goes quiet. Joe is dressed in pretty much the same thing he always wears: a dark blue golf-style Under Armor shirt. He looks like a health food commercial next to Chet.

"Unfortunately, we have not heard anything from Ashok, and given the recent events, the police are considering his disappearance as suspicious and have opened a criminal investigation. Once again, if you know anything that is relevant, please let us know.

"Chet and I had a morning meeting, and I spoke with our board again yesterday evening. We are going to have a couple of groups working on different things as we prepare for the prototype. Tom McAndrews, you will be the lead for the presentation at Zamtech. Get familiar with everything. Bill Milano, you will be the lead technical presenter, which means more of the actual presentation will fall into your lap. I am tapping Robert Dulaney to report directly to me and spearhead computer security for the company."

My heart stops. This is something I would have only dreamed of when I started my first job here, and now I'm reporting directly to the CEO. Sarah gives me a thumbs up.

"Bill, I would like you to educate Robert on every detail of what you are doing and have him be in position to present, if necessary. He will be your backup and will also be a part of the presentation for technical assistance if you need it. Tom, I will be working with you to help with the business aspects of the presentation. You should also be prepared to jump in if need be.

"Chet is going to lead the preparation team. We are going to assemble both the actual prototype and backup in here and go over it as Ashok requested. I need the presenters involved in the practice run, and we need to test everything. We will now plan to ship on Friday if we can, but definitely by Monday at the latest.

"Chet is 100% the lead on all staging activities, and he will have a group working with him here and then in California. If you are not involved in the prototype itself, please stay focused on your deliverables. We will need to beta-test the next release of the software on time, regardless of whether we win or lose this opportunity.

"If you have any questions, or if you have information about Ashok or the attacks on our company, please call me at any time. I am glad everyone wants to see this through."

Joe them walks out of the room. Sarah comes up to me and squeezes my arm and gives me a hidden smile. There is a lot of silence in the room, and then folks start talking in small groups. Generally, everyone seems serious, and they quickly head to work on what Joe discussed.

"Hey, I guess we will be working together quite a bit."

I turn around to see Bill standing there with a grin.

"Hi, I'm Bill Milano," he says, sticking out his hand to Sarah.

"Sarah Donnelly, nice to meet you," Sarah says with a smile. "Looks like you both have a lot to do."

"Should be fun and interesting. Robert, are you able to head to the lab now and just start jumping in?"

"What I really need a ten-minute union break for two cups of coffee and a scotch."

Sarah rolls her eyes and Bill and I walk down towards the lab area. When we get to the lab, we see boxes everywhere that looked like they had been packed and then unpacked again. I see the circuit boards that are being hooked up to the computer. It looks like they will be testing two of them at the same time as part of a block. My mind starts racing. Ashok was going to get me the circuit boards, and I was going to hook up the fiber-like tubes to them after he told me how to do it. I really hope he comes walking through the door soon.

I go over to the group where an engineer wearing shorts, a t-shirt, and flip-flops focuses his attention on the board. I watch him take a couple of sensors and hook them up directly to the circuit board and to the computer. It looks like he will be observing the heat coming into the board on the main channel directly from the source and seeing if it is the same coming out of the many tubes at the other end.

I remember Ashok talking about the fact that the high amount of energy that comes directly from the source needs to be broken up and transferred so that many components can take advantage of it. Ashok's algorithms did that with the help of the controller.

I point to the largest chip on the board and ask, "Is that the controller?"

"Yep," the engineer says.

He does not seem annoyed, even with his one-word answer, so I press on. "How hard is it to put the tubes into place on the circuit board?"

"Not very. They actually just slip right in. They're just commercially available parts that we just literally plug in."

"Cool stuff," I said as I walk away thinking, I'm glad Ashok walked me through it as well.

I walk over to the business development specialist, Tom, and introduce myself. He is talking to Bill. "Nice to meet you," he says. "I have heard good things about you."

I try to crack wise and say, "Not from anyone intelligent, I assume."

"If you think Joe and Ashok are not intelligent, you must be off the charts."

He says it jokingly, but it annoys me anyway, though I'm not sure why.

I ask, "When is the last time you have been to Zamtech?"

"I was there all last week, in and out of different meetings with product management and their system engineers. It is supposed to be kind of a quiet period, but they are talking to both sides. Basically, I just ask a lot of questions and then relay the answers to Joe and Ashok."

"Are their solar panels as good as we hear?"

"Everything I have seen indicates that they are better than we even imagined. Their engineers are saying they're seventeen times more efficient at collecting sunlight than anything we have seen before. Their energy converters are not quite caught up, but all said and done, they are probably fourteen times more efficient than anything on the market today. Wild stuff. There are literally press vans in their parking lots looking to interview anyone walking in there. It will be a zoo when we are out there."

I ask, "Have you seen an updated test plan?"

"Yep, sent one over last week to Ashok and Joe. I think Joe's admin is printing it out right now for everyone involved."

Bill jumps in, "Nothing really changed though, correct?"

Tom answers, "Not that I could see, but you will need to study it pretty hard for any technical nuances."

Nuances? What does that mean, technical nuances?

I just say, "I'm going to head down and see if they are printed out. See you guys in a bit."

All in all, there are about eight people going through setup, and I should hang in there and watch everything since I am going to set it up myself. I am now worried about the extra circuit boards that Ashok was ordering.

I walk up to Joe's office, and Chet is standing at the door talking. Joe sees me and says, "Come on in, Robert, Chet and I were just finishing up."

Chet says hi as I walk by, and I respond in kind.

"What's up?"

I keep my voice low and say, "Do you know where the extra circuit boards are that Ashok ordered?"

He answers, "They just got in last week, and the team has been taking them out of a box in his office."

Uh oh, now the team will know that Ashok ordered extra circuit boards. I say, "Okay, I need to grab two of the boards as discussed. Does anyone have the Zamtech prototype test plans they could send me? I would like to read them so I understand more of what we are setting up and what we need to show during the prototype."

"Yes, Brenda at the front desk should be finishing up printing these out for everyone. We wanted hard copies so we could physically check them off as we test them."

"Cool," I say and wander to Ashok's office. I just go in there like I own the place and beeline right to a box that is open in the corner. In it are smaller boxes, which I assume are each of the printed circuit boards from our manufacturer. I grab two and go straight to my desk. I lock them in my drawer, not that it will really stop anyone. I take the key. I then walk back to get a copy of the test plan.

I sit at my desk and try to read through this thing. It looks like they are going to be monitoring everything from the circuit board in "joules" marked throughout with a J. Oh, right—my basic engineering courses come back to me and actually help me remember that joules are a unit of measurement for energy. I quickly look it up on the internet and find that one kilowatt hour is equal to 3.6 million joules.

They request that the vendor provide the testing and measurement equipment to be able to read the energy levels and show it graphically. That must be the reason for all the computers, so we can simultaneously show the energy levels throughout the transportation process. They are going to test this with input levels of five million joules, incrementally going up through 200 million joules.

They note that they may decide during the testing to ramp to 800 million joules or above, but they will be checking for linearity of the energy to give them clues on whether the devices could handle spikes. Each board needs to be rated to handle 1,000 million joules. I do the math quickly on my iPhone; this means each board, and the corresponding energy tubes, needs to handle 277.78 kilowatt hours. Pretty crazy stuff.

They expect the vendor to be testing and showing that energy is not being dissipated, but they will provide their own equipment to test for heat increases on the circuit boards and energy structures.

There are a lot of schematics in the document showing where and how the circuit boards will be attached to the energy sources.

Very interesting; I wonder how we had tested for all this stuff here, but I remember that I've seen some fairly large and expensive systems for some sort of testing.

I write down some of the other specifications that sound important:

- Pilot testing should have controller board that is a total of five centimeters wide and twenty centimeters long.
- Each board should fit into a block of ten, but the pilot testing does not require this to be shown
- Each block must have the ability to break up the energy coming from the source into 600 separate energy sources with energy dissipation less than one microjoule

There is an entire section talking about energy dissipation in the form of heat, so they will be monitoring temperatures as well in nanojoules in and out of the tubes.

Okay, so that makes sense to me. They're breaking up the energy at the source to get to separate lines throughout whatever will be the consumer of the energy. Each board will have to break up into sixty channels, and that is where the multiple load-balancing techniques developed by Ashok will come into play.

I start writing down questions that I have, and then I close my office door and pull out one of the circuit boards. I look at it like I know what the heck I am looking at, but of course I have no clue. I do see where the energy tube will be hooked up and where the controller is. It is my understanding that the machine code language-driven software is installed by the manufacturer on the circuit board and the controller at the time of the integration, but I make a note to check into this.

I put on my computer security hat and have an "oh, crap" moment. Our complete schematics, software, and plans could have then be stolen from our manufacturer. They will not get the source code, but do they need it if they stole everything else?

I make another note to check into what gets installed and wonder if the hacking group chasing us has hit them. They would be dumb not to, but I had not really thought of this until now. Maybe they did not get deep enough to check into who we are using to manufacture this stuff.

I grab my papers, put away the circuit boards, and start heading out of my closet of an office.

"Hey, congratulations on your new promotion!" Great, it's David Rogers.

"Thanks David. More work, less time, no more money." I try to be funny to make him move along.

He responds, "Yes, but you are reporting to the CEO."

"Oh, joy," I say, trying to make light of it. "But, seriously, thanks." I am trying to brush him off because I have stuff to do.

"It was great having you work on my team."

Really? You never talked to me, much less worked with me. "Thanks David. I really appreciate everything that you have done for me."

We shake hands and I am able to escape back to the testing area. After reading the documents, I now feel a little smarter about what we have to do.

The rest of the day is basically me poking around the lab, asking questions and helping where I can. I am able to add some value here and there doing basic Unix system admin work.

That night I just go home, check on the equipment orders, email my brother with the basics, and catch some crap from George for not going out with him. Sarah had asked if I wanted to go for a long run, but I tell her I need to get some stuff done for the trip, and I ask her for a rain check. I'm getting old.

Chapter 28

Wednesday, May 13
Baltimore, Maryland

I am up early, and much to my surprise, so is George. He says he has some stuff to get done. I ask him if he wants to get a coffee and while we walk to the neighborhood Starbucks, I am able to catch him up on everything going on.

I get a medium cup of coffee and a delicious sausage and egg sandwich, and we walk back. George is all set for his trip. His flight will be going out on Monday, a day after I leave.

George is picking up all the equipment we ordered from ART's venture investment firm on Tuesday and setting it up his hotel room. We decide that I will plan on meeting him at ten on Tuesday night and that he will have all the equipment in the room by then. I have to be there for the real prototype setup, then the backup prototype setup, and then the secret prototype setup at night. That's a lot to keep track of!

I get to work around eight thirty and go immediately to the prototype lab. Things are really coming together, and there is one engineer in there looking at something he must have been testing. I have already received the last backup tapes for every single system in prototype from our freeze a month ago, so I am not too concerned with the software builds.

I walk around and see all the servers wired together with a router in the middle. Everything looks pretty good. I notice the ethernet cable is plugged into the wall as well. I thought this is supposed to be standalone system? I can't focus on it right now, so I bank it into my brain cells to ask someone about later.

I walk down to Chet's office and ask for the name of the integrator and any contact information he has. He looks at me and says, "What now?"

"Nothing, I'm just concerned that our machine language code on the circuit boards has been compromised or corrupted at our integrator's site."

He seems annoyed, but he looks down at his computer and says, "I'll forward you the contact information now."

"Thanks, man," I say as I leave and wander back to my desk.

I see the email with the contact info for some sales dude or partner guy for the integrator. They are in Frederick, Maryland, which is about forty-five minutes from where we are.

I shoot him an email and then follow it up with a voicemail that it's urgent we meet as soon as possible regarding the ART business.

He calls me back immediately. I figure he thinks I am some sort of big shot. He agrees to meet me in an hour. I do not tell him much—I just say I report to Joe Benfield and need to talk to him, throwing around my newly acquired status.

I want to talk to him at his office, because I now do not trust our phones or anything else in our offices, really. I drive up there and spend about an hour telling him what I need. I assume that they have also been compromised by the attackers, so there's no need to tell him about computer security. What I want is an old build of the circuit board; the last version is about two months old. I tell him to use our old ISO (which is compiled code) and build four of them (two potentially for the test and two for backup). I tell him not to email anyone about this request. I don't want any traces of this in any computers. If they need special authorization, I will get Joe to call their CEO.

He seems very eager to please for such a small order, but their company is probably smelling money and will also benefit handsomely if we win. I give him the venture capital firm's name and contact information so he can send the boards to them.

I get back to the office around two, and there is a group in the lab running the presentation. I walk in and listen to Bill and Tom walk through the different parts, and they really seem good. I am becoming genuinely proud of what Ashok had created here, and I have a pang of worry and fear for him. There's still no news on his whereabouts.

At the end of the presentation, Joe and Chet start pounding them with questions, and they handle them well. It seems like everything is working as planned. At the end, Tom asks if there are any more questions, and my habit of always saying weird stuff at weird times comes out.

I blurt out, "Why is this prototype connected to the network?"

Tom and Bill look at me like I had two heads. Finally, Bill smiles and says, "I'm not sure. Anyone want to take this?"

Chet looks pretty pissed at me but says, "Let me walk down and check with some of the engineers."

After he walks out, the silence is overwhelming, so I say, "Could you pull it out and try the demo again?"

Bill says, "Why not, let's give it a whirl!" and promptly walks over and pulls it out.

I like that dude. He then starts the process over. After a couple of minutes, he says, "Looks like it's good, but something's not quite right."

Chet walks back into the room. "Our guys have it going out to a time server to make sure all the clocks on all the computers are synchronized."

Now I'm the one looking at him like he has two heads. "Is it easy to take out?"

"No, I asked them, and it's an embedded URL all throughout the compiled code."

Are they really going to have the test relying on external connections? The guys we are up against are too good for us to mess with even if we shut down everything else. I ask, "Is there a way to fake it out and have our own domain name server and our own timer with that same URL?"

Bill answers, "Yep, we can fake it out. We will need another server. Chet, can you get us the exact URL?"

Cool, but in the meantime, I figure the bad guys have all the information from our tests being pumped out on a command-and-control channel. At least our test won't be connected. Joe asks if we can complete it and test it before sending it, and everyone agrees. Looks like it will ship Thursday afternoon.

Well, I have made enough people mad at me today, so I wander over to Sarah's desk and ask if she wants to see a ball game tonight. She is up for it and agrees to come down and have a little happy hour at a neighborhood bar before heading over. I tell her I will also check with George.

It turns out to be a very fun night. We drink some beer at happy hour, the Orioles pull off a 7-4 victory, I win a couple bucks playing home run derby, and I enjoy George and Sarah's company. It is a perfect spring night, but a sense of dread hangs over me; I can't forget that George and I will soon be gone for several weeks, and Ashok is still missing.

Chapter 29

Sunday, May 17
Baltimore, Maryland

The rest of the week whips by without incident. All the gear is packed up and shipped, and I have gotten a backup tape of the new time server from Bill. On Saturday I went home to dinner with Sarah and my parents, which was fun. I also had visited William in prison.

I get up on Sunday morning and hit the nine o'clock Mass with my parents, then I go back to my place and pack. Sarah is picking me up and dropping me off at the airport at noon for a one thirty flight into San Francisco.

When I come back to the apartment from Mass, I ask George to take a quick walk. We wander outside and head to the coffee shop. He is clearly looking around a little as we walk, and I ask if he thinks we are being watched or spied on.

"No, I'm just always paranoid, little man. These folks that you are messing with are serious. I learned in the army to be prepared, and they have definitely caught us unprepared a couple of times."

"When's your flight?" I ask him.

"Tomorrow night. I get in around eight, then I'm renting a car and will be in my hotel by ten. I will pick up both our new phones from the venture firm on Tuesday morning and give them to you when I see you on Tuesday night. I'll spend that day picking up all the stuff you ordered and getting it to my hotel room. I have a suite in Sunnyvale at the Marriott Residence Inn on Lakeway Drive. I won't send you my hotel room number or anything, just meet me at the hotel bar at ten on Tuesday night."

"Look at us, top secret and all: Lakeway Drive, Residence Inn, ten o'clock Tuesday, bar, done."

"Cool, man. Three weeks, and then hopefully you and I are going to cash some checks!"

I laugh; "That is the plan, my man, but we may have to wait for some of the options to vest."

We get our coffee and head back to the apartment. I throw some more stuff in a bag, and then Sarah is knocking on the door.

I yell, "Hey, come on in for a minute," and she enters. "How was your morning?"

Her eyes sparkle and she replies, "Good, I'm just thinking about how much I'm going to get done without you here."

I groan at the joke and reply, "Come on, it's just three weeks. I do wish you were going to be out there, though."

"I'll just hang out and watch baseball with George."

I forgot that she doesn't know George is going to be out there with me. He wanders out of his room.

"Sounds good, little lady, but I may head out to see some other friends. This lame bonehead won't be around to hang with, and I need to take advantage of my unemployed status."

"Really, you're taking a vacation from your vacation?"

"Potentially. It's one of the many advantages of being unemployed. You don't have to be anywhere."

I grab my bags and walk to the door. I had one bag to check and my new laptop. I give George a hug and say, "Later."

"Be safe, moron."

"Thanks."

Sarah and I walk out, and I get that creeping sense again that everything isn't going to be all right. Getting into the car, I say to Sarah, "I guess no one has heard from Ashok or they would call us, don't you think?"

"Yes, they would definitely call you. You okay?"

"Just a little paranoid about everything that is happening and worried about these next three weeks."

She asks a couple of questions about the trip, but in general we drive in a comfortable silence with each other to the airport.

When we get there, she gets out of the car and gives me a kiss and then a nice long hug. When we pull back, there are tears in her eyes, and she tells me she will really miss me. I tell her I will call as soon as I get there and text her all the time, and then we wave goodbye with a smile.

She is so sweet, and that gives me comfort as I walk to the ticketing area.

Silicon Valley, California

I get into San Francisco airport at four thirty and pick up a rental car. In San Francisco's airport, which I am clueless about, you walk to a little tram that takes you to the airport rental facility. I have picked up a Starbucks coffee waiting for my bags, so I am pretty fired up. It feels pretty amazing that it is four thirty and light and beautiful out.

I text Sarah from the car rental line to let her know that I am in safely, and she sends me back a smiley face. I get in my car and really don't feel like going straight to the hotel, so I decide to take a drive around and see the sights of Silicon Valley.

I'm not talking about the normal tourist sights. I want to see the geekish history of the place. To that effect, I start with

Apple. I want to see their headquarters, so I use Google Maps on my iPhone and head to the headquarters of the company that changed the world. When the iPhone first came out, I thought, who needs music on a phone? But they have proven themselves right—we can utilize everything on our phones, not just music, but cameras, calendars, entertainment, the internet, and more. I think they really set the mold and then were copied by every other company in the world that makes phones. Some companies not even involved in phones got into it the game after seeing Apple's success.

I park my car in visitor parking and walk around their campus, and it is overwhelming. It is located in Cupertino, which is another one of the Silicon Valley towns directly south of Sunnyvale. The campus is amazing. It looks like a college campus for tech, with green space all around and buildings surrounding a large open area in the middle. There is a road called Infinite Loop that circles the entire facility, but there also are a lot of buildings outside of the loop. I then get on Google Maps again and go over to their new facility about a mile away. Construction seems to be going on, and it does not look like it has been moved into yet. This is the one that you see in pictures that has a huge circle resembling a football stadium. Pretty cool.

Now I'm all geeked up and decide to head to Google's campus in Mountain View. I know Google is dabbling in some new innovative stuff, but everything about them comes from an amazing search engine. I like their maps better than the one that now ships on iPhone. And of course, it far outshines older online maps—anyone remember MapQuest? It was a great idea that did not change quickly enough. So I find their location and drive up there. Mountain View is just north of Sunnyvale, but traffic seems slow on this Sunday evening. I do not get out of the car this time, but I drive around their campus, which is neat as well. It's spread out, has lots of buildings, and is right next to a park. I think if I ever work in a big company, these two would be great to work for, although I am getting the feeling I am more of a small company or startup kind of guy. But I definitely have a better understanding now of how other huge companies have changed the way we think, work, and play.

I head over to the campus of Cisco Systems in San Jose, east of Mountain View, to complete my techie tour. Cisco has many, many buildings that really are not connected, so it is more of a drive, but really cool. They probably have at least thirty buildings throughout the San Jose area. There is a small train station right near their main campus, which looks like it is made specifically to get Cisco employees to work. Consumers don't know Cisco as well, but they provide the infrastructure that fueled the internet. All large tech companies know Cisco well.

It is now six thirty and I am hungry, so I head into Palo Alto and find a bar near Stanford University. I order a burger and fries, pull out my book, and have a delicious IPA shortly followed by another.

I figure enough is enough, so I finally head to my hotel in San Jose. This is where I am going to be working on the second prototype during the days before I go off to meet George to set up the secret prototype at night.

I finally check in, and I am exhausted. I text Sarah good night and that I wish she were here with me, but with the time difference, it's eleven thirty on the East Coast and she doesn't respond. I am shot and want to take a good look around the hotel. I have to get out of here almost every night without anyone seeing me and am happy to see there is an exit door that does not require a walk by the bar. It is a strange but interesting place that has the hotel check-in on the second floor.

I go to bed but cannot sleep. We have been targets of a sustained, systematic attack at many different levels. I have advised people not to bring in the FBI so our abilities to make the prototype on time will not be altered. But right now, as I try to go to sleep, that seems like a horrible decision—not that the FBI would have given too much thought to such a small company anyway, but maybe they could have helped us. Ah, well; they are probably overwhelmed with bigger cases.

As I lie here, I start getting angry. What will I do if I find out who the attackers are? My answer is: nothing. I am prepared to do nothing. A thought that I keep coming back to is to create some malware of my own to, at a minimum, find out more information. Something similar to what I did to Troy at ART, but better.

I finally realize I am not going to sleep, so I jump out of bed and immediately start into writing a program. The idea is simple:

- Create a software dropper that will wait for a certain time period before executing a process.

- There is a technique used in computer security called sandboxing that will try to execute software to see how it behaves. To evade this type of computer security, I write some code to make sure that the software I write will not execute if it is on a virtual machine.

- The software dropper's only purpose will be to create an executable and then erase itself; the next executable will do the same thing. This will make it very hard for someone to identify the software that is doing the damage.

- I then need a couple different versions of the actual malware depending on what I want to try to accomplish. The first one will be to send to someone that I want to spy on in an ongoing manner. It basically starts a simple keystroke monitor that will copy everything that is typed or clicked and put it in a file and compress the file, and then I leave an open spot to transfer it to. The purpose of the second version of the file is simply to compress and encrypt all the files on their hard drive and send it very slowly to an Amazon Web Services location. I could send it directly to a server I still have in my parents' basement, but I prefer to make it go somewhere to the anonymous cloud.

- I then use my company credit card to get an account on Amazon Web Services and create a fake LinkedIn site. Instead of using the normal URLs for LinkedIn, I alter it slightly so it will not be recognizable to anyone going there. I figure the way I can trap someone is to send them a fake LinkedIn request, but when they click on it, the request goes to my site instead of the real LinkedIn location. Once they click on my fake LinkedIn email, it will not only take them to my site but also download my malware on their computer to start monitoring them. I take a snapshot of my regular LinkedIn profile and use that as my landing page so it looks legitimate to the target.

It is two in the morning, West Coast time, and I am now officially exhausted. I crash almost immediately when I hit the pillow.

Chapter 30

Monday, May 18
San Jose, California

I wake up way, way too early, but I like it. It is five in the morning, and since on the East Coast it is eight, I actually get to call Sarah and say hey. She is doing well. Of course, she has already worked out and is on her way into work. I want to go back to bed because I know these days are going to go late, but I can't, so I actually go to the gym myself. Maybe I will impress Sarah and get in good enough shape to be able to go running with her.

The gym is standard issue, and I lift for a little and then go for a run on the treadmill. Bill shows up to work out and we talk for a while. We are supposed to meet in the room that ART has reserved at ten o'clock to start setting up the prototype, but Bill and I decide to meet for breakfast at eight thirty.

He is running a little late, so I am reading the paper when he walks over.

"Hey, how's the coffee here?" he says, interrupting my sports page catch-up. The Orioles lost last night, and they are two games behind the dreaded Yankees and tied with Boston early in the season.

"Good, it has caffeine. How was the end of your workout?"

"Not bad, feel a bit out of shape. And it's probably going to get worse."

"Yep, traveling and eating out is going to kill us for three weeks."

He asks, "Where are you originally from?"

"Baltimore born, raised, and stayed. My parents still live in the same house I grew up in. You?"

"Army brat, grew up all over the place. Also lived overseas for a while in Germany."

I think for a second and then venture, "That must have been pretty cool?"

"Not bad, but you miss having a place you call home. My parents live in Florida. I'm the youngest of six kids, all spread out all over the place. My brothers and sisters kind of settled near the colleges they went to, generally close to where my parents lived at the time."

I switch the subject on him. "How well do you know the prototype and the software that we will be working on?"

"I know it well; I came to the company very early on. I just got lucky, I guess, if we make it big here. If not, it's onto the next startup until one hits."

I am beginning to get really nervous about the prototype that I am going to set up without Ashok, unless something changes really quickly. "Can you set the entire thing up from scratch if you had to?"

"I think so, but it's lucky we don't have to find out. A handful of those real engineers we brought are a lot smarter than I am."

I say, "But you could if you have to? After all, you have to explain it to the customer, since we probably won't have the developers in the room."

"Yes, I don't know down to the coding level, but I do know the process at a layer a little higher up. Because of what I learned in the early days, I can even do a block diagram of which subroutines talk to which subroutines and how the hardware on the board interacts with the physical channels."

I blurt out without really thinking, "Can you show me and explain to me as much as possible what you see when we are setting up? I think what you do is cool, and I may want to try to do what you do someday."

Oh, jeez. Why did I say that? I don't know if he is the kind of guy who would see me as competition for his job.

He eases my tension a little when he says, "Yeah man, it's a pretty sweet job. You get out on the road and meet many different customers and see what they do. You also get to see a bunch of towns and meet a bunch of people."

He then changes the subject on me, turning the tables. "So are you dating that cute girl in software, Sarah?"

I laugh, "Yes, she's really great."

"Nice. You don't meet a ton of girls in engineering."

We finish up and pay and decide to drive over together. He drives, and I text Sarah in the car. She gives me a reply right away that she misses me already, which makes me feel good.

Zamtech has a Palo Alto address, and we have two hotel rooms in a Hampton Inn right across the street. The two prototypes will be set up in there, and we will bring over one of the prototypes and set it up at Zamtech for the tests the following week. We will replicate it with the second prototype in the hotel, just in case something happens to the first prototype.

We get to the hotel a little before ten o'clock and go up to the rooms where we are going to be doing the work. It is essentially two conference rooms that have a divider wall between them that is now pulled back to make one large room. There are tables and chairs all around. There are a handful of boxes in the room, but the main servers will not be there until the afternoon. The networking equipment arrived early, and two of our engineers are doing some basic wiring, and we make some small talk. It's good that Bill is here, as they seemed to know and respect him.

I help unpack some of the networking equipment and try not to ask dumb questions. Ashok had given me all the specifications of what to order, and I had ordered exactly off of that, so I am not too worried about the third prototype, but I have to catch myself a couple of times when I start asking too many questions. We are going to set up two exact prototypes in this room, so I will get my opportunity to watch.

My cell starts ringing, and I look down to see Sarah's name and picture on my phone. I decide not to answer it because everyone is around. A minute later it begins to ring again, so I grab it as I walk out of the suite.

I pick up the phone and say, "Hey."

"Did you hear?"

I try for a lame joke. "That you dig me?"

"No, I'm sorry, Robert. Listen to me for a second. They found Ashok yesterday." She pauses.

I say slowly, "I take it that this is not good news."

She says, "No. They found his body in a landfill somewhere in the Baltimore area. He was in a bag with his neck slit. Apparently, a foreman saw it as a truck was dumping into the landfill."

We're both quiet for a beat while I take the news in.

"I'm really sorry, Robert. I know how much you liked him. And now I just wish you would come home. I'm worried about you."

I am having trouble finding my voice, and I hear it kind of quiver when I say, "Do they have any other details or any suspects?"

"No, I actually heard about them finding someone murdered on the radio this morning, but they did not have names. Police and those investigators were here again this morning, and then Joe Benfield called a quick all-hands meeting ten minutes ago."

I don't know what to say, so I just choke out a little groan.

She says, "I'm so sorry, Robert. I wanted to be the one to tell you."

"Thanks, Sarah, for calling me. I really miss you and wish you were here now more than ever."

"Same. Please be careful."

I say, "I will. You too. Try to get a run in today. It helps clear the mind."

"Bye."

I walk back into the room and see Bill sitting across the room, talking on the phone quietly with a look of horror on his face. We make eye contact and nod.

What is wrong with these people? This has gone way, way too far. But now it has made me want to win at any cost. I think of the early information I had heard about all of this. This project could be worth tens of billions of dollars. People do strange things for money, even small amounts, and these profits could be astronomical.

Bill comes back over and addresses the engineers. "Hey guys, I have some really bad news..."

Joe calls me five minutes later, and I tell him I have heard about Ashok.

He says, "I'll see you in two weeks, but you need to be very careful. Don't tell anyone anything. I'm beginning to feel this is not worth it, but it will be over in three weeks one way or another."

I reply, "These people are insane. Why don't they just kill the entire company and be done with it?"

He answers, "They are mad. Call me as discussed if you need anything."

As I hang up, I think to myself that any conversations going forward at all with George or Joe will need to be on our unregistered phones. Joe gets away with that one, as he is just calling me to talk about Ashok, but if we are being monitored, there is no other reason the CEO would be calling a peon like me going forward unless we are up to something.

Bill has overheard the beginning of the conversation. "Was that Joe?"

I play it down. "Yes, as the computer security guy he felt I should know, not that there is a lot we can do about any of this. Clearly we need a physical security guy as well."

The rest of the day is spent unpacking in a disquieting silence. The engineers have known Ashok from the early days at the company, so they are very subdued. We unpack the gear, do some wiring, and get ready to receive the servers. The engineers are very neat and methodical with what they are doing, which is good. I start thinking about power. Will we have enough to run twelve servers for each setup?

We are mostly done as we wait for the servers, so I jump on the hotel's wi-fi and send my brother William a note letting him know of the latest developments. I do not care if someone is stealing my email, as I am not talking about anything the competition does not already know about or has actually caused. He emails back a reply about ten minutes later and says he heard about a body found on the news, but there is no mention of the way he was killed or what company he was from. I guess in the big house, you get some free time to look into things like this. He says that he has also looked at our competition and found that they desperately need this deal.

As I read on, I begin to better understand our scenario: "I have been reading about cyberattacks, and they define who is trying to break into you as your 'adversary.' Sometimes they also call them 'threat actors,' but I think that is more used for nation-state attacks. In this case, you are being targeted for commercial gain, and your adversary is definitely Hodophi.

"Hodophi's quarterly sales and profits have been down for six straight quarters. The company had to lower guidance on their future earnings the last earnings conference call, and they talked about new, innovative technology that was going to change the face of the company. They said deals were lining up around this technology, and they were looking to announce something over the next couple of quarters. Meanwhile, they lowered guidance again on earnings.

"The CEO is in trouble there for the first time in his career. He had been a rock star for most of his tenure there, as well as at a previous company. It looks like he is raising expectations to keep the stock price stable based on upcoming wins and technology while lowering guidance on actual earnings. This has worked to a degree, as the stock is only down about 10% after dropping six straight quarters. He is banking on something big, and you could be in the way of that."

As with everyone, he goes on to tell me to be careful. I sit back in the chair and think about it. This definitely helps explain some things. They are totally desperate, even whacking Josh, who did not really know anything. I wonder about Ashok and how they got him, how he died. Whatever it was, it's probably something similar to what they would have done to do to me if they were not interrupted, but who knows. Right now, they don't think I have anything they need. They may be watching me to see if I have anything else up my sleeve, but they don't believe I know anything about the hard drives, and I'm pretty sure they already stole everything else from our networks.

I say a silent prayer for Ashok, close my computer, and walk back to where everyone else is sitting. We sit around until about three, and then one of the engineers gets a call from the front desk saying a delivery is here. We all walk up to see the front desk person looking at the truck, saying, "This isn't a loading dock."

Bill goes over to her and nicely says that we can take it in through the side door, and we will be done quickly. He then goes and talks to the truck driver, and we walk to the side hallway door and prop it open. We spend the next ninety minutes carrying twenty servers to the room, and then we start the process to unpack them and set them up. With twelve servers on each side, well-marked for what they are for, it is not that hard.

Fifth-Floor Suite, Hampton Inn
Palo Alto, California

Three of the men that have done work on the East Coast meet up with the two professionals that flew in earlier in the month to do technical surveillance.

The leader of the group, Hans Tsugilva, is known as Andrew Buchanan to all but one of the group. Hans had done the work on Ashok in Baltimore with his right-hand man and childhood friend, Dima, who is known to the group as Brian.

Hans quickly establishes himself as the leader of the group, as he has not worked with these surveillance experts before. They have been hired based on the size of the contract and their reputation. He has direct contact with the end customer and has done work for them before.

The two surveillance experts walk the team through everything they have done since arriving three weeks ago. They have a fake company that is holding meetings in the Hampton Inn, with established credit cards, business records, and a legitimate website for anyone who decides to look them up. They are watching screens of the ART team setting up the prototypes right now. They have completely bugged all the rooms that ART is using with microphones and cameras.

They had had "meetings" in those same rooms the week prior. The technology allows them to turn the microphones up and down in each area, and they are able to listen to the computer security guys' conversations on the phone by turning down the engineers talking about the setup, and vice versa. Having worked with cell companies, they have both sides of the phone conversation being recorded on another computer.

Hans nods as they're going through and is pleased with the professionalism and the work that these two men have done. It's some of the best he's ever seen. They are definitely assets. The five men turn down the worthless jabber in the room and discuss the people they are watching.

All have been thoroughly briefed on all ART employees who are going to be there, and it is not believed that anyone of them could do any real damage. Right now, Hans knows that the malware placed on the main prototype will destroy ART's presentation to the customer. He is not sure if the malware made its way to the backup prototype because their command-and-control channel is cut off completely from that system. They also are not seeing any communication from their original malware on the main prototype because it has been cut off from the internet, probably during packing, so there is still a risk there.

Hans is the one who hired the hacker group out of Ukraine, and he is getting updates from his friend there daily. The computer security guy they had attacked is no longer really a threat. While he has been able to slow Hans and his colleagues down, Hans and his team are way too good to be stopped. He feels confident that they will be able to corrupt both prototypes and ensure that ART not only looks incompetent but also ultimately fails. Additionally, Hans has incentive along with the standard contract terms to ensure that Hodophi wins this deal.

Hans' contact with Hodophi is Kahn Lee, the chief of staff for and younger brother of Sinh Lee, chairman and CEO. Hans is going to have a call with Khan later tonight and will update him on the progress. He has worked with Khan before multiple times, and he knows Kahn is ruthless in his pursuits to protect his brother and his name. Khan is also working other channels and has mentioned that they have someone on the inside of Zamtech as well, but more for information than anything else. The beauty of working with Kahn is the professionalism, unlimited budget, and ruthlessness in getting any job done.

Hans has also gathered from conversations that there is a second team of hackers stealing information to copy it from ART, but they were hired by the engineering teams. Hans has no idea if that is successful, but he assumes it is not because of all the questioning of Ashok about the algorithms.

• • •

We unpack devices and wire them for most of the afternoon, and I am shot. I look at my watch and see it's only five. Eight o'clock on the East Coast. I ask the team if we want to keep at it or go grab some dinner and come back tomorrow.

I am happy that I get a willing "Let's get out of here" from Bill.

We look up some places to eat and learn that the engineers are also going to join us. We lock up the room and go to a sushi place that has good reviews and enjoy a couple of drinks and too much food. After dinner, we decide to work a few more hours, and we are actually able to bring up a couple of the servers on the main prototype side. We are all happy that they come up right away and that they have not been damaged in the shipping.

Around nine o'clock I tell the team that I'm exhausted and ask if we can start again in the morning. Everyone agrees, and Bill and I head back to our hotel in San Jose. Bill asks me if I want one more drink, which I figured I should take him up on, because I will not be able to really go out for the rest of the week. We sit there for a while and probably end up getting three or four drinks, toasting Ashok and talking about the craziness that we both are caught up in.

Chapter 31

Tuesday, May 19
Silicon Valley, California

The next morning, Bill and I meet for a run at seven. I wake up a little before then; it seems like I am beginning to adjust to West Coast time. We run outside and get a pretty good feel for the area. It's very flat, but there are good sidewalks and lots of good places to eat.

I talk to Sarah after the run and enjoy our bantering. She is really special, and I am now convinced I have fallen for her completely.

The rest of the day is really more of the same: setting up the prototypes, unpacking devices on both sides, making sure they communicate at basic levels, and moving to the next server. We are not really testing anything as far as actual tests, but we just want to make sure we have the basics down ahead of time.

This night we order pizza and keep going until around eight o'clock, and I am happy when one of the engineers requests we finish up. Bill and I go back to the hotel, have one beer, and then I head to my room around nine.

I shut my eyes for forty-five minutes. My alarm wakes me and I splash water on my face and put on a change of clothes. I sneak down the stairs to the back exit of the hotel and walk towards a Peet's coffee shop with a Walgreens across the street. I get on my phone and order an Uber through the app; I see that my driver, Ashim, will be picking me up in seven minutes, so I walk into the Peet's. They're in the process of closing, but they let me buy a cup of coffee anyway.

I might be paranoid, but I have a rental car, and if people start noticing it missing every night it will seem strange. Who knows if people are still trying to mess us up, but I really have a gut feeling we need to be careful. I make small talk with my Uber driver; he's only been doing it for two months, but he likes it. He works during the day for a construction company, and this is just an easy way for him to make some extra cash.

I get to George's Sunnyvale Residence Inn a little after ten. He is sitting at a tiny little bar with a beer in his hand. I am greeted with, "You're late, mule boy."

"You call this a bar, Jagular?"

We sit there and have a beer and basically don't talk about anything at all. His trip was good and he made a couple of stops—pretty uneventful.

I am tired already, so I say, "Let's go up and check it out."

When we get to the room, there are five large server boxes and a bunch of smaller boxes with the networking equipment and accessories.

"Uh, where is the rest?"

"Come on man, I have a rented SUV and it was packed. Those dudes are weird, by the way."

"How's that?"

"Just squirrely, that's all. One dude kept asking me questions about what we were doing and what the new company was all about. So I told him I didn't know squat, I was just a contractor told to pick up a bunch of stuff for a startup. He didn't even help me load stuff into the truck. Your phone is on the table as well; the numbers have been turned on, and everything is configured."

He stands there for a minute, looking like he is debating telling me something. I know George well, and I wait him out.

"Listen little man, I heard your buddy Ashok was killed. Your brother shot me an email. He does not know I'm out here, but he is worried. I was planning on doing this anyway, but I picked up a few things from one of my buddies, who's local." He pulled a pistol out from waistband of his jeans. He then goes over to a little case and pulls out two more.

I don't know jack about guns, so I don't ask him any questions. I just say, "Holy moly, how many do you need?"

"One is for you, but to answer your question, you can never have enough."

I said, "I don't want one."

"I figured your pacifist mind would say that, so my pal is getting me a Taser gun, which I will have to insist you carry."

"Are they legal?"

"Who knows and who cares? You think the dudes mucking with us care? I'm not getting surprised again. I spent years training for a lot of different situations, and then I allow myself to be jumped from behind—that ain't happening again."

I say, "Look man, I wouldn't even know how to use a Taser gun, and I wouldn't have been able to get it out in time during either attack anyway."

"Next time, you are going to pull it out in advance, because you never know."

I start unpacking the boxes and say, "The last time they came, they had two dudes. Do you think I would be able to get two of them at once with a stinking little Taser gun?"

"You only need to worry about one: anyone else will be dead with surprised looks on their faces, and a gun will be smoking in my hand. I am not going to help you tomorrow unless you carry the Taser and pull it out every time you walk back into your room." I swallow hard and nod.

"Alright, now help me with these boxes. We need power strips, and we will have to be careful not to surge all the hotel's power. We also have to keep this place cool. We've spent two days already on the real prototype, and we haven't even gotten them all talking yet. I need to restore images on these, which will take a ton of time. Our schedule is going to be very tight."

For the next three hours, we set up five computers and the limited networking equipment. I turn on two of the servers, and they come up. It does not really matter what software is on them because I will be doing a complete restore from a backup done about two months' prior at ART.

At two thirty in the morning, I tell George I am wiped and ask if he can drive me to the Peet's across the street from my hotel. He picks up two guns, puts one in his pocket and one in his waistband, and we walk out. Oh man, I cannot believe he is going to be walking around with them. He pulls up on the side of Peet's and tries to give me one of the guns. I just laugh and get out.

I wander back into the side door of the hotel and up the staircase to my room without seeing anyone. I go into my room and, thinking of George, I actually check under the bed before crashing.

Chapter 32

Friday, May 22
Silicon Valley, California

The week has gone by in a flurry, each day blurring into the next. Both the prototype and the backup are all connected, and Bill does a run-through of the entire demo, which is cool for me to see. He does it on both the setups and gives it to me the second time like I am the customer.

He is very good and has a natural way of explaining very complex issues. I let him run through everything, and then I ask him a bunch of questions about things that I am seeing. We are close to done; it will all be moved next week, and I am debating if I can sneak out and get to my prototype and do work, but that is too suspicious. I do tell Bill that I am heading down to meet an old high school friend over the weekend, so I won't have to be sneaking around then at least.

My prototype work with George is not going as well. Three hours of work a night after an already full day is getting old. We have a system set up where he picks me up at Peet's, and then we head over.

I find myself exhausted all the time, so I am looking forward to the weekend. I am also nervous about making the timeline on the backup, because I have a ton of stuff to do. George has been a big help and has done most of the physical moving of the servers and getting them unboxed and plugged in.

Friday night is finally upon us, and the engineers say we will see them on Monday morning. We plan on meeting here at the hotel and then Bill will walk us over to Zamtech so we can check in. We will be able to meet a couple of Zamtech's people, and then we can bring over the servers and start setting up the actual prototype.

Bill gives me a raft of crap for not hanging out with him for the weekend, but I tell him I am meeting an old high school friend at his place. I like the fact that my new friend Bill is able to dole it out a little.

I do have a beer with him back at the hotel, though, and he says he is just going to be hanging out here over the weekend. Once I get back to my room, I quickly pack a smaller bag of stuff and then go throw it in the car. I give a good look around the entire parking lot and try to remember the cars that are there and look to see if anyone is in any of them.

I then take a really different way to George's hotel. I basically take the longest route that Google Maps gives me and continue to look around to see if I recognize any cars from before. I think to myself that I am probably not good at this, but it feels good to try and use what I learned from watching too much TV and movies about spies as a kid.

I circle around the parking lot at George's hotel, but for some reason I decide to park in a neighboring hotel's parking lot and cut across two parking lots to get to George's place.

Fifth-Floor Suite, Hampton Inn
Palo Alto, California

Hans and his team have watched the location of Robert's car on a computer monitor via Google Maps. The small tracking device they put on Robert's car shows his location as he seems to wander around the area until he finally stops at a location fifteen minutes away.

They look at the area on the map and zero in, showing a collection of hotels surrounded by offices.

Hans says to the group, "If he is meeting a friend who lives out here, he would not be going to a hotel. So the question is: why would he lie to his friend Bill?"

The room is silent as they watch the location of the car, which has stopped.

His childhood friend Jan finally breaks the silence: "A girl or something else? I'll go down and watch his car and see who he is with and what he is doing. There is nothing going on here for the time being."

Hans nods.

Marriott Residence Inn
Sunnyvale, California

It's Friday night, and I will be working throughout. At least I have George; he has ordered pizza, and half his little fridge is filled with local IPAs and some Coronas for the evening.

I finally feel like I am making progress. All the devices are connected, and I have started the first restore from backup, which will go for about six hours. I crack my first beer of the day and grab a piece of pizza.

George sits there half-watching some Sports Center on TV and says, "Tell me exactly what we are doing here now, brother. We have a setup that you tell me is like the two other setups that are in the other hotel. Is this just in case they break in and bash those to pieces?"

"No man, much more than that. The restore I am doing on that device is from about two and half months ago. It is not the current code, and we know there will be some bugs that we will explain to the customer if we have to use that one, which I am assuming we will."

George answers, "So, we are going to use old code that is buggy. I thought you want to win this thing. I thought you startup dudes were actually intelligent."

"These guys that are breaking into us are very good. We noticed over a month ago that the attempts to steal data had slowed down. We think they either got what they were looking for or gave up. I think they gave up based on what you have been keeping hidden in Baltimore. The only thing they stole as far as the secret sauce was compiled code, and they cannot look into it to see how it works. We don't need the software that Ashok originally wrote, which is on the hard drives. That software was compiled into subroutines long ago, but if the other company gets that, they could replicate it. They compiled code, which we can assume they stole, but it cannot tell them anything."

I pause for a second before continuing. "What they need and want is the source code, which would then enable them to actually understand it. From their perspective, if they cannot get to our stuff, they can at least destroy what we have and make us look like idiots in front of the customer. Then they win, even if their product is not as good as ours."

I stand up and pace the room and say, "There is a good chance that in the last month they were able to access our prototypes and potentially plant malware that will destroy our demonstration. We looked through everything, and we cannot find anything at all, so we may be just paranoid, but these guys are really good. Maybe there is a piece of malware on there that looks like one of our regular programs and can spawn other processes at a set time—we just don't know."

He jumps in. "So, by going back two and half months, you are fairly certain you have code that worked before they changed tactics? There may be small problems in there, but the gist of it works?"

"Exactly."

George smiles and grabs another piece of pizza. "Okay. I just wanted to make sure I am on a good team."

Chapter 33

Monday, May 25
Hampton Inn
Palo Alto, California

The entire weekend is uneventful; I did restores from the backup disks onto the new servers, which created a lot of dead time during the process. We watched a lot of Sports Center and a couple movies. We went out once for dinner on Saturday night, and George and I hit Mass on Sunday morning at the Cathedral Basilica of St. Joseph, which is a neat old church in San Jose. We followed that with a big breakfast at a diner. He ran and got sandwiches and snack foods during the day, and I hit the gym on Saturday briefly.

I am now feeling good about how quickly the third prototype is coming along. My doing the restores has got the system to a working level. But I have nothing to test against, and I am sure if we had to pull this out, the engineers would have some work to do.

I get up very early and call Sarah, who is already at work. She is doing okay but says she misses me and that all the activity around ART's headquarters has quieted since we left. We have not talked much, so it is good to catch up. She asks what I did on the weekend and why I have not been in touch very frequently.

I say I worked a ton, worked out, and went to Mass—which is all the truth.

I meet Bill for breakfast, and we head to the Hampton Inn to walk through the prototype and pack it up for the big show. Everyone is excited when we get there, and Bill walks through the demo from start to finish on both systems. He does not have any real energy transfers to work with, but he practices what he is going to show anyway.

I put his steps in the back of my mind and plan on doing them when I get back to the secret prototype. Once we complete everything, we carefully shut down the computers and box everything up to bring over to Zamtech. We are very careful to label everything. The plan is to bring them into Zamtech and spend the day setting everything up tomorrow. On Wednesday, we will start the real tests.

Fifth-Floor Suite, Hampton Inn
Palo Alto, California

Hans listens carefully to Jan describe the fact that Robert is not in the hotel where he had parked and that he had come up to the car from a parking lot. There is another hotel across the parking lot, and he did not see anyone drop him off, so he assumed he is at the other hotel.

Hans thinks for a minute and then says, "Why? Why would he do this?"

Jan says, "I would have guessed he is seeing a different girl then the girl in Baltimore, but why would he be that worried about where he would park his car? She's not here with him."

Hans says, "He must be up to something. We need to start following him, taking shifts. We can't have any surprises."

Tuesday, May 26
Zamtech Headquarters
Palo Alto, California

I get up very early again and call Sarah at work. It is fun to hear her cheery self, and we talk about random things for a while before I have to run.

Bill drives me to an Enterprise Rental Car facility at eight, where we have rented a big van to move all the equipment. Then we head to the Hampton Inn. We spend the early part of the morning packing boxes into the van, and then we head to Zamtech. The engineering team is going to meet us there. We get to this new, modern-looking facility and tell the gatekeeper who we are and who we are visiting.

The four of us then start the process of checking in. They take our IDs, and then they take our pictures and place them on badges. We will, unfortunately, have to follow the same procedure every day.

Bill gives the name of the project manager for the overall prototype, Janine Campo, to the people, and they call her.

He looks at me and talks low, "I have met her once, and she's simply outstanding. Don't let her looks fool you, though; she is some sort of hot-shot working as a consultant from one of those big-four firms. Her role is project manager for the RFP process. She is one of those impartial facilitators or something. McAndrews says she is key if we can get her on our side. But he says not to bet on it, because she isn't known for helping anyone."

We wait about ten minutes, and then Janine walks through security and comes over to introduce herself. "Simply outstanding" is putting it mildly. She is absolutely beautiful. She is has long blond hair and blue eyes that would melt you into a puddle where you stood. There is something about her face that just makes you want to stare. She introduces herself easily, with total confidence, and she makes you feel like you are the only person in the room. She is dressed in a black suit with high heels that add to her height; she has white pearls down the front of her black dress and small diamond earrings. Did I really just notice all that?

She says, "Nice to meet all of you. Let me sign you in, and then I'll show you the room that you will be setting up in. We will have to bring in the equipment through the back of the building, and I have our logistics people set up to work with you."

As the engineers struggle to say hello, I decide to start a conversation and ask her, "Are you from around here originally?"

"No, I grew up in Ohio near Lake Erie, moved out to go to school, and never went back."

I stay very smooth. "Where did you go to school?"

"Stanford. I did move east for a while, but then I came back."

"Ah, where in the east?" Bill chimes in.

"Boston area, but it's too cold. Okay, put your security key badges on, and it will let you pass through the turnstiles," she says.

"'Badges? We don't need no stinkin' badges,'" I joke, but no one laughs. I thought you could never go wrong with *Blazing Saddles* jokes, but people probably don't know what I am talking about.

We walk through the long hallways, and she says we will be setting up in the "Lucerne" room. Apparently, all of the rooms in the entire campus of eight buildings are named after cities all over the world. There are two dudes that are introduced to us, and one of them walks back through the main lobby with me to bring the van around to the receiving area.

I ask the dude with me where he is from, and he says he's local, but he doesn't seem much for small talk, so I leave him alone. I have to say everything is very professionally done, and the building is enormous and awesome. The other guy is waiting for us on the loading dock with carts, and we quickly unload the truck onto two big carts and then walk to the Lucerne room, where the rest of the gang is talking to Janine.

The room is extremely large and very modern, like everything else. There are two sections of the room, one with a conference table and overhead projector built into the ceiling. The second half of the room has a glassed-in area with computers and some other strange-looking equipment, which must be the solar simulation equipment, as well as an area with what looks like a serving window at a hot dog stand and a couple of racks of routers (I assume that we will plug our equipment into these). There are also interfaces on what I assume to be power equipment. I guess that is to do the actual test. The last part of the room has empty computer racks in it and tables with power sources and flat-screen monitors.

Janine looks over at me. "Robert, sorry you missed some of the introduction, but we can answer any questions you have as we go. I am sure your team is ready to start setting up and running through any testing you have. The equipment will go in this room. Let us know if you need anything at all. I will be in and out, but here is my business card with my cell on it, so please call for any reason."

She walks around the room giving out her cards and making eye contact with each of us. The rest of the day is simply setting up the prototype in the computer racks, doing basic wiring, and actually booting up the machines to talk to each other. It goes much quicker than it did at the hotel because we have been through it before.

During the setup, Janine stops in every once in a while, and it looks like she and Bill are engaged in deep conversation off to the side in the room. I walk up to him later and say, "You were right, she is something."

He laughs, "I'm actually working, brother, trying to get some information."

"Anything interesting?"

"Hodophi set up on Friday; their walkthrough with the customer is next Tuesday and Wednesday. We have been moved to Thursday and Friday, which unfortunately means they get to set the table."

I say, "Why did that happen? I thought we were starting on Tuesday!"

"Don't know, I have to call McAndrews and let him know. He is coming in tomorrow. Janine is going to hit a little happy hour with us, if you want to join us for a couple of beers."

"Absolutely. You going to invite our engineers?"

He replies, "Not sure, probably not tonight. We'll get them another day."

"Sounds good. Do you want to leave from here?"

"No, let's go back to the hotel, then Uber it out so we can have some cocktails."

I laugh. "You are always thinking. What time are we out of here?"

"Let's bail at four o'clock since you and I are not adding any value here. We are meeting her at five at a place called Nola; it's supposed to have a good outside area in the back."

I reply, "Done and done. I could use a beer."

I go back and hang out watching the engineers continue to hook up everything. This is good for me, as I really get an understanding of what is going on. I feel I now have the system set up completely back at the place, though I see that we will still need to do some work when and if it is needed. I am not sure what the plan will be—if it will just remain as backup or if it is actually going to be used. Oh well, I'm sure I will find out. My double-secret phone basically has not rung at all. George is hanging out during the day, getting some naps in and working out, I'm sure.

I tell George that we are going out tonight and that I probably will not be over to work. I think we are pretty much done with everything that can be done at this point.

Bill and I get to Nola's about fifteen minutes early and get a table out back on the patio. We both order Lagunitas IPAs on tap. I have learned that the company started in Lagunitas, California, and though it is now brewed in Chicago and California, it is always looked at by locals as a West Coast beer.

I really am enjoying Bill's company. He constantly makes light of everything; laid-back is probably the description that fits him best, but he is on the far spectrum of laid-back. I also get the feeling he is very, very talented, based the questions he asks about the prototype and the relationships he seems to have with everyone around him.

We are laughing about a group of young professional men sitting across from us because of all their designer clothes and how many times they play with their hair when Janine comes in. All eyes seem to follow as she walks over to us. She throws her keys down on the table.

She says, "What, no beer waiting for me?"

Bill answers, "I figured you for some sort of fruity drink, but if you want to hang with the big dogs, we can order you one."

She laughs, and the waiter comes over and she says, "I'll take whatever these two are drinking."

She looks right at me, "Robert, how was your day? Are you enjoying being out here?"

"Standard issue, you?"

She replies, "Busy. How is your setup going?"

I answer, "It's good, but as you can see, Bill and I don't really do anything all day; we are just here for our good looks and our winning personalities."

"I know that is what Bill is here for, but I heard you are the computer security guy—that seems pretty important."

Bill laughs, "Robert is the man at ART. He does a little of everything."

She says, "I figured. Probably not too much for a computer security guy like you to do."

Time for me to change the subject. "How long have you been working at Zamtech?"

She smiles. "I have been here for about twelve months, just working as a project manager across the RFP process. I'll probably move on to another company once this is all done, but who knows. If they like the work I do, maybe they will find another project for me to help make my company a lot of money."

I ask, "So what does a project manager on an RFP process do?"

"I just make sure it's fair to all parties involved, from the initial request down to the selection: did people respond to the questions properly, did they cover all the areas and make sure one company does not get an unfair advantage over another, that kind of thing. We received seven written responses, a couple of which had multiple companies involved teaming together. From there, we had to get it to two or three companies that we wanted to test. "

She lowers her voice and says almost secretively, "You both are probably pretty aware of how much attention this has, within my company and across many industries. It's pretty cool that a company as small as you guys are in the hunt. My lead partner wants status updates once a day from me; it's crazy high-pressure, even though I'm not really doing anything."

Bill says, "Sounds like you have huge responsibility."

She smiles again, "Don't get me wrong, I do, but it's not really imperative to the outcome of the project. You guys have the technology, that is key; I can easily be replaced."

She then says, "Are you guys going to be able to win this without your CTO?"

Bill answers, "The CTO's work was done early. He was important at the current stage, but he's not critical to the outcome any longer. What are you hearing?"

"Just that it was tragic; we really have not talked about it."

Bill stands up, swallows his final sips of his beer, and says to me, "Get me another? Where do you suppose the bathrooms are?"

I look around and tell him to try back by the bar. When he has gone, Janine smiles at me and leans in a little and says, "So, you really aren't going to tell me why it is so important to have a computer security guy out here with the team? Have you guys been hacked?"

My heart starts racing. What do I say here? If they think we have been hacked, will they not pick us? Is she working right now?

I say, "I came into ART about four months ago, first building servers for them. I took it upon myself to become the computer security guy, because it's really interesting to me, and I believe every company is under attack. At the end of the day, my real job was just to build servers, and I've built a ton of them since I have been here." I am hoping I'm not sounding defensive, but rather more matter of fact.

Janine puts her hand on my knee in a friendly sort of way and says, "I think you are downplaying your job and your role. I think you are more important then you say, and more interesting than most people I meet."

Sirens are definitely going off. No one thinks I'm interesting. I lean back and laugh and signal to the waiter. "Two IPAs, and can we get some nachos? Janine, did you want another?"

"No, but I'll have a water, thank you."

Bill is back and he says, "Why don't you get an Uber with Robert and I? We can drop you off."

"I don't want to leave my car out there in the parking lot."

I look down and see her Mercedes key fob sitting on the table and say, "You ought to drive crappy cars like I do, then you don't have anything to worry about."

She smiles. "I grew up with everything crappy; now I like things nice."

We talk a bit more about the San Francisco area and what she likes about it. She does like going to baseball games in the newer stadium downtown, and I am jealous of that. She has been to a 49ers game in the new stadium in San Jose. I tell her if we win this and are out here a lot, both of those would need to be on the agenda.

She finishes her beer and is sipping her water. She goes for her purse and says she needs to go before she is inclined to have more beer.

Bill tells her to put away her money, but she says with a smile that she does not want any gifts from one of the competitors and throws a $20 bill on the table. She has eaten about two nachos and Bill tries to give her back a ten, but she refuses.

She brushes my knee again when she gets up, and I have to ask myself if I am imagining things. Like I said, this never happens to me—but maybe she is like that with everyone.

She says, "Great to see you guys! I'll see you tomorrow at the office, and thanks for the company—I have not had the chance to hang out with a lot of folks our age."

She shakes our hands and melts us with her eyes as she rolls out of here.

After she leaves, Bill and I do not say anything for a couple of minutes. Then he says, "Wow."

I ask him, "Do you think she could get in trouble for hanging out and drinking beers with one of the competitors?"

"Don't know; maybe she hung out with them last week when they set up, but she definitely did not hang long, and maybe the fact that she needs to be impartial is the reason."

I think for a second and say, "Do you think there is an advantage for Hodophi to go first in the prototype and presentation?"

"Good question. Normally in these situations I like to go first; you can set traps for companies based on areas you excel at and they do not. That is normal during the pre-sales phase, but this is really based on performance and whether we meet the requirements or not. If we both do, then it will fall into some of the softer areas like features. Cost is normally an issue, but it won't be the main issue here, as I think they need something that meets their requirements so Zamtech can get to market with their new solar energy systems as fast as possible."

We have a couple more beers and some sliders and then Uber it back to the hotel. By the time I hit my room, I am really tired, but I decide to try out the burner phone and call George. We talk for a couple minutes; he is kind of bored, and I tell him I will hopefully be over to work tomorrow night. I tell him about Janine and later look her up on LinkedIn. She is a premium user, so she will definitely know that I have looked her up, but I do not send her a LinkedIn request. I find out her "stint in Boston" must have been when she received her MBA from Harvard. Interesting; I thought all people that went to a school like that had to mention it to you, but maybe since she mentioned Stanford she did not feel the need to.

I then email my brother and tell him about how we set up today and how I am doing. I know he wants to help me, but even though we are using another email addresses, I cannot share anything secret that we are doing.

Chapter 34

Wednesday, May 27
Silicon Valley, California

Wednesday starts pretty much the same way as every other day out here. I get up, do some sit-ups and push-ups, and call Sarah at work. We talk for about twenty minutes; she is fine, and she asks a bunch of questions about how the prototype is being received. I tell her nothing has started yet. She asks if it would be weird if she went to meet William in prison while I'm away. She constantly amazes me—I can't believe how thoughtful she is. I say it would be awesome and that he would love it. I text her William's information and how to go about a visit.

Bill and I meet up for breakfast, and then we head over to Zamtech. Some of the big dogs are getting in today to begin going over things, but they have morning flights, so they probably will not be over until the afternoon.

At Zamtech, the engineering teams say they are mostly ready and show Bill and I how the interfaces are working with the real energy sources. It is pretty impressive how it has all come together.

The circuit board, which is ART's design, has the controller with all the algorithms that Ashok had come up with in a glass container that Zamtech has provided. The energy tubes are connected to the circuit boards, each with sixty magnetic channels. There are two batteries connected in parallel to each other with dials and meters on them. I assume that is the way they will provide the energy to our devices. There are monitors all over the place with sensors connected to different areas. Those sensors will be reading many variables from before and after the energy is transferred. They will be showing the audience two of the boards, but they fit squarely into a block that can handle as many of ten of them. They have been built according to Zamtech's specifications.

I went over some of this with Ashok, and I know that basic electrical wiring will not work at all, as there will be too much heat. Even the slightest loss of energy will be devastating to what Zamtech is trying to accomplish. When the sun rises into the sky and again around two in the afternoon, the energy output from their new solar panels will be massive and cause way too many problems with normal wires. The energy tubes that they built also can effectively store energy by a loop in which it will travel if it's not needed when it is collected.

An engineer from Zamtech is in the room as well, and he explains to our engineers how to use the testing device and warns us to make sure we are 100% ready before turning it on. He also checks the connections to make sure everything is where it's supposed to be.

Bill asks if we are ready for a test run and the engineers say we are, so we turn on the device to its lowest level: five joules. He and the engineers then begin to look at the monitors. Seven of the eight monitors read 4.99999999 joules—exactly what we are looking for. The monitor watching the power at the very end of the tubes reads 0.00000000.

This does not really scare anyone; we would panic if we actually thought it is losing energy. The fact that it is reading 0.00000000 tells us something is probably not connected correctly or the software meant to monitor what is happening is having issues.

They turn down the power source, and the engineers begin banging away on the keyboards of the computers that are monitoring the end of the wires. Bill signals to me to take a walk with him, and we wander over to the other side of the room.

He says, "No real issues; they need to figure out what is going on, but we have seen this before. I figured we shouldn't be standing there looking over their shoulders. We should let them work in peace."

He pulls out his laptop, turns it on, and sits down on one at the conference tables. I do the same, but there is really not a ton of stuff for me to work on. I clean out a little email, but people are generally leaving me alone. I actually want to stay over there with the software engineers so I can understand what the problem is and potentially be able to fix it on the computers in George's room.

The day wears on with nothing much happening other than the engineers talking to each other. They call back to the main office and ask some questions of some people there. I listen in and understand what they are talking about. I know that the software is the same on each of the monitoring servers, but I do not want to let them know how much I know. They can't know that I am actually building and installing the software from backups.

Our key badges let us walk around the first floor in the demonstration areas and into the cafeteria, so Bill and I go down to the cafeteria and get some Red Bull for the engineers. We sit and drink a cup of coffee, just out of complete boredom. We also bring back some sandwiches in order to let the engineers work through lunch.

After lunch, Janine shows up with Tom McAndrews, Chet Hartley, and Joe Benfield. Chet immediately starts talking to the engineers about what is going on, but they seem baffled. He then goes and makes a phone call. Tom and Joe ask us how everything else is going and if we think it is a major problem.

Bill's answer is what I am thinking. "If it's with the monitoring software, no big deal; if it's with the controller board and what is going through it, that is real. If it's with the energy tubes, we can build them again if we have to, and we also have backups of everything in the hotel, so we should be fine, regardless. We also have time to figure this out."

"Not too much time," Joe says.

I walk over to Ryan, who seems to be the lead engineer. Ryan is a huge man in more ways than one, and he seems always to be panting and out of breath. He is a good guy, though, from what I can tell. He mostly keeps to himself except when he is having a smoke, which seems to be every hour on the hour. He is standing near where Chet is on the phone.

I do not want to show him up by stating something in front of the team that he should have figured out. I say to him in a low voice, "Can we use one of the other monitoring computers with the monitoring software that we know works to take a look at the joules at the end of the tubes? That way, we could start narrowing down if we have a monitor problem, a board problem, or a tube problem."

Ryan looks down at me, thinks for a second, and says, "Good idea. Let's try that."

He walks over and simply starts shutting down the computers, which he needs to do before he physically moves anything. Chet walks over and asks him what he is doing.

Ryan answers him, "We are going to use the monitoring software that we know is working to test that back link that is currently not working. That way we can figure out if the problem is with the monitoring software, the tubes, or the boards. It was Robert's idea, and a good one, too."

Wow, I'm flattered. He does not need to say that. I told him privately in the first place so I wouldn't make him look bad.

For the next ten minutes, we all sit there and watch them move things around. Janine stops by again and asks if we need anything, and Joe walks off with her to get a cup of coffee.

Finally, they have everything hooked up, and they start turning everything on. Once the software is showing on the monitors, Ryan walks over and says they're ready, and then he turns on five joules of energy.

The graph immediately spikes to five joules and reads 4.999999999 on the screen. Everyone pats him and I on the back, and Ryan says, "Great call, Robert!"

I smile and say, "It's about time I did something. I've been standing around here and drinking beer and eating food on the company's dime all week."

Everyone laughs, and then we start discussing how we are going to fix the two servers that are having trouble. We end up doing a backup from one of the good servers and then simply restoring it to one of the bad ones. Bill and I agree to go to the hotel and bring backup servers from the second prototype in case the problem is hardware.

When Janine and Joe walk back in, Joe says, "Working?"

Chet answers, "Yes, well, at least we diagnosed the problem. It was Robert's idea to use the monitoring software we knew was working to help diagnose the problem. It turns out those servers are having issues; this will be fixed today by either a restore or using backup servers."

Joe says, "Awesome! I actually did not expect that after just going for a cup of coffee."

Janine gives me a look that is somewhere between a smile and something like a "I told you so," or at least that is the way I read it. She is sure something.

That night we have a full-team dinner at a steakhouse in Palo Alto. It's fun catching up with everyone, but the talk turns serious when Joe talks about the investigation around Ashok. The police are thinking it was a kidnapping/murder, but they have no real progress at this point. We get back to the hotel around ten o'clock, and I can't just bail to go see George, as everyone wants to grab one more beer at the bar. I have never figured out a way to say no thank you to that, and it would seem strange with everyone in town anyway.

Tom McAndrews turns out to be a good guy, very down to earth. He talks about how he and Ashok approached Zamtech when there were only five people at ART, as they had approached a lot of different customers in the very early days to get companies interested in what they were doing. They knew early on that the product that Ashok had invented would be a feature of something bigger, and they could not exactly go out and sell it to the masses themselves.

They had targeted a lot of companies in the beginning, which was only eighteen months ago now, but Zamtech took early interest and became their primary target because of the scope of what they were doing. McAndrews has three kids under five, so he is a busy man at all points in time, whether at work or at home. He understands the technology and is excited about what makes ART different. It's amazing what you can learn about folks if you listen and ask pointed questions.

He is also very interested in how I got into computer security, so I tell him I really only became interested four months ago, which probably does not instill much confidence. I quickly correct and tell him that it was something I worked on for many years on my own growing up.

Joe Benfield walks up and says, "Robert, can I grab you for a second?"

I say, "Sure. I'll talk to you in a little, Tom."

Joe says, "Let's get a breath of fresh air."

We walk outside, and he starts walking across the street towards Peet's, which looks closed. I wait for him to start.

He asks in a low voice, "Everything good with you and George?"

I say, "Yes, everything is up and looks good; unfortunately, I can't test it against anything."

He says, "Plan on having all the equipment at Zamtech next Thursday morning at kickoff. We may leave it in the van as we start with the real prototype, but I want it there just in case we see anything strange. I am debating just starting the presentation by detailing the attacks on us and then bringing in the equipment from the van and starting fresh with that. I'm not sure how I'm going to play that yet, but I want to be prepared in any case."

He continues in a quiet voice as we both look down. "The more I think about it, the more I think you are correct in your assumption from several weeks back. If they could not steal what they were looking for, they will sabotage any of our systems that they know about. What do you think?"

I keep my head looking at the pavement as we turn around at Peet's and start to walk back towards the hotel. I say, "I like your idea about being up front about the attacks with the people we will be presenting to at Zamtech. They will be astonished if they hear about everything that has gone on in our little company. I am convinced that the two prototypes that Hodophi knows about will have malware on them that will act as a time bomb and will blow up right in our face."

We walk back, just making small talk and talking about Ashok.

Nothing much exciting happens before the end of the evening; I do have one more beer and hang a little with Bill, but then we both bail at the same time and call it a night. I had texted George on our burner phones that I am busy with dinner tonight, so I am happy to call it early for a good night's sleep.

Fifth-Floor Suite, Hampton Inn
Palo Alto, California

Hans picks up his cell phone.

"Jan, anything going on?"

"The CEO walked up to Robert and asked to talk to him, and then he said he wants some fresh air. I walked out after they left to get a smoke, and they had gone across the street and were outside the coffee shop talking. They just walked back in now."

Hans says, "Thoughts?"

"We are missing something."

Hans hangs up the phone and looks down at the email he has up that has been forwarded from his handler from an unknown source.

Subject: Fwd: RD

No info. RD had 2 phones, which I thought was strange. One he looks at and texts someone with. One I have not seen him use at all, but he pulled it out once to look at it.

Hans thinks for a couple of minutes and starts a new message to his contact in Ukraine with his email specifically for this project and for this week in May. They have been using a different email every week, starting on Sundays, as they go through this project.

> Subject: Investigate
> High Priority: Standard contract
> Need to find out about any new phones that the company has purchased over the past 60 days. If none are associated with RD, work on any partners associated with them or any contacts.
> RD has more than 1 phone.

He thinks about the team in Ukraine. They will figure that out quickly by looking directly at the telecom provider records or back through ART or their partners. They always have ways in and out of networks, and the team has never let him down.

Chapter 35

Thursday, May 28
Silicon Valley, California

I have a standard-issue morning: get up, hit the gym, call Sarah. Man, I miss her, and I wish I could tell her everything that is going on out here. I keep having this nagging feeling that something bad is going to happen. Bill and I head over to Zamtech together a little after eight, which has become our pattern.

That morning there is a lot of activity in the room. Bill, Tom, and Joe walk through the flow of the presentation.

Joe will start off and explain the background of the project, who ART is, and the brief history of the company. He will talk about the history of the energy load-balancing project and Ashok's innovative ideas. His slides are 90% there, he says.

Tom will then talk about the project requirements put forth by Zamtech and walk the Zamtech executive and engineering teams through their own guidelines so they knew that ART understands their requirements. I think this is a really interesting segment and approach, and I like it. His slides seem to be complete.

They have then marked on the agenda slide a fifteen-minute break, but they agree not to start until the entire Zamtech team is back in the room.

Chet will then present ART's engineering design that offers the solution to Zamtech's problem of passing the collected energy to storage devices. Chet's slides break the components into blocks and show what technology is talking to what technology as the energy moves through the system. He has several slides on the load-balancing techniques involved in the process. It is interesting to me that he can present this clearly without actually giving the algorithms that do the work.

After that, Bill will walk through slides of what ART is going to show in the prototype. He will then move to the prototype and actually show everything. They will start by turning on the energy source and showing the energy that is input into the system and then go through the different stages that Zamtech requires be shown. He will make this very interactive and try to draw Zamtech into asking any questions that they may have. He will be backed up by Chet and the two engineers that set up the prototype.

In the end, they have about five hours of material to show for an eight-hour session, but they figure once they jump into the prototype, there will be many questions that will take them through the rest of the day and into the next one.

Joe shows some conclusion slides but doesn't think they will get to them. Basically, if I can sum up all the presenting materials, I would say: Zamtech told us what the requirements were, and ART met them 100%. We then agree as a team to just shut everything down until after the holiday on Monday and come back on Tuesday and do the dry run before the actual event on Thursday of next week. Everyone feels good about the work, and we call it a day early.

I am walking down the hall towards the restroom while everyone is packing our bags and getting ready to go, and I run into Janine walking down the hallway towards our room.

"How are you guys doing?"

I answer, "Good; I think we are packing up for the day, but the boys in the room are calling the shots."

She leans very close to me and says, "Maybe you and I can grab a drink together. I don't want everyone there, because I could get in trouble for hanging out with one of the companies and not the other."

We are in the alcove where the bathrooms are, but no one walking down the hallway can see us. I leaned back a little and say in a noncommittal way, "That might be fun."

She puts her hand on my hip, leans in closer, and whispers, "Don't blow me off, Robert. I can assure you I am not used to that. I'll call your cell later, and I can drive in my SL convertible if you would like."

She then pushes me away and strolls down the hall towards our demonstration room.

We all go back to the hotel, and I excuse myself from the dinner planning and say I am going to meet up with friends locally. I go up to my room and fire up my Mac.

I know Janine has a Mercedes from her keys on the table, so I Google "Mercedes SL convertible." What came up shocked me.

"2015 Mercedes-Benz SL-Class 215K (Mercedes-Benz SL65) AMG base includes AMG 6.0L V-12 621hp engine twin turbo, seven-speed automatic transmission with overdrive, four-wheel anti-lock brakes (ABS), base price $250,000."

She is driving a $250,000 car? She mentioned she grew up without means, so if I am reading this correctly, the money is not old family money. She probably has some student loans from Stanford and Harvard as well—you don't have to be an Ivy League genius to figure that out. How can she afford this car?

I spend a little time finalizing the malware that I have been working on and then send Janine a fake LinkedIn invite to download the software.

I decide I need to talk to Joe. I walk out into the parking lot towards Peet's and call him on the burner phone.

"Joe, it's Robert. Do you have a minute?"

"Sure, just getting some email done."

I say, "Can you walk out of your room and to a safe place?"

He replies, "Give me a minute."

A minute later he says, "Okay, good."

"A couple small things I think you should be aware of. The biggest is that Janine has asked me out, and women like that are definitely not interested in guys like me."

Joe laughs. "Is that your problem?"

"Well, a little more than that. She has been asking a lot of questions about computer security and why would we need a computer security person here. She also mentioned that she grew up without anything, and she also went to Stanford and Harvard for graduate school, but I just looked up the model of her car, and it's a $250,000 Mercedes. My guess is with that much debt and a desire for expensive things, she is an easy target for our competitors to get someone on the inside."

Joe is quiet for a minute. "Okay. Maybe there's another explanation, but I have learned I need to go with your gut. What are you going to do?"

I say, "You don't know this, but I am trying to do a little investigation of my own. Also, I'm thinking about going out with her tonight when she calls to try to figure out what she is after. I'll plan on doing a lot of listening, but I may need you to back me up with my girlfriend at home that this is work-related."

He chuckles again. "Man, the problems of youth. Anything else?"

I reply, "Yes; I would not do the last walkthrough on Tuesday."

"Why?"

"Well, that was the day that we were going to originally give our demonstration. If they have malware on the prototype, it may be time-activated to wait for that day."

"What do you suggest? Everything works now."

I answer, "It's your call. If you blow it up, then we have to move the backup into place right off the bat, which may blow up too. So, I don't know how you want to play it. Maybe they just stole everything but didn't plant malware on the prototype, as we assumed. Maybe we are overthinking it. I don't know."

He says, "Okay, again, I'll think about it. I'm scared to ask, but anything else?"

"No, have fun tonight."

"Thanks Robert. Everything good with George and your other project?"

"Yes, but we can't really test it, so the engineers may struggle on my backups if we have to use it."

"Understood. See you."

I call George on his burner phone and take a bunch of insults for leaving him again tonight. I tell him what's up, and he just keeps asking, "Wait a minute—how pretty is she again?"

I tell him I will be over this weekend and we should pack it all up and be ready for what happens next week. He tells me to try to take a picture of her and send it over to him, and I assure him that I would not be heading out with her if it wasn't for the good of the cause. I am trying to be serious with him to tell him how much I like Sarah, but he would have none of it.

I then grab a twenty-minute nap, take a shower, and check my email. Janine has accepted my invite for my false version of LinkedIn. I will be seeing real-time updates of what she is doing, sent hourly to my computer, which I can remotely log into. I am starting to wonder if she is actually going to text me, though, when the text comes through: "Meet you at six thirty at the same place we went before, or do you want me to pick you up?"

I reply: "Done, since you are not used to taking no for an answer. ☺ I'll just meet you."

And that is that. I know I'm continuing to get in over my head, but I think I am in a good place. I walk over to Peet's and order up my Uber. One is here in seven minutes, as advertised.

I get to Nola's early again, sit at a table where I can see the parking lot, and order a Lagunitas IPA draft. Five minutes later I see a red convertible Mercedes pull in, and I know it is her by the fact that five guys having a smoke literally walk over to stare at her and the car.

Janine walks into the bar to even more turned heads. She throws her purse and keys on my table and says, "Drinking alone?"

"Not scared to," I reply.

"You didn't order me one?" she pouts. She motions to the waitress and orders one.

"What type of Mercedes is that again?" I ask.

"An SL. It's really nice; I'll have to give you a ride one of these days."

I change the subject. "So, how is the competition going from your eyes?"

She laughs easily. "Nothing has started yet. Everyone is just setting up. I'm just the facilitator really, but I will be sitting in on the presentations next week."

We then just talk about nothing really for the next thirty minutes. She is easy to talk to; she grew up in Ohio outside of Cleveland. Her father worked installing wiring for one of the Midwestern telephone companies, and her mother was a stay-at-home mom but had passed away when she was nine from breast cancer. She has one older brother and one younger sister. I do like her personally; she's very outgoing and seems fun.

I am on my second beer, and I go to the bathroom once when she has to take a call. When she returns, she starts in on me again about why a computer security guy is on the trip. I am getting the feeling she knew anyway, so I figure it won't hurt to respond.

"I was originally in charge of setting up servers. I am supposed to be a software engineer, but they had no one else to do the server setup when I came to ART, so I ended up doing system administration work as well. When I was doing it, I immediately noticed someone scanning my servers when I turned them on. When I drilled down into it, I found that the scans were coming from the outside, so by default I started putting in measures to tighten up our security on the servers I was building. Then I just expanded it to the entire company."

She responds, "Wow, pretty interesting. Did they steal anything?"

That's quite the question, I think to myself. "I don't know. The thing about computer security is technically you aren't stealing anything, you're really just copying it, so there's nothing to notice missing. I suspect they did get what they were coming for, or I guess it could have been just a random targeting of a bunch of companies to take whatever data they could. Who knows; it had just been announced that we received a round of funding, so they may have been looking specifically at us to see if we had any IP of value."

She replies, "Hmm. Do you think it had something to do with this project?"

I answer, "I'm not sure. I guess it could have been due to anything. Anyway, that is what got me into computer security, but as I said, I am doubling as a sys admin, so I'm doing a handful of roles, none too exciting."

All of a sudden, I feel completely woozy, almost like I am drunk—but I have just been sipping my second beer of the night, so I know I am not.

Janine is talking about something, and I stop paying attention. In fact, I'm just kind of staring at her. She is very pretty, and I'm not sure why I thought she could have anything to do with all this craziness. I am beginning to feel very, very good, if a little out of focus.

She then looks at me and takes my hand and says, "Robert, are you okay?"

I start to say something, but the words do not seem to be coming out right, so I just pick up my beer and take a large swallow until it is gone. I try to signal to the waitress for another beer.

Everything then starts getting fuzzy, and I hear Janine ask for the check. The waitress remarks, "Good, because I would not serve him anything anyway." I start to protest, but it seems funny, so I kind of laugh and then start getting up. To my dull surprise, I fall off my stool.

I feel arms grab me and hear Janine on one side as I am walked out the door. There is someone else on the other side holding my arm, and my legs are kind of working. I am placed into a car and hear whoever is helping me tell Janine that she must really like me, because she is crazy to put me into a car this nice in my condition.

We then start moving, and I feel the wind blow over the top of my head. I remember Janine's nice car and try to tell her how nice her car is. I enjoy the speed and watch the lights go by fast. We stop, and again Janine's hands are there, pulling me out of the car this time. She is closer now and asks me to help her by trying to walk, which I do. I know that I am not walking straight, but she takes me to the back door that I have been sneaking in and out of. I try to tell her this is my secret door, but again I'm not sure how it comes out. She asks what I mean, but I can't find the words to answer her.

We are now out of the elevator and into my hallway, and I tell her my room number. She is very close now with her head leaning up into mine. She smells fantastic. She asks me for my room key, and as I am reaching for it she seems to push me up against the wall. I feel her cheek on my cheek.

I pull out the key, say, "Found it," and make it to my door. I look down the end of the hallway as I am telling her this and see someone standing at the far end. I ask Janine, "Who is that down the hallway?"

As she turns to look, I slip out of her arm and through my slightly open door and slam it shut as fast as I can. She starts to try to open it, but I have engaged the lock quickly, as alarm bells are going off in my head. I add the security deadbolt and chain.

Though I'm slurring my words, I say, "Janine, thank you so much. I am sorry, but I am sick. I will talk to you tomorrow."

I drop the key on the floor as I try to get it into my pocket and stumble to my bed. The last thing I remember is trying to get the bed to stop spinning as I roll onto my side.

Chapter 36

Friday, May 29
San Jose, California

I wake up to a pounding headache and nausea. I look at the clock and it is a little past five in the morning. What the hell happened to me last night? I try to put it together, but I can't. There are data points but not a continuous view of the night. I go back to sleep, and the next time I look at the clock, it is almost eight o'clock.

I stumble to the bathroom, fill up a glass of water, and drink it. My head pounds, and I find two Advil, but I am also nauseated. I wish I could throw up. I close my eyes for a couple of minutes, sitting in my standard-issue hotel chair, and then I pick up my burner phone and call George.

"Hey rock star, how did it go last night?"

"Hey man, not good. I got hammered, but it's not what you think."

He laughs, "Sure, okay. How is getting hammered not what I would think?"

"I drank two beers, and it was the weirdest thing. All of a sudden, I totally lost it; I felt so drunk. And right now I feel like I'm going to get sick, but I didn't have any more than the two beers last night."

He answers, "Are you kidding me? I always knew you were a lightweight, little man, but that pretty girl turned you into a major one."

I say, "George, I'm serious. Thinking about it, I had to be drugged last night with something. Is there anything you know about that can make someone that drunk, that quickly?"

He is silent, and then his tone changes when he says, "Yes, there is stuff. Did you leave a drink for a while?"

"I did get up and go to the bathroom."

He asks, "Did the Wicked Witch of the West do this to you?"

I answer, "She is actually alright. She took care of me, and thinking about it, she was on the phone outside when I was in the bathroom."

He says, "Dude, just because you got to hang out with her and had fun doesn't mean you shouldn't trust your gut about her. Someone did something to you. Even if she did not slip anything in your drink, there is probably a good chance she knew it was happening. Tell me everything."

I walk him through everything that happened. When I am finished, he says, "Wow, that's my boy, with a strong move at the end. You did not tell her anything about what we were doing, did you?"

"I don't think so. I think I remember saying something about her bringing me in my secret door, but that on its own could mean anything."

He says, "Okay, pretend she is a bad guy. She could have gone through everything you had in the room and your personal computer, which you have not been leaving in the room. Do I have to remind you about the Baltimore occurrences? We are under attack. You know this. You should have Tasered that dame. Every college kid knows not to leave a drink on the table."

Ugh, George is right. This is a rookie mistake. I then call Joe on the burner phone and tell him the same story.

I go back to bed on and off for the entire day. I talk to George once and check in with Sarah. I do not tell Sarah my whole story; I just say I am not feeling very well, that we have to wait until next week to get rolling, and that we have everything set up.

Janine texts me at some point and asks how I am feeling, and I just say, "Rough. Sorry I was so out of it."

She responds that it is okay and to let her know if I want to grab a cup of coffee.

I also log into my server at home and go through everything that Janine has written or sent on her computer all day. Nothing. Bummer—she is either not using this computer or she is not involved. Who knows? My head hurts.

Fifth-Floor Suite, Hampton Inn
Palo Alto, California

Hans finally receives an email on the phone situation.

> Subject: Phones as requested
>
> 4 phones were purchased by company's original investor along with 2 credit cards.
>
> Locations: 3 are in your general area; 1 is not turned on.
> - Phone located in Marriott Residence Inn in Sunnyvale—cannot tell specific room number, but tracking and a layout of the hotel looks like it is in a room ending in 06. There are 5 floors to the building, so room would be 106 through 506
> - Hotel Valencia, 355 Santana Row, San Jose—room ending in 18 from layout of the building
> - Hotel Valencia, 355 Santana Row, San Jose—room ending in 31 from layout of the building
>
> Credit cards:
> - Registered to George McCarthy
> - Registered to Robert Dulaney
>
> Have not been able to obtain credit card records for transactions yet but will be able within next 4 hours. Also working on hotel for specific room numbers. Let us know what else you need.

Hans knows the Ukrainian team will have a handful of "zero day" vulnerabilities that they can use to break in virtually anywhere. These are vulnerabilities that the manufacturers of the systems do not know about yet themselves, so there are no patches released that can be used to protect anyone using the application or operating system that is a target.

Virtually no one—neither the vendors nor the customers—actually knows about a particular zero day vulnerability except the people who find it, so there are no defenses against it and no patches for it. The Ukrainian team did their own research on operating systems, applications, web browsers, and databases to find ways to access them that other people have not figured out yet. They have also purchased exploitable zero day vulnerabilities from another organization for high dollar amounts. Four hours is not unreasonable to be able to break into a major American credit card company with your own zero day attack, but it still depends on what types of systems are being utilized by the target.

Hans looks up at Jan and then at a pile of pictures on his desk. "These are worthless to us."

Jan thinks the same thing, but he has put them in front of his boss and friend anyway. "Yes, there is not enough in the pictures. Besides, the target is not married and may not care."

"Yes...it was worth a try, though."

He slides over about ten pictures of Robert and an attractive woman at the restaurant, in the car, stumbling back into the hotel, and in the hallway of the hotel where the woman and him appear face-to-face leaning against the wall by his room. The thought is they could blackmail Robert for some quick information at risk of exposing the pictures to another relationship, but while they know he likes the woman in Baltimore, he is not married to her. He also slammed the door shut in the hallway, so the pictures ended there. Robert does not seem the type to take a bribe, and he will probably be making a lot of money anyway if the prototype is successful.

Han's says, "Robert's friend from Baltimore is here and is the one staying at that hotel in Sunnyvale. He is who Robert has been visiting. Look at this email."

Jan looks up after reading the email and says, "This confirms what we have suspected: there is something else going on. I'll grab one of the guys and head over to that hotel. I will look for target there and try to get a fix on his exact room. If they get into the hotel's systems, can you get electronic keys to the room?"

"We can figure something out there."

He looks back at his email inbox and sees another from Ukraine.

Subject: Hotel
Into hotel registry—Sunnyvale room number is 406.

He replies back:

Subject: Re: Hotel
Can you add Joseph Baker as a registered guest on the same room at the hotel so he can pick up a key with an ID?

Joseph Baker is one of the aliases of the other men that Jan and Hans are working with, and it will be better not to expose Jan to the front desk.

Chapter 37

Sunday, May 31
San Jose, California

Well, my head has finally stopped pounding every time I move, so I go to Mass early after grabbing some coffee. I continue to have a nagging feeling in my stomach and anxiety about the upcoming prototype, but going to church helps me put it all in perspective. I need to do the best that I can and release my anxieties about all of this.

I call Sarah, and we talk for a while. I do tell her I believe I was drugged, but nothing happened; I just got sick. I decide not to relay this to my parents, though, based on Sarah's alarmed reaction. She is worried and also believes that after our multiple attacks in Baltimore, something bad is going to happen.

I am looking forward to putting this entire thing behind us and getting back to my normal life in Baltimore. I email my brother and tell him how I am doing. He has emailed me several times with articles about hackers targeting American companies.

I call George on the burner phone, and he gives me some crap for lying around all day Saturday and tells me how bored he is. I agree to meet him in the afternoon at his hotel room to start boxing up the servers and get them ready to be moved.

I make it there by two o'clock, and we spend the next handful of hours catching up and boxing up all the servers. I hope I have configured them properly, but since they are mainly restores of systems from several months ago, there is not much I can do or test.

We are able to finish boxing up all the equipment by six, and then we go out and grab something to eat.

Monday, June 1
Hampton Inn
Palo Alto, California

The hacking team has identified all the room numbers connected with Robert's new credit cards that are linked to the investor. They have also watched Robert walk into a room of the hotel, and they have all the credit card transactions made with his cards. It seems as though Robert and George have been busy purchasing a lot of computers.

Hans sends a note to their main handler with the suggestion that they destroy the computers and end the threat of Robert and George if they get in the way. They are waiting on the reply and also making plans to exit the country by Thursday afternoon.

Hans and Jan will trade in their car at San Jose International Airport and take separate cabs to San Francisco International Airport, where they will catch a redeye to Washington Dulles International Airport and then over to Eastern Europe the following day. The other two will drive to Oakland International Airport and fly to Los Angeles, where they will transfer to their international flights. The tickets are expensive, but the cost is easily absorbed by the amount of money that they are getting paid.

Hans keys a note to the hacking team in Ukraine that he wants a text of the location and time of any transactions on either of the credit cards.

Wednesday, June 3
Hotel Valencia
San Jose, California

I wake up early and energetic. Finally, we are almost there as far as showing ART's technology and heading back home. I believe that there is no way that our competitors can know about the third prototype and that it is going to work when and if we are called upon, and then this will all be over. I have a nervous energy and feel my adrenaline already kicking in.

I work out and see Bill, who is excited as well, in the workout room. I call Sarah and talk for a while. She can update me on the Orioles with the same enthusiasm that she has when she talks about the weather, and I enjoy every minute of it. She also tells me about her visit to William, which was just a nice thing to do. She is getting to know my brother even though he is serving time. She was able to go during a weeknight with visiting hours between seven and nine. I didn't know you could do that.

Our entire team had taken Memorial Day off because we are just waiting to go forward, and George and I had taken off for a day baseball game at San Francisco's downtown stadium against their archenemy, the Dodgers. It was a great day, and I didn't worry about work once. Yesterday, we met at Zamtech, but it was basically folks going over slides and timing, as the Zamtech team was involved with the other vendor.

I have a little time before I have to go over to Zamtech, so I log into my server that I had spun up on the cloud for my special operations and am able to start going through outgoing email from Janine. One is very interesting. It is a note to someone in her own company as a reply to a question on how it is going. This feels a little bad, because I am actually spying now on her, and it is unrelated to anything she may or may not be involved with against my company. Anyway, I do not care because of the war waged against us, but I do not want to get caught.

The email talks about how Hodophi's day had gone: "Hodophi's presentation was flawless, very well prepared and impressive to the executives here. Their actual testing was strong but not perfect. They seemed to be able to successfully move 98.4794% of the energy. They did lose some to heat, but they were able to reduce the risk of the heat in innovative heat dampening techniques.

"The Zamtech execs met briefly at the end of the day without Hodophi in the room, and I was able to sit in the meeting. They were disappointed Hodophi could not capture more of the energy through the channels, but overall, they were impressed with the ways they managed the movement of the energy to the storage devices. They believe they can go forward with this if ART cannot do better, and they feel they need to jump on this because of their nervousness about their timelines for getting to market before their competition. They were very impressed with the counter-measures that Hodophi put in place to reduce the effects of the heat and believe they could embed that strategy to move forward with their partners looking to put Zamtech's solar technology into technologies used every day in society."

I pick up my secret phone and call Joe, asking, "Do you have a minute?"

"Sure, Robert. I'm going to see you in thirty minutes, but what's up?"

"Yesterday Hodophi did 98.4%, but they had some innovative heat-dampening techniques. They win if we don't perform."

"Where are you getting this information?"

I answer, "Call it spying on people that are spying on me."

There is silence on the other end. Finally, Joe responds, "Robert, do not do anything unethical, period. No compromises in who you are and who we are."

This makes me kind of angry. "I'm not! These people have tried to kill me. I am trying to get ahead of them a little, that is all. This information was practically seen by mistake when I was trying to figure out the next attack. Anyway, another attack is coming. Zamtech believes Hodophi will win unless we can beat that 98.4%, and I'm pretty sure this information got back to Hodophi."

Joe says, "Robert, I understand, but we really need to be careful here. Stay above reproach. If you see anything about their technology, don't read it, don't forward it, and don't give our team any feedback...but if you can see an attack coming, obviously we need to protect our people."

I answer with a very intelligent "Yep."

He continues, "Plan on getting your equipment here tomorrow at eight thirty in the morning, right when we are supposed to start. I will ask Zamtech's CTO at 8:25 a.m. to walk with me to the front desk and authorize new equipment coming in. They will be mad that we won't start on time, but I will explain."

We hang up and I look at her email some more. There's nothing too exciting, but she forwarded the message she sent to her boss to a personal email: jc4791@gmail.com.

Gotcha. She is probably using that to communicate with whoever she is talking to at Hodophi. Not really hard evidence, but it's enough to confirm other items for me. Why would she send an email she sent for work to her personal email address? Also, this is not her personal email address that she uses on LinkedIn, so maybe it's just used for this one thing.

If I had more time, I would get some malware to that email address to find what has to be another computer with which she is communicating to the outside. She just made a mistake, and I picked up on it. She probably did not want to rewrite everything to Hodophi, so she just pasted from what she sent to her company. That's enough circumstantial evidence for me. I grab my computer and go down to meet Bill to head to Zamtech.

Fifth-Floor Suite, Hampton Inn
Palo Alto, California

The team has just finishing the morning's impromptu planning meeting. Jan will go to Sunnyvale with "Joseph Baker" and wait until George leaves his hotel. Then they will use the key they have received to go in and destroy all the computers in the room. They will open each box and steal hard drives or pull wires or whatever they need to do to wreck them completely.

They all agree that this is easier then stealing the equipment or lighting a fire. If it does not appear George is going to leave the hotel, they will wait until the middle of the night and stage a burglary. They will take out George if necessary.

Hans is now getting texts with the time and location of each transaction made on the credit cards; Robert is not using his at all at this moment, but George seems to be using his for everything.

Zamtech Headquarters
Palo Alto, California

Wow, talk about boring. I have never been part of this type of agonizing discussion, where our folks go through every single slide and comment and make changes. We seem to do this all day long.

Bill really wants to run through another test of the equipment, but Joe says no, that it worked the last time we tested it and he does not want to mess with it. I am proud of the way Joe handles it, because I believe there is a time-based trigger on malware that will totally blow up the day after we were supposed to start.

Anyway, the day passes quickly. I walk outside at some point and touch base with George on the burner phone. He is just hanging out in the hotel, working out and doing nothing. I quickly tell him that Hodophi wins if ART fails, so be careful, as they will certainly do something if they are on to us. I doubt they are and hope they aren't, but we still have to be careful.

Later on in the evening, our team eats a short dinner at our hotel. Everyone is anxious, yet we all focus on what we have to do. I let Bill know that I am going to drive tomorrow and that I will meet him directly at Zamtech.

I call George and let him know that I will be over around six in the morning to pack the van with him, and then we can grab some java and head to Zamtech at exactly 8:25 a.m. I will call Joe in the morning and ask him to put George's name at security so he can get in.

Chapter 38

Thursday, June 4
Marriott Residence Inn
Sunnyvale, California

George cannot sleep at all. He is not sure what it is; it could be as simple as him trying to finish all the beer in his little fridge while eating a chicken wing dinner. It also might be the statement that Robert made about Hodophi needing to do something. He looks at the clock, and it reads 2:13 a.m.

He picks up the gun that is sitting on the double bed beside him and fusses with it. His stomach hurts, and he thinks to himself that it figures—it's the first time he has to wake up early this entire trip. He goes to the bathroom and then goes to his door. He hears someone walking slowly down the hallway, and he looks through his peephole. Two guys walk by, and one glances at his door. He has seen the one guy before, though he's not sure where. Maybe in the lobby? He has actually been watchful because of past events. He goes to the bathroom, turns on the shower, and pulls the curtain closed.

• • •

Jan and the guy he knows as Joseph walk down the hall again. Joseph is the fifth member of the team, and he has worked with Hans before. He is more muscle than brain, but he is also a very talented hired killer. The hallway is empty. This is a hotel where consultants stay after being on the road for the week. They drink beer with dinner, but everything quiets down by about ten o'clock. Their target has not given them any good opportunities today; he has stayed in the hotel to work out and eat dinner. They have not risked anything during that time, as people are all around and in the hallway.

Jan gives the signal to Joseph, and within a second both of their guns are out as Jan uses the room key to ease open the door. The security latch isn't on, which saves them from having to wake George up. They slowly walk into the room. The shower is on, and a light coming from the slightly ajar bathroom door gives them a little illumination. The computers are stacked up on the far side of the room next to a double bed that looks slept in.

Jan signals to Joseph to walk towards the bathroom. He waits for a second and then follows.

Joe eases the door back and peeks in. The shower is running, and the curtain is shut. He steps into the bathroom, and Jan walks in beside him. Joe looks at Jan and Jan nods. Joe shoots five consecutive shots at different angles through the curtain into the shower. He then walks up, grabs the curtain, and pulls it open.

• • •

George waits until he sees the lighting in the room grow and then become shadowy. He eases out of the closet just as he sees the second man enter the bathroom. He levels his gun with the silencer on and walks up behind him. He needs to see both men clearly if he is going to get out of this without shooting. All of a sudden, he hears shots ricocheting in the bathtub. He sees the man then walk toward the shower curtain and pull it open. The guy sees that there is no one in it and turns quickly with his gun raised. George shoots twice and connects on two head shots, and the man tumbles into the tub.

George has the drop on the second man as well, and he sticks the gun to his head and tells him to slowly drop his weapon. The man does as George says but at the same time cuts upwards with a knife into George's extended arm and slices across.

George shoots as the knife cuts into his right arm, but the shot goes high and the man ducks. George has never seen such speed, and the knife finally comes out of his arm, but it forces him to drop the gun. The man is coming at him fast, but he seems to lose his balance and slip a little. George takes this opportunity to throw a hard left-handed punch, catching him on the side of the head; the punch seems to knock him further off balance. The guy slips and slams his head into the door jamb. He falls to the floor and seems to black out.

George is not sure if it is a trick. The guy seems to have hit the door pretty hard. He realizes in this moment that he is so lucky, because that guy would have been on him if he had not slipped. He cannot believe he has messed up this badly. He is shaking, and the gash in his arm has arced down towards his hand. He picks up the gun with his left hand and keeps it on the man. He kicks the knife that the guy threw across the floor towards where the computers are.

There is a fair amount of blood from his injury, and he walks into the bathroom, gets a towel, and tries to tie it around the injury to stop the bleeding. He looks at the man in the shower. He had not taken chances with the first guy with the gun. He had used his training to shoot to kill, aiming at the middle of his forehead with both shots. These men did not expect George to be armed but fully intended just to kill him and then deal with the computers.

The towel tied sloppily on his arm seems to have helped some, but it is not a good job, and he's bleeding pretty heavily. The man is still out on the floor, and George checks him for other weapons. He finds two more: a knife in the small of his back and another crazy-looking knife with a small handle and a short, curved blade that looks like a miniature sickle. He has to be really careful with this guy based on what he has seen. He realizes that he is truly lucky to be alive.

George walks back towards the computers and grabs the tape they used to pack them up. He walks to the man on the floor. He tapes his hands together as tightly as he can behind his back and leaves him lying on his stomach.

He picks up his burner phone and calls Robert.

Hotel Valencia
San Jose, California

Ugh, I feel like I just fell asleep, and now my phone is ringing. I see it's George's line. I pick up.

"Yo," I murmur sleepily.

"Hey man, I need your help big time. Two dudes just came in here to kill me. One of them is dead, and the other is some sort of crazy psycho, but he is knocked out for now on the floor. He stabbed me in my arm, so I couldn't do a good job of taping him up. If he wakes up, I may have to shoot him."

I feel my heart pounding, and I do not know what to say or do. As my head quickly comes out of my sleep haze, I say lamely, "Are you okay? Should I come over? Did you call the police?"

"Hold up. Yes to you coming over. No to calling the police. I need you to bring one of the luggage carts from downstairs for the computers, bring your Taser, and knock on the door five times. Any more or any less and I'm going to shoot you through the door. If someone from the other team is there with a gun on you, knock three times."

"Got it, five times if alone, three times if not."

I hang up the phone and throw on a pair of shorts. My heart pumps in my chest as I grab my keys, my Taser, and a baseball cap. I then throw my computer into my backpack and pull the cap down and walk out. No one is in the hallway. I run down the exit stairs to the back of the hotel where my car is parked. I haven't seen anyone, but I really can't worry about that now, anyway.

It is a good time to be driving in this area, as you can actually get around without sitting in traffic. I cover the twelve miles in about ten minutes.

Marriott Residence Inn
Sunnyvale, California

When I get there, I decide to leave the computer bag in the car, which I hope will not come back to haunt me. I use the key George has given me to go in through the back door of the hotel. I look around as I grab a luggage cart from the lobby with one hand holding the Taser in my pocket.

I go up the elevator and down the hallway to George's room. No one seems to be around. I knock on the door five sharp times. George opens it, and I see a big red towel taped poorly to his arm. I walk in without saying anything. George is holding his gun with his good arm and pointing it at a man on the floor. The man is moving slightly and George says, "Dude, I just told you, if you move again I'm going to blow a hole in your head like your buddy. Don't pretend you can't speak English. If you don't understand me, I'm just going to shoot you. I have no patience for people that try to kill me."

George then looks at me and says, "Robert, grab that packing tape and tape his hands up more securely. Then tape his ankles. I am going to kneel three feet from you, and if he or you make any sudden movements, I'm just going to shoot him in the head. Be careful: he is extremely fast. I had the drop on him and he still almost got me earlier. I just got lucky."

I walk over to the boxes and see a weird-looking four-inch knife on the carpet and blood all over the place. I pick up the tape and walk up behind the man on the floor.

George kneels down three feet from the man and steadies the gun with his left hand as he aims at his head. I quickly start taping his wrists together as tightly as I can. I am using a ton of tape.

The man on the floor says in accented English, "Too tight. Cutting off circulation."

George looks at me and says, "Tighter," and I pull as tight as I can. I then use the rest of that roll on his ankles. I go and grab another roll, and George tells me to tape his mouth shut as well, which I do. I make sure his nose is clear so he can breathe. I don't think George cares either way.

He then says, "You need to fix my arm, and then we need to get the hell out of here."

I have known George since first grade, and he is a goofball 99% of the time, but the other 1% of the time, he is extremely focused on what he has to do. He is in that mode now and seems to have a plan.

I go into the bathroom and see a bloody mess on the mirror and in the bathtub, which I try my hardest not to look at as I grab two clean towels. I step over the man's legs that are on the bathroom floor but manage not to look at his face.

I pick up the strange-looking knife on the floor, wipe the blood on the bed cover, sit next to George in a desk chair, and cut off the tape holding the towel in place. There is a ton of blood, and I tell him we need to clean it. He says no; his eyes are focused on the man on the floor. I wipe it to see a deep, jagged cut going up his arm. George grimaces in pain. I then wrap his arm with a fresh towel and tape it firmly. The tape works, though there is still quite a bit of blood making it hard to stick on there, but enough of it keeps the towel in place.

George gets up slowly and walks over to the man. "Were you just moving your feet?"

I am nervous. George definitely wants to shoot this guy. I quickly start packing computers on the luggage cart. It looks like it is going to take two trips. George says to pack it in his minivan and that the keys are on the nightstand. I grab them and walk out the door and downstairs.

The night attendant looks at me as I walk out and says, "Working late?"

I answer, "You always are when you're in IT."

I quickly pack the van, grab my laptop out of my car, and return to the room, knocking five times. George has thrown his stuff together in a bag, and he is pacing back and forth by the man on the floor. He has put a light jacket on so you can't see the bloody towel covering his arm. I refill the luggage cart with the rest of the equipment, and George and I head to the minivan.

· · ·

Jan lays on the floor with his face down. He is truly surprised that his target had been armed and is embarrassed he had lost control of the situation. He rolls onto his side and kicks back with both of his feet as hard as he can against the wall.

Nothing happens. He tries it two more times until he feels a small capsule break.

The device on the tip of his shoe has electronics in it that will spill the liquid from a capsule that is broken into a chamber. The liquid then acts as an electrical connector between the circuitry and sends an electronic alert to Hans that he is in trouble with his exact location. He is sorry he could not have done it earlier, but the target would have clearly shot him if he kicked his feet.

Fifth-Floor Suite, Hampton Inn
Palo Alto, California

Hans receives the alert from Jan on his phone with his location. He has been waiting for an update and is distressed to see the alert come across. Jan had broken a capsule once before on another operation, ultimately saving his life. Hans shoots a quick message to his team in Ukraine to be ready to help over the next twelve hours, grabs the other two men, and heads for the door.

Silicon Valley, California

I look over at George, who is lying back in the passenger seat, and say, "I should take you to the hospital."

He answers, "Not yet, little man, they will be all over it. They are more formidable than we think. In fact, we should not be using any of the phones or the credit cards. We also have to ditch this car."

I still feel like I am in a haze, my ADD taking my mind from one thought to the next at lightning speed. My adrenaline is pumping, and I am soaking wet with sweat, but I keep getting chills. I say, "Ditch the car? What are you talking about? You have lost too much blood, and I think we should go to the police or the hospital."

George replies slowly and calmly, which settles me slightly, "They came in the night before we were going to deliver that equipment. They did not care that I was in the room. We have told no one about that equipment, so the way they knew we had it was either by following us, tracing our transactions, or whatever, which means they know the car as well. Who knows what type of resources they have, but they seem to be better than us."

George reaches into his pocket and pulls out his phone. He dials a number and waits while it rings. Finally, someone picks up. George says, "Jeff, I'm having an emergency here. I need to borrow your SUV. Yes, I'm serious. Meet you in the same place as we met last time. I'll be there in twenty minutes."

He hangs up. "I served with Jeff. He's good people. He probably saved my life by lending me those guns." He plugs in an address on his phone and starts telling me which way to go.

We end up at a Chipotle in a strip mall about a mile from the new 49ers stadium near San Jose. All the stores are closed, but there is an SUV hidden from the street near a bunch of trees.

We get out, and George's boy jumps out too. George introduces us really quickly. Jeff is a shorter guy, but he looks like he is solid muscle. He's not the bulky weightlifting type, but he's a guy that looks like he has done a thousand pull-ups and push-ups. He has a buzzcut that makes it look like he is still in the military.

Jeff asks how he can he help. George answers, "My arm is a little messed up, so if you could move the computers from that minivan to your SUV, that would be great."

Jeff answers, "What the hell happened to you? You need me doing more than just moving computers and borrowing my ride?"

George says, "No, that's it. We need to be quick, though, and you may want to get an Uber or cab from here. That minivan is definitely a target," George says.

Jeff replies, "Maybe I'll drive it around for a while to take the heat off you. I'll be fine."

We move the computers quickly and say goodbye. It is totally business, and I am happy to have George as a friend.

George yells after him, "Call if you have problems! We'll try to get this back to you tomorrow."

Jeff laughs, "Jennifer may mind if you scratch it all up, and this is not exactly an even trade!"

George says, "Remember, you need to ditch that minivan before too long. Don't wreck it; I will need to bring it back to the rental place at some point."

Chapter 39

Thursday, June 4
Marriott Residence Inn
Sunnyvale, California

Hans looks around at the mess in the room. Jan is sitting on the bed. He is not hurt, except for some blood dripping out of the side of his head. He is upset, though, and wants to move quickly.

Hans says, "No problems. We have people on the inside, even if they make it." He sends an email to the team in Ukraine:

Subject: Top priority

Do first: Break into the Santa Clara County, California, police and put an alert in to watch for a dark blue minivan, California plates XHK-574. Stolen computer equipment, two assailants believed to be armed and dangerous.

Do second: Get into the phones and give locations, their personal ones as well.

Do third: Monitor any hospitals in San Jose area for someone coming in with a deep cut in the arm and advise us.

If the police detain them, you need to let us know when they have them and where they are taking them with any other details. Also, relay any credit card use.

He receives a message a minute later:

Subject: Re: Top priority
Sixty-minute estimate on Number 1—we can work all three in
parallel. Will confirm when complete.

Han's remaining team is already cleaning everything up. They
go about their business efficiently. The body is a problem, but
they have the keys to the room, and no one is coming back. They
do not want to leave it here and will return for him with a box
and wrap it up.

Hans goes up to Jan and says, "Give me the details again."

"He seemed to know we were coming and tricked us. He turned
on the shower and was hiding somewhere, probably in the closet.
He came up behind us. He had a gun with a silencer and shot
Joseph right after Joseph had shot into the shower. He had the gun
on me, but when I dropped mine I was able to fool him and come
up with my knife. I got his arm good, but I slipped as I was going
for his body. He caught me in the side of the head with a hard
punch, and my head ricocheted off that doorjamb, which must
have knocked me out. I came to taped up with a gun on me. This
guy actually knew what he was doing, which is also a surprise."

Hans tells the team, "Let's go. We will come back for Joseph
with a big enough box if we have time."

He places the Do Not Disturb sign on the door as he receives a
text from the Ukrainian team: "All tasks completed—Last call on
George's personal phone in San Jose at 3:14 a.m. to a Jeff O'Neal,
whose primary residence is in San Jose."

Hans thinks to himself as they are walking out that the police
will find George and Robert and arrest them soon. They will
impound the vehicle with the computers, so they won't make
their meeting tomorrow, and the computers will be destroyed
where they are impounded for good measure.

Silicon Valley, California

We are driving back toward Sunnyvale as George's phone rings. He leans up in his seat, hits the speaker, and says, "Hey."

"George, it's Jeff. I just got pulled over by the police. He's not out of the car yet. What are you guys into?"

George answers, "Crap, nothing. The guys after us are computer hackers, they probably called something in. Be very, very careful, and show your hands at all times. Tell them the entire truth, everything except that you gave us your car. Say we have another car, but we need you to return that car to Hertz at San Francisco International Airport. Say you took an Uber to the parking lot. Are they coming up yet?"

"No, it's weird. He's just sitting there with lights on."

"Both hands on the steering wheel, Jeff. We need to get off the phone, as they are probably tracing my phone by now."

Jeff says, "Another cop just pulled up in front...and a third just pulled up behind as well."

"Tell them our names, everything—all the truth, except for that we are in your car. Tell them your friends believe the hackers were going to put in an arrest warrant."

Jeff replies, "The police are out of cars, guns drawn."

George says, "I owe you. We are hanging up. No sudden movements."

He hangs up and says to me, "Give me your phones." He pops the batteries out of the burner phones and takes our personal iPhones and puts them in airplane mode and says, "What time do we need to be at Zamtech tomorrow?"

"Eight twenty-five," I say. "What now?" I look at the clock on the dashboard. 3:40 a.m.

"Can you get us to San Jose Airport without your map on the phone?"

"Yes, I have seen the exit before, but we're not going anywhere, are we?"

He answers, "No, we are going to go to long-term parking
there and take a little nap until about seven fifteen. Then we are
going to wake up, get some breakfast, and make our delivery.
I have enough cash to cover this, since we can't use our credit
cards anymore."

I say, "You sure? You should hit a hospital. I can drop you off
and finish this."

He replies, "You have to be kidding me. First, they will probably
off me in a hospital. Second, this is fun."

I find the San Jose Airport and follow signs for long-term
parking. I find a nice spot between two other SUVs in a remote
area. We put our seats back and close our eyes. I am worried I will
not wake up in time without my standard-issue iPhone alarm,
but I figure the light will probably do it. And I am too tired to
worry about it anyway.

It takes me a while to go to sleep as my mind is racing,
but the next thing I know I am waking up. The sun is up and
getting brighter I look at the clock: 6:15 a.m. I do not wake
George, but I want a cup of coffee really badly. I manage to go
in and out of sleep again until exactly 7:15 a.m., when I wake
him up.

Once again, I am a little lost without my phone, but we
stumble on a Starbucks and get breakfast sandwiches and large
cups of coffee, which hit the spot. George seems okay, although
his bloody arm contraption does not look good. He really needs
to get to a hospital, but he once again refuses.

We take the exit off of Route 101 to get to Zamtech in
Palo Alto, and George asks if there are guards at the gate at
Zamtech. I say yes, and he asks me to pull over. I ask, "Why,
what's up?"

He says, "Zamtech is not going to have me on any registered guest list. Pull into this shopping center, and let's get things set for me to hide in the back."

I reply, "I asked Joe to put you on the list."

He says, "If he forgot, that is a problem we don't need. This is not a normal day where we can risk sitting around waiting for someone to realize it's okay to let us in."

I pull into the shopping center, and he lies down between the seats in the middle gully in the center of the SUV. We put some boxes around him so you can't tell he is there from any angle.

Chapter 40

Friday, June 5
Zamtech Headquarters
Palo Alto, California

At 8:15 a.m., we pull through the guard gate, and the guard asks me my name and verifies I am on the guest list.

As I drive through, I peer in my rearview mirror and say, "You can get up now; he's gone."

George replies, "Nope, not until I'm sure we are 100% safe and your CEO has a little nametag with my name on it."

• • •

In the conference room, Zamtech scientists, engineers, and business folks gather around the coffee setup and are having small discussions amongst themselves. Bill and Tom are chatting with some of the groups.

Joe walks up to the CTO and asks if he can have a word with him privately, and they walk out into the hallway and then down towards the front desk.

• • •

As I pull around back, I see one of the guys that helped us move the equipment in earlier motioning to me where to pull in. Joe must have told them earlier, as I expected, to wait there. I turn on my phone to let Joe know where we are. I turn the SUV around and back into the spot.

He says, "Hold on one second," and walks up to the passenger door.

He opens the door and jumps into the seat next to me with a gun pointed right in my face. This guy looks like a weight lifter. Stinking meathead.

I say, "Seriously, another gun right now?" I hope George can hear it from his hiding place.

He says, "Drive slowly out of this alley and straight through the guard gate."

I want to keep him talking, so I say, "What is in this for you and Janine?"

"Shut up and keep driving."

"Why? You're not going to shoot me until we get out of here. That would be a pain for you." I keep talking. "So what is in it for you, money? Lots of it? How much money is enough money to do something like this?"

I finally hear George's voice and look over to see the gun against the back of the dock worker's neck. "Took your finger off the trigger didn't you, you arrogant idiot? I would love to blow your head though this window, but I won't if you slowly drop that gun onto the middle console next to my boy there."

He does what he is told, and I pull the gun over to me and put it down between the door and my seat so he can't reach it if things go bad. Then I do a big U-turn and head back to the spot we just came from. I park and then reach into the middle console, pull out my burner phone, and put the battery back into it.

I call Joe, who picks up on the first ring. "George and I are out back in the loading dock. Bring security with you. The dock guy just had a gun to my face, but George got it away from him."

Joe is in shocked silence for a second, taking it all in, and then he answers, "What?! Okay, I will have them call the police, and we will be there in a minute."

A couple minutes later, Joe is there with two security guards and another guy. We are still in the car, but I get out, walk around, and cover the dock guy while George gets out of the car.

The two security guards do not have guns, but one does have handcuffs, so they cuff the guy and make him sit on the curb .

Joe goes to shake hands with George, but George motions to his arm that he can't, and Joe sees the blood-soaked shirt inside George's jacket. "Nice to meet you, George. Are you okay?"

"I had some visitors in my hotel room last night who planned on killing me and taking the computers. My arm took a knife... but they were the worse for wear."

Joe looks horrified, and he stands there with a blank stare. He then paces back and forth and looks at George before saying intensely, "I am so sorry this happened to you. We would have never involved you or Robert out here if we thought there was this kind of a risk. I guess I should have realized this could happen after what we found out about Ashok. I just didn't believe it was this widespread. We should have all walked away." He looks down and says quietly, "After what happened with Ashok, I guess I felt that they were through...that they had thought they had won."

George smiles and simply says, "Well, I'm not sorry to have been involved."

Joe looks at the man standing with him, who I now recognize as the CTO, and says, "Can you also have them call an ambulance, please?" The guy then walks away and makes a phone call. When he comes back, Joe introduces him as the CTO of Zamtech, Jonathan Jacobs, and asks him if we can wait to get started for thirty minutes. Jonathan is dressed in a sharp suit without a tie. He is my height and has an air of intelligence, like Ashok had. Joe also asks if it is okay if his team of engineers unload the equipment to the room. Then I call Bill.

When Bill comes out, he takes one look at me and George and a wild expression comes over his face. He walks up quickly and says, "What is going on?"

I answer, "Long story, but we need to get this gear in and start setting it up. I will be inside in a couple of minutes, but do not connect the prototype to the internet or anything for any reason. Also, leave the gear that is currently set up in there the way it is—I'm not sure how Joe wants to play this."

Bill grabs a cart and quickly starts loading the computers onto it with the engineers. The police and an ambulance show up, and I quickly give George a hug before he is taken away to the hospital.

Jonathan tells the police that the dockworker pulled a gun on me and tried to steal some very expensive computer equipment by carjacking the SUV. I answer a few questions, but I keep my answers limited to what happened here at the dock. Jonathan and I agree to go into the police station later that day for statements.

And now it's time for the big show: the presentation I have been waiting for and what, it turns out, a lot of people have risked their lives for. We walk into the room, and everyone stops milling around. Joe goes up to the podium at the front and brings his presentation up. I see Janine, who looks startled to see me, and I wink at her. She looks away quickly.

Joe's slides are just bullet points that he expands on:

**ART Has Succeeded in Transferring the Energy
with Virtually No Loss (99.9999%)**

- This test was done last week using the equipment provided by
  Zamtech in testing

- We do not believe, if we attempt to do this same test, that
  we will be able to repeat it with the same equipment

The crowd is really listening. They are wondering what kind
of presentation this is. I look around the room, and the only one
fidgeting is Janine.

**ART Has Been under Continuous Cyber and
Physical Attacks for at Least Four Months**

- We believe the attacks came from our competitor, who has
  been attempting to find our ability to dissipate heat

- A new employee responsible for building servers was key in
  understanding the attacks, and we put up defenses accordingly

- Our CTO, Ashok Ready, was kidnapped and murdered, we
  believe to get to the algorithms that he came up with to load
  balance the transfer of energy

- We have had two other employees murdered during this short
  run-up to the pilot

He looks up after going through these slides and points to me,
saying, "Robert, who originally found out about the hacking, also
was attacked four times, including an attempt on his life just this
morning by one of Zamtech's dockworkers, trying to stop us from
bringing in the new equipment here." He points to the computers
George and I built. "The person staying with the equipment was
stabbed last night, but he is okay and is on his way to the hospital

right now. It is clear to us that this technology is so innovative and transformative—and that it has the ability to make a lot of people a lot of money—that our competitor has gone to great lengths to ensure we don't succeed." He moves onto the next slide.

Why We Believe This Current Equipment Will Fail

- Ashok had coded the algorithms, known as his "secret sauce," on his home computer before he asked me to launch the company
- We moved the hard drives containing the algorithms from Ashok's house to a safe location
- Ashok's house was then robbed and ransacked before he was kidnapped
- We believe that our competitor, unable to find the hard drives, then changed tactics to destroying our prototype instead
- We think that the equipment here may be infected with malware that will be timed to disrupt the prototype

---

He says, "It is up to Zamtech what you would like us to do. We restored the equipment just brought in from backups that we believe would have been from before the competitor decided to attempt to bring down our prototype."

He hits his next slide.

Zamtech's Decision

- We do not know what harm the potential malware will cause
- We can run it to see what happens
- If we are incorrect, then the worst thing that you will see is the success of our prototype
- We have equipment that we believe will work, but we will need several hours to set it up

---

The CTO asks his group, "Is this connected anywhere to the rest of our offices? Can we isolate this test?"

A gentleman towards the back says, "This is isolated, but this equipment is very expensive. We have more of it, but we really don't want anything to damage it."

The CTO thinks for a minute. "Can we get a Zamtech private meeting in the conference room across the hall? We will be back in ten minutes."

We all sit there and look at each other for a couple of seconds. Janine hides her face behind her computer and pretends like she had some very serious work to attend to. Finally, I stand up and say, "Bill, can you help me start unpacking this stuff? I think we will need it one way or another."

Everyone gets up and starts helping me unpack.

The Zamtech crew comes walking back in about twenty minutes later, all with very serious looks on their faces. Their CTO says, "We have decided to let you run the test. We would like to see what happens. We have other equipment that we can use to test the equipment you just brought in if we need to."

Joe turns to Bill, and says, "Your show."

Bill is more rattled then I have ever seen him, but he slowly walks everyone through the setup of the ART system and explains that the "secret sauce" is in the load-balancing algorithms that Ashok developed to manage the energy going down each tube. After talking about the design and testing process that ART has gone through, he then asks the engineers to give it five joules.

Quickly the monitors all read 4.99999999, which makes everyone in the room gasp. I am not sure if I should breathe a sigh of relief or not.

Within five seconds, the numbers start switching quickly and then read 3.2. All of a sudden, the connection mechanism between the energy-producing machine and our prototype starts smoking.

Bill notices it as well and says, "Shut down all power! Pull plugs if you have to!"

He goes immediately to the testing equipment producing the energy and shuts off the power. By this time there is a small fire coming from where the energy tubes meet our circuit board.

Someone comes running up with a fire extinguisher and is about to blast it before I step in and say, "No, hold on!"

I grab someone's thick cloth laptop bag and pat the fire out. I said, "Sorry—sometimes the cover up is worse than the crime."

People look at me blankly and have no clue what I'm talking about, so I say, "I think that fire retardant would have caused more damage to all of this equipment then the little fire."

The CTO says, "Team, I would like everyone in this room to help bring the computer equipment ART just brought to the room that we used last week to test the Hodophi solution. Don't unplug the Hodophi computers yet; I would like to be there and make sure we document what we did."

Immediately Janine walks over and grabs two small boxes. These are the small boxes that I brought with our backed-up circuit boards in them.

I walk up to her. "Janine, I need to carry those boxes."

She locks eyes with me and smiles. "I have them, no problem. They are light."

I lean close to her and hiss, "I must insist, or I will make a scene. Quick question for you: when I email you, should I use your company account, your personal one that's on LinkedIn, or that third Gmail account starting with 'JC' that you use for other special projects?"

The look on her face is priceless— it goes from denial to anger to looking like she might throw up.

She sets the boxes down on the table where she got them and says, "I don't know who you think you are or what you are talking about."

I step between her and the boxes and say very lightly, "I think you do. I lost a very close personal friend at the hands of your other employers, and I almost just lost another one. Think about that when you are spending your money, if I decide not to disclose what I know."

Again, she comes back at me with a quick statement of denial. "I still don't have a clue as to what you are talking about."

I take the boxes, hand them to Bill, and then say, "Make sure these are the circuit boards that plug into the tubes."

By then most of the equipment is being walked down the hallway on large carts. Janine walks out of the room right before me, and I follow her down the hallway. She makes a left towards the bathroom, and I say, "Make sure you have some mints for after you throw up. You're going to have a long day."

Chapter 41

Friday, June 5
Zamtech Headquarters
Palo Alto, California

I walk into the new room, which looks very similar to the old one. The CTO asks his engineers to disconnect all the Hodophi equipment and move it to the side. We stand there and watch as they go through this process. Janine walks in and looks the worst I have seen her look. She stands in the back of the room, does not make eye contact with anyone, and looks like she is in a daze.

I think about her for a second. I should probably give her the benefit of the doubt; she was probably offered a large amount of money for a little bit of information. They probably targeted her specifically, and they would not have told her about the other things going on elsewhere in the country. I will have to debate whether I try to rat her out later, but I really do not have much to go on in the first place.

The equipment is all moved, and now it is Bill and our engineers setting up my equipment from the backup. We all stand there like idiots, drinking coffee and watching them set up.

Joe walks up to me and quietly says, "So, what happened to George?"

I say, "This is probably better-suited to a discussion over a beer later, but we need to get him more stock. They tried to kill him in his hotel room last night. He ended up killing one of the attackers, and he taped up the other. They were foreign dudes. We will have to alert the police after we get through this. They also hacked into the police system and put an APB out on our car to arrest us. We ended up getting one of George's Ranger buddies arrested last night. We'll need to help clean that up, as well."

Joe now looks horrified, so I continue, "Also, don't look at her, but I have a pretty good reason to believe our project manager over there, Janine, is working for Hodophi."

Joe, to his credit, looks straight at me and says, "You suspected that before, but you really know now?"

I answer, "I don't have hard proof, but I'm pretty sure."

He says, "Wow. This is just absolutely nuts. I have never experienced anything remotely like this in my life."

The next hour is spent just standing around. Jonathan, the CTO, walks over to me and asks, "So, you have been through a lot?"

I answer, "I'm not sure if you really want to hear this story."

He says, "I do, believe me."

So I tell him. I start from the beginning and tell him about my first week at work and the fact that I noticed an outgoing command-and-control channel sending everything off one of my servers and that I and our networking guy had found malware on about seven servers that were connecting to a service provider down in San Antonio.

He listens intently, asking questions every once in a while. I go on to tell him about all the attacks, the targeting of our VP of Marketing using a fake website for a conference she was going to, the USB drives showing up for free, and all the probes and exploit packs run on our stuff. I tell him about my first mugging, when they realized that I was causing them problems as the computer security guy. I explain that I had suspected Josh and Troy as moles, and then they both ended up dead. As I am spelling this all this to him, I realize how foolish we were to keep going with this thing, given just how much we were up against and what we had been through. Twenty-twenty hindsight is a powerful thing.

I then tell him about the attack in my apartment by the men with guns and silencers but that I then believed they had started leaving me alone because they no longer thought I had the hard drives. They must have been following or monitoring me, because we had brought this equipment to my friend's apartment, all on the sly, and somehow they still found out about it. They went in there last night to wreck the equipment, and they could have cared less that they were going to have to kill George.

Jonathan continues to ask questions and actually starts taking notes during the discourse, and I end by explaining what had happened on the dock this morning. Then I say to him, "We were really lucky that the hard drives with the source code for the heat dissipation algorithms were not in the company's system, or you would have seen Hodophi succeed with an inferior design. I am also lucky I have a friend who happened to be an ex-Army Ranger. Thinking about it now, we are really lucky to be here. I want to finish this for Ashok—I'm not sure if you ever met him, but he was a great guy."

He answers, "I did know him; he is the reason ART is in this bake-off, and I'm sorry for your loss."

When he walks away, I can see Janine staring at me. She has no idea what I know or what I would say, which is kind of satisfying. I think I will just let her stew in her worry for now.

This is taking a while; the engineers are actually running tests before they hook it up. Zamtech has sandwiches brought in, and I eat too much, as usual.

Finally, Bill walks up to Joe and tells him we are ready. Jonathan texts a handful of people, and in the next ten minutes, the room is packed—even more crowded than the original room.

Bill once again explains the equipment, what it does, and what should show at each monitor. He then goes into a small spiel and says that we needed to go back two months to ensure a safe setup and that there are some known bugs in this version that have been fixed in the subsequent release, which we will detail and give to Zamtech.

Joe, Chet, and Bill have been talking for a while, and I think that this is a great move. Just be up front: tell them what's broken but that we know how to fix it.

Bill seems to be enjoying himself now, and I think to myself that he is a showman and this is right up his alley. I feel a tinge of guilt that we didn't bring him into the third prototype, but it wasn't my call to choose who would be involved.

Finally, Bill says we are going to turn on the system. As he does, for some reason I look down at some discarded boxes on a table. I see the circuit board boxes and think that something looks strange. What is it? I cannot tell, but something is different. I can hear them beginning to power on the systems...

Wait, I know what it is! The boxes I had taken from Ashok's office and had just taken away from Janine had blue box tape on them. These had white tape. I look at Bill and then look over at his laptop bag, which is resting close to where he is standing.

I yell at the top of my lungs, "Wait! Shut down immediately!" The engineers look at me like I am a psychopath, but they start doing it.

I walk across the room, grab Bill's bag, and unzip it. Bill asks, "Robert, what are you doing? What's up?" He tries to grab the bag from me.

I turn my back to him and yank the two small boxes, taped shut with blue tape, out of his bag. I say to the engineers, "Use these boards." Then I say, "Chet, I think you need to do this presentation instead of Bill."

Bill glares at me, and Joe says, "Robert, are you sure?"

I reply, "Yes. I just gave these to Bill this morning and told him to use them, and I don't think it was a simple mistake that he didn't."

Bill says, "Joe, it was an honest mistake. We have so much going on here, I just got confused."

The Zamtech people are now looking at us skeptically, so I say, "Regardless, let's use these boards, and we'll be fine."

Bill steps away as the engineers spend the next ten minutes changing out the boards, and then Joe pulls him to the side so they can have a hushed conversation. Every once in a while, Bill looks look at me as though he could kill me.

Finally, Chet alerts the crowd that we are ready to go, and they power on the devices. I look at Janine, and she just looks at me like I am an idiot. I think I may have made a mistake about her.

The power turns on, and Chet asks the engineers to power up five joules. They do, and I finally smile as I see four computers with four readings of 4.99988888. There is another screen that reads 100%, and there is a circle graph all filled in at 100% as well. All of the energy has been transferred!

Wow, the stuff actually works! We are making technological history! Chet then says, "I'm going to raise this to 250." And there it is, 249.99988888 once again across the board. Again, the percentage graph says 100% with a large red circle graph showing full transference as well. Joe walks up beside me and looks at the systems like he is going to cry. I really think he is about to.

One of the Zamtech engineers comes up wearing blue jeans and an untucked white collared shirt. He says, "This is unbelievable. Can you raise it to ten megajoules?"

Chet smiles and says, "Yes; if your backend systems can handle it, these systems can handle it." He slowly moves the dial until it reaches its highest level. Once again, four monitors read 9,999.99988888, and the percentage monitor is at 100%.

I think to myself that Ashok was a genius, and a tear almost comes to my eye remembering the passion with which he explained his algorithms to me.

The room is silent. Finally, Jonathan breaks the ice. "I may be giving away a negotiating position, but these results are unbelievable to me. This completely complements the abilities we can deliver with our solar paneling systems. We have never seen results this impressive when transferring energy—we didn't even think they were possible. I am sure you know we tried to do this ourselves for most of last year."

He is actually exuberant and runs around shaking everyone's hand, both Zamtech employees and ART employees. He should be happy; his project depends on the successful transfer of energy that they can now do. His project and his company will now be extraordinarily successful.

Joe walks over to shake my hand and says quietly, "Do you think it could have been a mistake with Bill?"

I say, "I just took them away from Janine and handed the correct boards to Bill. And then the next thing I know they are hidden in his bag? One hundred bucks says the ones he had plugged in would have melted as well."

I feel sick to my stomach; I really like Bill. I think of him as a friend, but somehow they had gotten to him. He probably just got in over his head and did not realize people would start showing up dead. Maybe he was just getting himself paid, regardless if we succeeded or not.

We stand there for a minute in silence as engineers from Zamtech circle around Chet and the demonstration, asking questions and moving the energy around as it continues to match their inputs every step of the way. I say to Joe, "Just do me a favor and take care of George. He risked his life many times for me and the success of this project."

He looks at me, nods his head, and smiles. "You got it. Done."

Epilogue

It's early December in Baltimore, and it is bitingly cold. I am with my parents and Sarah waiting in the Baltimore City Correctional Center lobby.

Finally, William comes out with a small bag of personal items he had walked in with over two years ago. He first hugs our mom and dad, and then he hugs me. He even gives Sarah a hug, too. He simply says, "Thank you."

There are plenty of tears in our eyes as we walk out, and I am really happy, especially for my parents and for William.

Sarah and I are both now Zamtech employees. Joe and the board eventually sold ART to Zamtech for $1.2 billion. Yes, billion. They originally had offered $900 million, but Joe had negotiated hard; he would have just gone public and sold them the technology for each product they shipped. They also had to be thinking that we could have gone to their competition. I am working directly for the chief security officer at Zamtech in an advisory and innovation role. I have learned an incredible amount playing with new cyber security technology that Zamtech can afford.

Joe was as good as his word. He ended up giving George and I more stock before the sale of ART went through. All of the stock vested upon any transfer of ownership of ART, which meant it turned into cash. This was good and bad. The bad part is I was going to have a huge tax bill this year, and so was George. But I guess that is a good problem to have.

Joe and the board of ART also had taken care of Ashok's parents, vesting all his shares as if he was alive and giving them the profits.

I would definitely work for Joe again if he hits another startup, which I am sure he will—not that he needs the money. Right now, he is a VP at Zamtech in charge of the ART product line and hiring people all over the world.

Bill disappeared after the project, and I saw from his LinkedIn account that he is working for another small company in Baltimore. He did not make any money on the ART sale, as he had quit the company. Oh well. He made his dirty money up front from our competitor, though we had no real proof to go after him. I still cannot believe that he was on the inside for them, and I would hate to see what would happen if George ever ran into him in a bar.

I had really messed up by accusing Janine, and I found out from another employee of her company later on that she had won a twelve-month lease on that nice car for being the top producer among all project managers in the country for her firm. I did send her an apology, but I never heard back. She definitely would not be sending me any holiday cards, but oh well.

After the presentation, George had turned over Ashok's heavily sought-after hard drives to Joe, and we had gone out for a celebration dinner. We toasted to Ashok. George told Joe he had just left them in the trunk of his parents broken-down car in their garage. I am pretty happy that I did not know that during all of this.

Zamtech had shipped the first beta of their finished product to one of the largest companies who had preordered the technology. Their sales and engineering teams hear all products are working as designed, and there is media buzz in tying Zamtech's work to the future of sustainable energy sources.

In further news, I am actually looking at engagement rings, though I have not told anyone about it yet. Not my parents, not my brother, and not George. George may be flat-out angry with me if I move out. Sarah does not know either, but I think I am going to chance asking her. She is such an amazing part of my life and so intimately connected to everything I've been through this past year. I think she might even say yes.

Acknowledgements

I would like to thank my beautiful wife, Mary, for being tremendously supportive in everything I do, as well as being my best friend and the love of my life. I would also like to thank my children, Elizabeth, Patrick, Megan, Kevin, and Johnny, for bringing me so much joy and laughter. I have been so blessed.

I would like to thank my parents, Mary Ann and Michael McCormick, for giving your four boys an amazing childhood and teaching us to focus our lives on faith, family, and education. I would like to thank my brothers, Mike, Brendan, and Eamon, for being the best friends a guy can have. I would also like to thank my wife's parents, Eli and Eileen Dabich, for welcoming me into such a tremendous family.

I would like to thank my many business colleagues and the friends I've made along the way, especially John Czupak for being a great friend and mentor and giving me numerous opportunities. I would also like to thank Tom McDonough, John Negron, and Ron Partridge for their friendship, trust, and guidance. I cannot name all the wonderful people that I have had the pleasure of working with over the years, but I am lucky to have had the benefit of working with some of most hardworking, ethical, and intelligent people in the business.

I would also like to thank my friends growing up, my college friends, and my Rockville friends for always making life fun.

Once again, I cannot begin to name all of you, but you know who you are.

Lastly, I would like to thank all my new friends in publishing: Todd Sattersten for getting me started, Kate Sage for an unbelievable job developmentally editing this book, Sarah Currin for her copyediting and proofreading skills, Robyn Crummer-Olson for bringing the book to market, and Gene Kim for some great advice along the way.

About the Author

Matt McCormick serves as Senior Vice President of Corporate and Business Development at ThreatQuotient, Inc. ThreatQuotient is a venture-funded software company focused on cyber threat intelligence operations and management.

Prior to joining ThreatQuotient, Matt was Vice President of Business Development for Sourcefire, Inc., for eleven years prior to its $2.7 billion acquisition by Cisco Systems, Inc. At Cisco, he was responsible for strategic alliances and running Cisco's global security channel. Prior to his work with Sourcefire, Matt ran strategic alliances at Axent Technologies, Inc., which was purchased by Symantec Corp. in 2000. Matt's work in the cyber security industry has given him over 20 years of experience as a programmer, cyber security consultant, and sales engineer. He has a Bachelor of Science in Engineering Science from Loyola University and a Master of Science in Electrical Engineering from Bucknell University.

Matt is married with five children and lives in Rockville, Maryland, where he enjoys spending time with his family and friends.

23582474R00166

Made in the USA
Columbia, SC
09 August 2018